ASSASSIN'S CREED
THE GOLDEN CITY

The man who'd been watching them from above was crossing the roof, heading in Hytham's direction. He decided to let the man get a little closer, in the hope he might be able to take him unawares with a clean and silent kill.

Crouching low, Hytham breathed in deep and slow. He would find every shadow, make his body small, his steps silent. To fade away and be no more present than the gentle hiss of the wind – that was his gift, hard-won and practiced for years until he could hide in plain sight.

The man shifted slightly as a tile wobbled beneath his boot, and Hytham seized the advantage. He leapt into the air, exploding over the peak of the roof, wind whistling in his ears. His target must have sensed the movement at the last minute, for he spun, but he was too late.

MORE ASSASSIN'S CREED® FROM ACONYTE

Assassin's Creed: The Magus Conspiracy by Kate Heartfield

Assassin's Creed: The Ming Storm by Yan Leisheng
Assassin's Creed: The Desert Threat by Yan Leisheng

Assassin's Creed Valhalla: Geirmund's Saga by Matthew J Kirby
Assassin's Creed Valhalla: Sword of the White Horse by Elsa Sjunneson

ASSASSIN'S CREED

The

GOLDEN CITY

JALEIGH JOHNSON

ACONYTE

First published by Aconyte Books in 2023

ISBN 978 1 83908 221 4

Ebook ISBN 978 1 83908 222 1

Cover art by Alejandro Colucci

Distributed in North America by Simon & Schuster Inc, New York, USA

Printed in the United States of America

9 8 7 6 5 4 3 2 1

ACONYTE BOOKS

An imprint of Asmodee Entertainment Ltd

Mercury House, Shipstones Business Centre

North Gate, Nottingham NG7 7FN, UK

aconytebooks.com // twitter.com/aconytebooks

To Tim, for introducing me to Altaïr and Ezio and always knowing the right video game to give me at the right time. My gamer heart is yours forever.

CHAPTER ONE

The olive grove was gray and cool in the pre-dawn light, an uncaring host for the two Assassins who'd come to find each other on its shadowed paths.

Mist threaded the uneven ground at waist height, a thick white river that Hytham shredded as he walked. The silence was heavy but not complete. Faintly, there came the sounds of birds waking and the soft hiss of wind barely rustling the branches along the rows of trees. In the distance, the city's massive inner wall curved away from him, octagonal guard towers rising to mute the emerging sun and delay the heat of the oncoming day by a few more precious minutes. The air carried the faint tang of smoke from morning fires and breakfast being prepared, but the grove was empty, so Hytham enjoyed a brief moment of peace that wasn't destined to last.

He wondered if there existed a more secure place in the world than where he stood at this moment, in the quiet fields of New Rome. Nestled on a triangular peninsula, with the natural protection of the Bosphorus, the Golden Horn, and the Sea of Marmara, Constantinople was also fortified by a moat and three separate, intimidating walls built on rising embankments, studded with guard towers large enough to house an impressive display of artillery when needed. Many an army had tried to breach the city's walls over the centuries, despite these extensive deterrents, for the promise of the bounty that lay within. None of these had managed to conquer the great city.

A figure materialized from a cluster of trees and strode toward Hytham, a darker shadow against the gray, moving with the soft tread of a predator. Basim Ibn Ishaq walked with unhurried steps, and Hytham took this opportunity to study the man, though he could see few details of Basim's features beneath his peaked hood. His robes were white as the mist, the traditional, distinctive garb worn by the Hidden Ones. The only spot of color visible at this distance was the red sash that marked him as a Master Assassin.

Something about the way Basim walked struck Hytham as strange in that moment, dreamlike, though he couldn't put his finger on what unsettled him until the man came closer. Only then did it dawn on Hytham – Basim walked like a man aged far beyond his years. Not the stooped, unsteady gait of infirmity, but the way a man walked when he has trod the same stretch of earth for decades or longer. Basim moved through the world as if he'd done all of this before.

As if he were a ghost, insubstantial as the mist.

The Master Assassin glanced up then, meeting Hytham's gaze, and the moment was dispelled. He was simply a man again, out for a morning stroll to become acquainted with the place they'd been assigned to work in together for the next several months. What a strange flight of fancy to have. Hytham blinked. He must be more tired than he thought.

"'Come spar with me,' your message said." Hytham kept his stance relaxed, but it was as much a deception as his cheerful tone. He was on guard. Basim's version of friendly sparring often drew blood and was never dull. "Maybe now you regret leaving behind your comfortable bed."

A light came into Basim's eyes at the joke. The accommodations they'd been given were anything but luxurious, not that they'd expected any different. They were here to work, not relax.

"You were staring at the defense wall with an affectionate look," Basim replied, his voice smooth and measured. "I hated to disturb you. Tell me. What were you thinking about?"

"Security," Hytham said, sweeping a hand out to encompass the limestone and brick cutting across the horizon above the treetops. "I would not want to lead the force set to attack this city. A fool's mission, I think."

"A death sentence," Basim agreed. He'd stopped several paces away from Hytham, standing easily, relaxed, which put Hytham even more on edge. "To be a soldier looking up at these walls when the mysterious Greek fire of Constantinople rains down upon their heads – it must be to them like the vengeance of God, or the end of the world."

Hytham suppressed a shudder. He'd heard stories, of course, about the strange alchemical substance that had helped defend the city from attack by sea. Explosive projectiles of fire and death launched in the night, the recipe a closely guarded secret by the emperor and his successors. Many people would kill to have the means to make the powerful weapon.

Their own brotherhood among them.

"But there are other ways to control a city than taking it by force," Hytham said, casually feeling the ground around him with the toe of his boot. It was disconcerting, not being able to see the terrain for the mist, but he thought it would burn off soon with the rising of the sun.

"Exactly." Basim flashed a quick smile, and there was something equally playful and dangerous in his eyes, like a fox in reach of a hen. "So, this security you speak of is a carefully crafted illusion, is it not? We're never truly safe."

And with that, he fell into a crouch, disappearing completely into the mist.

Like a ghost.

Hytham cursed under his breath, his heart beating hard as the thrill of the impending fight kicked in, but he forced himself not to react to the surprise of Basim's move. He stood still, listening for the sounds of footfalls, an indrawn breath, anything that might give a clue as to where Basim approached to strike. The mist-softened ground dampened sound, giving the Master Assassin the advantage, but Hytham had learned from his own mentor Rayhan the skills of listening and patience. He trusted the land to tell him what he needed to know about his opponent.

To his relief, he was rewarded. A tiny shift of pebbles disturbed by a foot – that was Hytham's only warning, but it was enough. Basim emerged from the mist behind and slightly to Hytham's right, an impossibly fast shadow, his Hidden Blade springing free from the sheath at his forearm. It was a maneuver designed to end the fight before it began, an elegant and lethal attack.

Hytham had observed the move many times, had performed it himself on countless unsuspecting targets. Still, seeing it from Basim froze him for the barest instant, either in fear or in admiration, he couldn't have said. Then he snapped back to himself and reacted.

Mirroring Basim's opening move, he let his body drop into the mist, rolling to the side into the underbrush. Basim landed next to him, boots inches from his face, blade whipping down. Hytham's hand shot out, deflecting the oncoming strike with his own Hidden Blade. The shriek of metal meeting metal was loud in the morning stillness. Somewhere above Hytham, a cluster of ravens burst from a tree in an agitated flap of wings and plaintive cries. Hytham surged up, mist hanging off him like a torn shroud, using his momentum, forearm against forearm, to drive Basim back, slamming him into a tree.

The light had changed, just in those brief seconds Hytham had been down on his back. Gold spilled over the wall and across the grove, burning away the mist in slow rolling heat and casting dappled shadows over everything.

"One less hiding place," he remarked to Basim, pleased that his breath wasn't yet labored. A thin sheen of sweat clung to his neck, and he grinned, unable to help it. The pure joy of being alive and testing himself against an opponent he respected coursed in his blood like a small taste of immortality. He might have been made of Greek fire himself in that moment.

Basim gave a nod of acknowledgment and shoved himself off the tree into Hytham's space, faster than he'd disappeared in the mist, so quick that Hytham was briefly disoriented, but his arm went up instinctively to deflect the Hidden Blade again, a gesture so rooted in survival he no longer had to think about it. He shoved, twisting around Basim, putting the tree between them, and they broke apart, movements like a dance just interrupted.

The partners reassessed each other. But instead of launching another attack, Basim took a second to gather himself before drawing the elegant, curved scimitar he carried.

Dawn light flashed off the blade's edge, aching to draw the eye under its hypnotic spell, but Hytham couldn't afford to let his focus waver. He drew his own sword, and then it was a very different kind of dance. Thrust and parry, and again he marveled at the way his opponent moved. They were closely matched in strength, by Hytham's estimation, so between them it became a contest of speed and maneuvering as each player tried to move his opponent where he wanted him on the field like a piece on a chessboard.

At the moment, Basim was driving him toward a small cluster of trees bordering a worn footpath. The ravens had regrouped there to search out food, mistakenly thinking they'd be undisturbed. Hytham felt the land sloping gently downhill, forcing his attention briefly away from Basim's blade to attending to his balance, making sure he wouldn't fall – ah. He felt it then, the patch of mud pulling at his heavy boots, slowing his reflexes, making his feet slide. No chance to keep pace with the fight if he couldn't find reliable footing. Basim knew this, had driven him here on purpose.

Hytham met his eyes, saw the bright spark of triumph. But the fight wasn't over yet. Basim may have the grace and speed Hytham lacked, but Hytham compensated with sheer physicality when called for.

He lunged, digging stubbornly into the mud, blade aimed

at Basim's flank. The other man parried, and Hytham ducked low at the same time. It left his neck exposed to Basim's blade, but Hytham snagged the other man by his calf and pulled, knocking him off balance.

"Into the mud with me," Hytham said, and this time his breathing *was* labored, the sweat dripping into eyes half closed by the brightening light.

Basim laughed – an ominous sign, and not the reaction Hytham had been hoping for.

But the move worked. Basim went down, catching himself on his hands – he kept hold of his sword somehow – and kicked out with the leg Hytham had snared. It clipped his jaw, and Hytham saw stars. Cursing, Hytham rolled away, collecting more mud for his efforts, but he gained his feet and aimed his sword in a downward arc. Basim caught it with the scimitar, the impact jarring Hytham's arm. A wide smile stretched Basim's face.

"Good," he murmured, leaping back to his feet. His chest rose and fell visibly with the exertion. He rolled his shoulders and raised his blade again. "Would you like to hear a story about the great walls of Constantinople, since you find them so fascinating?"

"Because we have nothing else to occupy our attention?" Hytham feinted, but Basim didn't flinch. They tapped blades and paced back from each other, circling, moving on to ground that wasn't choked with mud. This was another interesting thing about Basim. He could go from sparring to lecturing as quickly as the light had swept away the mist.

Basim pointed to the walls with his curved blade, then brought it quickly back into a defensive position. "Impressive as they are, they aren't impervious to the tremors of the earth," he said. "The story goes that the ground shook, in centuries past, and the walls crumbled in the wake of the disaster, raising vast clouds of dust that blocked the sun."

"You wouldn't know it to look at them now," Hytham said, but he did not look. Never take your eyes off the wolf, even when it seems to be at rest.

"It was in the time of Theodosius II," Basim said, and indeed he appeared very much a wolf on the prowl as he wove in and out of the trees. "Though I'm certain the emperor wished it had happened in any other time. Perhaps he thought God punished him, opening his city to attack by the gathering Huns and their leader Attila. Or perhaps he saw it as a test of his leadership, put before him by the Almighty."

Despite Hytham's training, something about Basim's voice, rich and smooth as honey poured over warm bread, made it easy to fall into his story, to let his stance relax and tense muscles slacken. Hytham thought Basim belonged around a fire spinning tales when he spoke like this. With an effort, Hytham refocused and tightened his grip on his blade, but Basim had stopped moving now with the sun at his back. He seemed content simply to talk.

"Under threat of invasion, the emperor ordered the praetorian prefect, Constantine Flavius, to repair the walls with haste," Basim said, shaking his head. "Can you imagine being given such an order? Repair in haste something that took near a decade to build."

"So, it was more a test for Constantine Flavius," Hytham said, "rather than the emperor. Myself, I would prefer to face the Greek fire."

"As would I, but the prefect was a canny man, by all accounts," Basim said. He was circling again, letting the tip of his sword drag a light track through the underbrush, which here barely grew past the cuff of his boot. "He had the workers he needed at his disposal, but they weren't moving as fast as the Hun army and were not half so well motivated."

"Not motivated by the desire to save their own lives?" Hytham said in disbelief.

Basim shrugged. "To them, the enemy was far away, and they had been secure behind their walls for so long, perhaps they believed it would always be so. In any event, the work was proceeding too slowly for Constantine's liking – and the emperor's – so the prefect hit upon a scheme to make the work into a competition." He glanced in the direction of the palace, though it was too far off to see from where they stood. "The chariot races in the great Hippodrome are nothing like the grand spectacle they were in those days, with the teams of red, white, green, and blue competing so fiercely for their faction that there was often more bloodshed outside the great circus than within. Constantine, as I said, was a canny man, and knew he could use that bloodthirsty spirit to his advantage. Each team and their supporters were put in charge of repairing a certain section of the wall."

Hytham raised an eyebrow. "Let me guess. The team who finished first was handsomely rewarded?"

"And increased their prominence within the city," Basim confirmed. "The work of years was finished in months, as the story goes, and the city was saved. When the enemy heard the news of the grand achievement, the Huns turned back from their march upon the city, and Constantinople stayed at peace."

Hytham tried to picture it, but in the end, he shook his head. "I don't believe this story. Surely, the people were motivated more by a desire to save themselves and their homeland, than by a competition for bragging rights in the grand circus."

"Ah, well," Basim shrugged again, "whether the story really happened or not, I believe there is truth in Constantine Flavius's knowledge of human nature and what truly motivates people."

"Is that the point of this sparring match, then?" Hytham asked, tapping his blade against Basim's to show he wasn't quite ready to call a halt to the battle yet. "Proper motivation?"

"Perhaps," Basim said, and fell smoothly back into his fighting stance. This time Hytham struck first, refusing to start on the defensive again. His muscles were burning, blood pumping – he was ready. Ready to show Basim what skills he possessed, and ready for wherever this mission together in Constantinople would take them.

Blades sang as they moved through the grove, heat intensifying as the sun climbed steadily higher in the sky. Hytham spared a thought to wonder what it was that motivated Basim. He knew little of the man who was his superior on this mission, except that some event in his recent past had resulted in questions about Basim's loyalty. He gave every appearance of being committed to the Hidden Ones' cause, but some members of their brotherhood suspected that Basim harbored personal obsessions that threatened to cloud his judgment. Hytham didn't know what event had taken place to cause these suspicions. As an Acolyte, he was not yet trusted with such privileged information, so he hadn't been able to question it when his mentor Rayhan had ordered Hytham to watch Basim.

"*See that he stays to the task at hand – advancing the influence of the Hidden Ones in the city, as far as the emperor's palace, if you can.*" A tall order even for a Master Assassin, and Hytham was still an Acolyte.

He'd strayed too deeply in his thoughts. Hytham snapped his attention back to the battle, but he saw too late the gleam in Basim's eye. Hytham's foot caught on a tangle of spiny underbrush and upthrust tree roots – again Basim had led them toward an obstacle without Hytham noticing – and he lost his footing for an instant.

It was more than enough.

Basim's blade screeched along his own, and with an elegant twist, he forced it from Hytham's hands. He raised the scimitar to Hytham's throat, where it caught the light again and shone in Hytham's eyes.

"Your head wasn't in the fight this time," he said, but there was less of an admonishment in Basim's tone than Hytham might have expected for letting himself be led so easily into the trap. He seemed more curious than anything. "Were you thinking about the story I told you?"

"Yes," Hytham said ruefully, retrieving his blade from the underbrush. It was only half a lie. The story *had* sent his thoughts off in this direction, after all. "Your distraction worked well."

"It wasn't meant as a distraction," Basim replied, but he waved it away when Hytham would have questioned him further. "Come, we have plans to discuss, and we should clean up as well."

Hytham sheathed his sword, wiped some lingering mud from his hands, and fell into step beside the other man as they made their way through the trees. Deep in the grove, they were still alone at this time of the morning, except for the waking birds.

"This mission we've been given will not be accomplished easily or quickly," Hytham said. "Not if the information we've gathered about the emperor and his allegiances are true."

"Rest assured, the stories you've heard are as true as they are strange," Basim said. "It will be an interesting sojourn here." He didn't sound intimidated. In fact, Hytham could sense the excitement in Basim's body language. It wasn't just the leftover exhilaration from their sparring. Basim was looking forward to the challenge of advancing the Hidden Ones' cause here.

But Hytham wasn't wrong. Nothing about the mission would be easy.

In the short time Hytham had spent in Constantinople, he'd learned much about Emperor Basil I and his unusual rise to power. His parentage uncertain, born to neither wealth nor status, Basil was described as handsome but coarse, an uneducated but physically imposing man, who had been at various times in his life a slave, a wrestler, a beggar, and a horse breaker before catching the eye of the previous Emperor Michael III.

The young Michael, "the drunkard" as he'd been called by his detractors, by many accounts had been a capricious ruler, more interested in his own amusements than in making his city prosper. Despite that reputation, the Hidden Ones had worked for years in secret to build an alliance with Michael, to set him on a path that would strengthen Constantinople and further the Hidden Ones' agenda at the same time.

Then one day Basil came into Michael's sphere, and everything changed.

The young, impressionable emperor took an immediate liking to Basil, elevating him to the position of horse master, then chamberlain. The Hidden Ones warned Michael repeatedly that Basil, though handsome and charming, was an ambitious man who saw a clear path to power through the young emperor. Michael didn't listen, and ultimately, his unlikely alliance with Basil resulted in Michael making Basil co-emperor, a move he would quickly come to regret.

When their relationship eventually soured and Basil fell out of favor with the emperor, instead of disappearing, he conspired to have Michael assassinated in his own bedchamber one night, leaving himself in sole possession of the throne and the riches of Constantinople.

Basil did not come into such power by his will alone. He'd had help.

It was whispered that the Order of the Ancients had aided Basil every step of the way in his rise, and with Basil's ascension to emperor were situating themselves to become the true power behind the throne.

This was not a situation that could be allowed to stand.

As the new seat of the Roman Empire, its successor and the gateway between East and West, Constantinople was too rich and well situated a prize to be left for the Order to seize. Though it had been often besieged, the city had never been conquered by land or sea, but as Hytham had pointed out, there were other ways to take over a city, and the Order excelled in this form of insidious control from within. They were already at work.

Hytham and Basim had been assigned to rip them out at the roots by any means they could find. A vital mission to entrust to a Master Assassin whose trustworthiness was in question.

So, as much as Hytham wanted to share Basim's enthusiasm for the task ahead, he couldn't ignore the sense of uncertainty that gripped him when he considered again Basim's place on the chessboard.

CHAPTER TWO

There were logistical considerations to establishing oneself in a new city, beyond just getting settled in living quarters and sparring with your superior at dawn. Hytham also needed to familiarize himself with the geography of the city itself. To walk its streets, listening to the people speaking Greek and, occasionally, Latin, and in general get a feeling for the place he would be calling his new home.

He'd expected to do most of these explorations on his own, but Basim had had other ideas. He took Hytham on a tour of the city without ever proclaiming that he was doing so. Hytham first suspected it when he glimpsed the great dome and buttresses of Hagia Sophia emerging from the surrounding architecture, a sight to steal the breath and give one pause, even in the middle of a crowded, noisy street.

Constantinople was sometimes known as the Golden City, and Hytham had seen the truth of that name on mornings like these as the sunlight gilded the water, sweeping across the great harbor and holding the city in a moment so brief and lovely as to make artists reach greedily for brush and canvas. The light that touched Hagia Sophia was no exception, transforming the great building into a treasure box that Basim described as being ablaze with candle and lamplight within.

The city itself was not hard to navigate, with fourteen regions connected by well-kept avenues. There were rolling hills, city parks, and many public squares decorated with sculptures and columns. Life here was busy, vibrant, and rife with possibility. It was the only way Hytham could describe the energy he felt. He was glad that Basim had taken the time to show him these sights. Hytham knew he must get to know this city, but he also needed to get to know Basim.

Eventually, Basim led him into the courtyard of a small wine bar. Tables and chairs had been set up in the shadow of the building, and they sat, their backs to the cool, shaded wall, a good view of the streets and passersby in front of them.

A woman came out of the bar with some dishes on a tray. She smiled at them in greeting and put down bowls of spiced nuts, figs in honey, and peeled oranges. Basim asked for water for the two of them, and the woman nodded and went away again.

"Is there someone you're looking for?" Hytham asked as he watched Basim eyeing the foot and cart traffic passing by. It was growing warmer, the late spring days bright and fair with the promise of summer coming soon.

"I've been here before," Basim said, popping one of the figs in his mouth and licking honey from his fingers. "It's a good place to see the city, to watch its people." He glanced at Hytham. "As I noticed you doing as you walked the streets with me. You're very observant."

"I would not be very skilled at my chosen profession if I weren't," Hytham said with a faint smile.

Basim laughed. "True enough. So, what do you think of this New Rome?"

The question caught Hytham by surprise. He hadn't expected Basim to ask him anything about his personal observations, only to speak about the mission at hand. "This is my first time in Constantinople," Hytham said. "It's everything I thought it would be and more, although with so many people living in one place, it takes some getting used to when compared to my time in the wilderness or in less developed settlements."

"Ah, so you're still readjusting to city life," Basim said, waving a hand in invitation for Hytham to eat. "Anything else?"

Hytham thought of the more practical details he'd seen during their impromptu tour. "I can see why this city is difficult to besiege, and I'm speaking beyond the strength of its walls and the water that protects it," he said. "The city's aqueduct system and its many cisterns ensure a plentiful water supply, and its capacity for grain storage is something I've not seen anywhere else in my travels. A long siege, even over several winters, would wear down any attacking force before it substantially weakened the city."

"And it has done, for many an attacking army," Basim said, as Hytham took a handful of the spiced nuts. "So, it would be foolish and costly to try to take the city by force, which, of course, the Order of the Ancients knows well. They were wise to make the emperor the target for their campaign to gain power in the city."

Basim spoke softly, though there were no other patrons

at the wine bar this early in the day. He paused in their conversation as a tall, slender man with a shaved head came to their table with a jug of water and two cups.

"I apologize for the wait," he said, pouring their drinks. "My son was supposed to be up early to help me in the kitchen, and I swear I still hear him snoring all the way downstairs." He gave them a rueful smile and a shrug of his broad shoulders.

"We're in no rush," Hytham said, returning the man's smile. "We're just here to take our ease for a bit."

"You've chosen a good time for it," the man said as he walked back toward the kitchen. "It's a fine day to sit idle and watch the people pass by."

When they were alone again, Hytham said, just as quietly, "Is it certain they've made the emperor a permanent ally? If so, it's going to be difficult to root them out if they're already entrenched in the palace."

"Nothing is certain," Basim said. "Emperors are often the target of assassinations in this city. The power structure has changed and destabilized many times over the centuries. There are opportunities we may be able to exploit, but there are dangers we need to be aware of as well."

"Did you have specific dangers in mind?" Hytham asked curiously. He took a drink of water, the cool liquid feeling good on his parched throat.

"Perhaps," Basim said. "Tell me, are you familiar at all with the Varangian Guard?"

"A little," Hytham said. He'd been briefed with some information about the government structure and palace life by his superiors before coming to the city. "I know they're the emperor's personal bodyguards, recruited from the same

Viking clans that once raided the coastal settlements and farms."

A rare example of an emperor turning his enemies into allies, Hytham thought. The story he'd heard was that instead of squandering soldiers and resources to wipe out the Viking raiders, the emperor had instead sent missionaries to learn more about the fierce warriors and their clans, and offer them the chance to serve Constantinople and acquire more wealth and prestige than they might do burning villages and destroying crops.

"Another canny move from a ruler who understood human nature, I think," Basim said, giving Hytham a meaningful look. "Rumors spread far and wide of the ferocity and rage the Viking clans displayed in battle, the absolute commitment they have to their cause. They showed no hesitation, no fear of dying. Perhaps the emperor thought that earning the loyalty of such a force would discourage any from attacking his person or his family."

"It would also help him avoid betrayal from within," Hytham said. "He would surely feel more secure recruiting outsiders, those untouched by the complex political forces at work in Constantinople."

"True," Basim said. "Thus, any plan we undertake to challenge the emperor must take into account the power of the Varangians and the strength of their loyalty to the emperor."

Hytham nodded solemnly. It was yet one more reminder, as if he needed one, that this mission would be complicated. He took one of the honey-soaked figs from the dish and put it in his mouth, savoring its sweetness as he considered their options. He also considered the fact that Basim never spoke of anything idly. It was one of the things he'd observed about the man in their limited time together. His words always contained a purpose or a lesson, and Hytham sensed now was no different.

"Why did you bring up the Varangian Guard specifically?" Hytham asked. "Do you see an immediate threat from that corner?"

Basim looked pleased that he'd caught on. "It's something I'd considered, in light of recent events."

"Recent events?" Hytham prompted, but Basim just shook his head, ending the thread of conversation. Hytham suppressed a sigh. The man could also be infuriatingly opaque sometimes.

Basim stood, leaving some coins on the table to pay for their food. "Come," he said, gesturing to the busy street. "There's another part of Constantinople you must yet experience before you can say you're fully acquainted with the city."

Hytham rose and followed Basim out of the courtyard and back to the sun-dappled streets. He was thankful for the water and the brief rest after the early morning sparring and the winding tour of the city, but he wondered what Basim wasn't telling him.

The man was intelligent, experienced, and his fighting skills were unmatched. Hytham knew there was much he could learn from Basim that would in turn help him survive and rise in the ranks of the Hidden Ones. But if he could not penetrate the shroud of secrecy that seemed to cling to Basim, he would not be able to accomplish his personal mission and prove himself worthy of his mentor's trust.

Still, Hytham couldn't say he was afraid of the challenges

that had been presented to him. The Hidden Ones had taken on greater foes and emerged triumphant. Theirs was often a long game played from the shadows and back alleys. Hytham knew the game well, and he was more than prepared to do what must be done.

Chapter Three

The markets of Constantinople felt to Hytham like the beating heart of the city. He could see why Basim had saved them for last on his tour. Even more than the great dome of Hagia Sophia rising in the distance, or the crowded streets and decorative columns, the religious icons gleaming from churches along the thoroughfares, the markets were where gold and goods flowed, the clink of coins making you the object of every avaricious merchant's attention. The colorful mounds of fragrant spices were like splashes of paint on an artist's palette, teasing the senses and giving way to incense and perfumes. There was olive oil in abundance, wine, and the sharper tang of fish sauce that Hytham didn't care for.

Jugglers and street musicians moved through the crowds dressed in flamboyant tunics, wearing wide grins and tipping their hats or an empty boot for coins. Hytham tossed an offering to a particularly impressive baritone hitting a long note with one endless breath while a skinny cat walked across his shoulders.

The markets were where the sweat and dirt of dozens of cultures mixed, the languages of east and west mingling with other words Hytham had never heard, curses and praises and laughter in a cacophony of sights and sounds. It was a heady place, exhilarating, the complete opposite of the quiet wine bar they'd just left.

It was also an excellent place to get robbed blind, if you weren't always alert.

Hytham moved with ease through the crowded market, letting the dense foot traffic flow past him like water even as he kept Basim in sight walking a few feet ahead of him. The sun was overhead now, warming his back and enhancing all the smells of humanity and livestock around him, though it wasn't an unpleasant mix. At either end of the long market street was a set of stairs to discourage wheeled traffic, leaving the people more space to walk freely from stall to shop and to gather for conversation and gossip with the various sellers.

Out of the corner of his eye, Hytham caught furtive movement as a beggar boy of about twelve or thirteen slipped up beside him, nudging his shoulder gently, and then his hip.

A fairly clumsy attempt, as far as pickpocketing went. Hytham caught the boy's bony wrist in a firm grip and casually led him out of the flow of people. The boy yelped a protest, but Hytham squeezed just hard enough to shut his mouth and make him drop the stolen coin pouch into Hytham's waiting hand.

"You're lucky this time," Hytham said, looking the boy in the eye. His dirt-streaked face had gone pale as he tried to twist out of Hytham's hold. "Leave the market. I don't want to see you here again today." He pressed some coins into the boy's hand and then released him, watching him dart quickly back into the sea of people. The boy cast a bewildered glance over his shoulder as he ran, as if to make sure Hytham wasn't going to change his mind and chase after him.

"Never a dull moment here," Basim commented from behind Hytham.

There was an odd note in his voice, a false lightness, but when Hytham glanced over his shoulder, Basim had turned away, already dismissing the incident.

Hytham tucked his remaining coins back in his pouch and fell into step beside him. "I assume you brought me here to show me something besides the city's petty crime?"

"You liked the singing too."

"True."

Basim chuckled. He pointed to a market stall across the way that dripped with silks of every color, dazzling in the light and gracefully billowing up in the breeze that helped to break the heat of the day. The seller was clever. He knew exactly how to hang the fabric to its best advantage, naturally drawing the eye to the impressive display. "Do you see the woman haggling with the merchant there?" Basim asked. "And the men with her?"

Hytham looked. The woman Basim indicated wore her hair in many long, steel gray braids, her mouth pinched in a severe expression as she examined a bolt of fabric, though the silk merchant didn't seem intimidated. There was likely some intense bargaining going on, but it seemed to be an honest exchange. Still, the woman was armed and armored, carrying two hand axes that appeared well used and cared for. Two men stood on either side of her similarly armed, their hair shorn so close to their skulls the veins stood out against the pale blond. They watched the rest of the market warily while the woman made her selections.

"Norsemen," Hytham observed, taking their measure in dress and armor. "At least as far as I can tell. I don't see clan symbols. Looks as if they're here for the silk trade." He shot a curious glance at Basim. This was the second time that Basim had drawn attention to Viking warriors. "What's your interest in them?"

"The men with the Viking woman have been following me," Basim said easily, "ever since I made it known through our whisper networks that an outsider – namely myself – has come to Constantinople seeking to undermine the emperor."

It took a second for his words to sink in, but then Hytham stared at Basim in disbelief. "*You* made it known?" His thoughts reeled at the implications. Assuming this wasn't a joke, it meant Basim had as good as revealed the Hidden Ones' mission to their enemies. "You've all but exposed us as targets to the Order of the Ancients!" he hissed.

Basim shook his head. "Only myself. *Your* name and presence in the city I kept out of it, and whatever risk I took has borne fruit. You'll recall our conversation about the Varangian Guard? I suspect we're about to find ourselves meeting them. Whether it be for good or ill, I can't say yet, though I confess I find myself fascinated to know more about this woman and her clan."

Hytham was only half listening. He was watching the rooftops around them, the darkened alleys, and the crowd itself with new eyes, looking for something more than a beggar coming at him with a clumsy pickpocket attempt. What was

Basim playing at, only telling him this now? Was it some kind of test?

"Are you angry with me?" Basim asked. Again, he seemed curious, almost amused. Certainly not concerned. Hytham ground his teeth.

"Did you bring us here hoping to draw out the emperor's supporters?" Hytham asked, ignoring Basim's question.

"In part, but I also hope to see the faces of some of the Order here in the city," Basim said. "It will be helpful to know who is acting against us."

In other words, Basim not only expected an ambush here today, he had walked into the marketplace with his arms out in welcome. That wasn't the way of the Hidden Ones. They acted from the shadows, taking strength from anonymity. Uneasiness stole over Hytham at the idea that Basim might have lost sight of that fundamental mantra. If that was the case, what other compromises might the man make?

They continued walking, but now that Hytham was actively waiting for an attack, he no longer absorbed the sights and smells of the market with the same pleasure. He ignored the fortune tellers, performers, and merchants who competed for his attention. Now their presence here was entirely about measuring threats and trying to anticipate where and when their enemies would strike.

His vigilance was rewarded a short time later when a shadow moved on the rooftop just to his left.

"You saw that," Hytham murmured. It wasn't a question. In response, Basim moved a hand casually across the hilt of his scimitar.

"There are two more waiting in the alley ahead," he replied.

"I've been tracking them since we entered the market. I wasn't sure they were after us at first, but I believe they're lying in wait for us now."

Hytham nodded minutely. "I'll follow you into the alley then and go up on the roof from there."

"Be careful," Basim said. "You'll be more exposed on the roof."

About thirty feet in front of them, a narrow alley broke off from the main market. It was choked with crates and strewn with trash – refuse from the merchants' stalls to be collected later and disposed of. The reek of piss and rotting food filled Hytham's nostrils as they ducked into the shadows of the alley.

Two cloaked and hooded men waited for them, just as Basim predicted. They tensed when Basim's sword hissed out of its scabbard, and he tossed the blade casually from hand to hand.

"Gentlemen," he said, and with that same explosive movement he'd used in the olive grove, Basim set upon them.

Hytham spared a glance to make sure Basim wouldn't be overwhelmed, but he engaged both men confidently, disarming the first one with a dizzying strike and twist that Hytham had been on the receiving end of just that morning. But he had no sympathy for the man Basim was about to kill.

Hytham leapt lightly atop the stack of crates to his left and grabbed the edge of the roof tiles, the rough stone scraping against his calloused fingers. Muscles flexing, he hauled himself up, landing in a crouch on the slanted roof. Some of the tiles were loose, grinding loudly against each other, but the shouts and bustle of the market overtook the sound, just as they hid the swordplay going on below him. Hytham was confident he could still catch his target unawares.

The man who'd been watching them from above was crossing the roof, heading in Hytham's direction. It could be that he awaited a signal from his fellows in the alley and, seeing nothing, had come to see what was going on and what was keeping them. The man's attention was turned away from Hytham, but as soon as Hytham moved, he knew he would surely be seen. He decided to let the man get a little closer, in the hope he might be able to take him unawares with a clean and silent kill.

Crouching low, Hytham breathed in deep and slow. He held his right arm close to his chest, checking the mechanism on his Hidden Blade to make sure nothing had jammed in it during their earlier sparring session in the mud. He felt the blood pumping in his ears, his heartbeat quickening, even as a layer of intense calm settled over him.

He would find every shadow, make his body small, his steps silent. To fade away and be no more present than the gentle hiss of the wind – that was his gift, hard-won and practiced for years until he could hide in plain sight.

It was the gift of the Hidden Ones that their enemies would not know how near the threat was, how deadly the danger, until it was too late.

Hytham waited, observing his target. The man was also cloaked and hooded, head bent slightly to watch his footing on the loose tile – he was close enough now that Hytham could see a faint scar at the base of his neck beneath curling blond hair, his skin darkened by the sun.

The man shifted slightly as a tile wobbled beneath his boot, and Hytham seized the advantage. He leapt into the air, exploding over the peak of the roof, wind whistling in his ears.

His target must have sensed the movement at the last minute, for he spun, but he was too late.

Hytham landed in front of him and released the Hidden Blade which slid smoothly between the man's ribs. He would barely feel it in those first few seconds. Then the man's breath hitched, eyes going wide, and he started to crumple on the tile. Hytham guided his body down and made to step back, but the man found some last bit of strength and lunged for him even as he coughed up his life's blood, grabbing a fistful of Hytham's robe and yanking him off balance on the uncertain tiles.

There was a dizzying instant where Hytham thought he would tumble off the roof, sky and ground tilting crazily around him, but he caught himself on the tiles, scraping skin off his palms. Ignoring the intense burn, Hytham shoved the dying man away from him, sending him rolling down the tiles and off the roof into the alley where he'd left Basim.

Hytham lay flat on his stomach, taking a second to regain his equilibrium. From below, there came the sounds of fighting in the alley. Basim hadn't yet finished off his opponents.

With the blood still dripping from his blade, Hytham sprang up, ready to jump back off the roof to help.

An arrow hissed by him, catching a bit of his sleeve and trailing a stinging line across his flesh. So much for equilibrium. Hytham dropped to his belly again and let himself slide down, putting the slant of the roof between him and his unseen attacker. A second arrow shrieked by overhead, burying itself in a wooden sign attached to a building on the other side of the alley.

There were more attackers than they'd realized. Shouts and

footsteps echoed from the alley, signaling Basim was about to be hit with more enemies as well. Depending on how many of his opponents he'd already dispatched, Basim could be seriously outnumbered, and Hytham was trapped on the roof by an archer that had him pinned.

Carefully, Hytham crawled back up to the peak of the roof and risked a glance over. To his shock, his attacker was in plain sight two buildings away, slumped over the edge of a roof, his bow dangling from slack fingers.

There was a hand axe buried in his back.

As Hytham watched, one of the Vikings from the market appeared on the roof. He pulled his weapon free of the archer's back and kicked the body off the roof, very near to the market stalls at one end of the street.

Hytham winced. Not exactly subtle, but he wasn't going to spit on the unexpected aid. He got back to his feet and made his way down the roof to drop into the alley. There was a body on the ground nearby, but to Hytham's relief, it wasn't Basim's. The Master Assassin was crouched beside it, wiping his blade clean.

The Viking woman they'd been observing at the market had the second of Basim's opponents pinned against the alley wall by her two hand axes – one in the man's neck, and the other in his gut. As Hytham watched, she yanked the weapons free and let the body slide down the wall. Turning, she met his gaze briefly, the fever of battle flashing in her eyes, sweat glistening on her skin.

"I see you also had some extra help," Hytham commented.

"It was a battle well fought," Basim said, nodding to the woman. "May we know you?"

The Viking woman didn't immediately reply. Stone-faced, she dragged the bodies deeper into the alley to hide them from the sight of the market patrons. Judging by their simple clothes and armor, they looked to Hytham like mercenaries rather than members of the Order of the Ancients. A small force hired by the Order and sent to test them, perhaps.

When the woman returned to them, she inclined her head. "My name is Thyra of the Varangian Guard," she said, "leader of the Eagle Clan. May we speak?"

So, Basim had been right. The Vikings were Varangian Guard, but they had not attacked them, as Hytham had expected. Instead, they'd helped kill the mercenaries and spoiled their ambush. What was going on here?

For his part, Basim looked pleased at the Viking woman's question. Hytham hesitated, a sudden suspicion filling his mind.

Had Basim orchestrated this meeting by opening himself as a target in the market in the hopes of attracting the Viking clan leader's attention? It seemed a stretch, especially since he had warned Hytham the Varangian Guard were a danger to them and their mission. Yet the foxlike expression of satisfaction on Basim's face was difficult to ignore. But for what purpose was he doing this? To expose himself so brazenly – whatever Basim was up to, Hytham hoped it ended up being worth it.

Hytham felt as if he'd been on the back foot ever since this day began, and he didn't like it. His mentor had asked him to watch Basim, to make sure he stayed focused on their mission and didn't let himself be distracted by personal agendas. But it felt as if Basim was already ten steps ahead of him, and

Hytham was simply struggling to keep up. He had to stay sharp in the man's company.

But for the moment, he forced his attention to the woman – Thyra. "Thank you for your aid," he said. "What is it we can do for you?"

Thyra looked at him and Basim narrowly, as if she could measure their worth with just a glance. She must have been satisfied by whatever she saw, because she gave a quick nod.

"We've heard you talked about in the city," she said, addressing Basim. "You're the outsider who would challenge the emperor. Foolish words, I thought. This man courts his own death." Her lips thinned. "Then I heard it said you represent a greater force, one that works from the shadows to invoke change. It gave me hope that your bold words might be more than simple bluster. If this is true, then I'm here to ask for your help." She glanced around. Though they were standing in the shadows of the alley, they were still very much in a public venue. "Is there a safe place we can speak?"

Hytham and Basim exchanged a glance, then Basim said, "There is a man – Demetrios Hestiun – an aristocrat who is also an ally. We'll take you to his house. Is that acceptable?"

She considered, then said, "Yes, my men and I will accompany you."

They were a strange procession fading back into the bustle of the market, weapons safely put away, pretending for all the world as if nothing had occurred and that no bodies had been concealed in the alley to be discovered long after they were gone. And they'd been fortunate. No one had heard the sounds of battle, and no one gave them a second look.

The Vikings stayed several paces away from them, and the

men accompanying Thyra were watchful, shooting suspicious glances at Hytham and Basim more than once.

"Not all of them are as friendly as Thyra," Hytham said under his breath, his words meant only for Basim. "Are you sure about this?"

"If they meant us harm, they could have let the Order's mercenaries carve us up while they watched," Basim pointed out.

"Have a little faith," Hytham said with a grin. "I would have gotten around to helping you eventually."

The comment earned him a booming laugh. "I appreciate your consideration," Basim said.

That was the other thing about the Assassin. Basim could be all charm when he wanted to be, easy to like and very much a creature of the moment, flowing from one situation to the next with an easy confidence born of long experience.

And sweet mother of Christ, he fought well. Hytham knew he would not have needed his help, and they would have finished off their foes without the Vikings' intervention. Basim was being gracious, and he was obviously deeply interested in whatever Thyra had to say, if he was willing to take her to the house of an ally to speak.

But what could the Varangian Guard possibly need their help with?

Chapter Four

The house of Demetrios Hestiun was a large two-story building constructed around a spherical inner courtyard filled with colorful flowers and stands of carefully cultivated olive and fruit trees. So many fragrant plants were crammed into the enclosed space, it was almost unpleasant. The servant who'd greeted them at the door led them along a swept stone walkway to a comfortable seating area in the back of the courtyard. A sculpted fountain bubbled nearby as multiple servants tended the garden in silence.

Stepping off the loud, dusty streets to this peaceful setting was jarring to Hytham. He would have preferred to stay among the people in the market who felt more like him than this obviously wealthy household.

But Demetrios's hospitality was unquestionable, as was his discretion. Once he was summoned by yet another servant, he gave quick, whispered instructions, and the courtyard cleared out, the gardeners taking themselves off elsewhere, leaving the visitors and their host alone with only the buzzing of insects and the wind moving through the plants.

Demetrios served them wine himself, and if he thought it strange that Hytham and Basim came in off the street with bloodstains on their clothing and a group of Viking warriors in tow, he did a decent job hiding any reaction. Hytham thought he was on the younger side, with lapis eyes and a firm enough build, but his hair had gone prematurely white, almost colorless, making it hard to judge his age. He spoke pleasantly to Thyra and her men, his voice deep and measured, and Thyra relaxed fractionally in his presence.

But before they sat down on the benches and divans arranged in the center of the courtyard, Thyra leaned in to whisper to one of her men. He made a gruff sound and nodded before leaving the courtyard, heading back toward the entrance to the house.

Hytham exchanged a glance with Basim, both of them remarking on the departure without words. Basim gave a small shake of his head, apparently not wanting to question it for now. Again, Hytham hoped Basim knew what he was doing. He himself still wasn't sure they should be trusting this Thyra and her clan, no matter how helpful they'd appeared in the market.

When the drinks had been handed around, Basim got straight to the point. "You can speak freely in this house," he told Thyra, with a nod to Demetrios, who also gave his assent. "What is it you want from us?"

Thyra turned her cup in her hands, watching the deep red liquid swirl and leave thick tracks in its wake. "As I said in the market, I have heard rumors of a man come from Baghdad, an outsider intent on moving against the emperor. Are you that sort of fool?" she asked bluntly.

"I believe the rumors give me too much credit," Basim said, leaning back slightly on the divan, though his relaxed posture was as much a deception as his self-deprecation. Hytham noticed as he spoke that Basim never took his eyes off either of the exits to the courtyard. Perhaps he wasn't as trusting as Hytham had feared. "Our organization is dedicated to the preservation of free will in any city on Earth, not just Constantinople," Basim continued. "If the emperor is interested in these same principles, I see no reason why we should ever come into conflict." He waited a beat, taking the barest sip of wine. "On the other hand, if the emperor were to have allied himself with certain parties wishing to suppress the will of the people and exert control over the government of the city, then I would be very concerned indeed."

"As should any conscientious citizen of New Rome," Hytham put in.

Demetrios raised his cup in acknowledgment.

Thyra considered them. "In that case, I will tell you I work for an individual who is concerned about the emperor's bloodthirsty tendencies, especially in regards to the way he attained his power," she said. "I assume you know to what I am referring?"

"Basil had his former co-emperor assassinated," Hytham said.

"It's not a well-kept secret," Basim added, "though of course there's no proof."

Did Thyra or the individual she represented have some connection to Michael the drunkard? Hytham wondered. It didn't seem likely, not unless the Vikings had been in the city a long time. What was Thyra getting at, then?

"There is no proof of what I would accuse him of either," Thyra said grimly, "but–"

"Proof is what we need you to obtain," interrupted a tall, broad-shouldered woman who loomed in the doorway to the courtyard. At her back was the man Thyra had sent out of the house a few minutes ago. That solved the mystery of his errand. The woman wore a hooded cloak that covered her hair and much of her features, but she tossed it back as she approached on the stone walkway, and though Hytham didn't recognize her, there was something undeniably regal about her bearing that made him rise to his feet automatically along with the others.

It was Demetrios who spoke first. "Pious Empress, you honor us with your presence in my home," he said, his voice gone faint with disbelief. He bowed deeply and then rose to pour more wine with hands that managed to shake only a little. Clearly, the man had not expected to be entertaining such guests today.

Hytham felt just as blindsided. The *empress* was the individual who wanted to meet with them? Uneasiness clawed at him. What had they walked into here? He suddenly felt how exposed they were, standing in this open courtyard.

But Basim didn't seem perturbed, or if he was, he hid it well. He offered his own bow as Demetrios placed a cup of wine in the empress's hands and guided her to a seat on the bench nearest him.

Thyra said, "May I formally introduce Empress Eudocia Ingerina, wife of Basil I and mother of Leo VI. Members of my clan and I serve the emperor and his family as part of the Varangian Guard."

"Would you care to sit?" the empress asked, when none of them moved. "I don't want to drink alone, and I'd rather not spend the rest of this conversation looking up at all of you."

There was an unmistakable note of amusement in her voice. It made Demetrios's shoulders loosen, and he smiled as they slowly resumed their seats.

"I'm sorry to have to employ such deception in arranging this meeting," the empress went on. She nodded to the Viking woman. "Thyra can be overly cautious, but in this case, I believe she was justified. I needed to know that you were the men I have been looking for and that you were trustworthy. I also deeply appreciate your hospitality, Demetrios, in providing a location that is safe from the eyes and ears of the palace." Her expression clouded. "Such places are becoming harder and harder to find these days."

Basim's lips curved in his own amused smile. "With respect, Honored Empress, you can't truly be sure that we are trustworthy. You took a great risk coming here."

Thyra spoke up. "If her faith turns out to be misplaced, the Varangian Guard will ensure that she comes to no harm from it."

It was not quite a threat, yet Hytham was keenly aware of the Viking warriors flanking Thyra, their hands on their weapons.

"I take you at your word," Basim said lightly, raising his hands. "Your reputation for your loyalty to the emperor precedes you." His look turned sly. "Yet, obviously, you're not here serving the emperor today."

Thyra's eyes narrowed, but the empress's husky laughter broke the tension. "I would ask that the two of you wait to draw blood until you've heard what I have to say." She turned to address Basim. "You're the troublemaker, then. The man I've heard whispers about. The man come to challenge the emperor." She sipped her wine, a gleam in her dark eyes. "I have been called a troublemaker myself, you know. I'm not well loved within the palace."

"That makes you all the more interesting," Basim said, and Hytham felt his jaw go slack. With an effort, he composed himself.

But the empress didn't seem to mind Basim's boldness. "'Too spirited', they say of me. 'Not the demure wife that will define the emperor's legacy.'" Her gaze sharpened on the two of them. "And yet I am here today – at great risk, as you observed – to serve the legacy of my family and the future prosperity of this city. I have cultivated allies among the Varangian Guard – Thyra most prominently – to help me work toward this end."

"You spoke of accusing the emperor," Hytham said, his gaze moving between Thyra and the empress. "What is it you believe he has done?"

He felt the weight of the empress's gaze on him. "Not what he's done, but what he intends to do," she said, her voice dropping. She set her wine cup on the bench beside her. "I believe the emperor intends to murder our son."

CHAPTER FIVE

"Murder a *child* – and his own heir?" Hytham's voice had risen, but he didn't notice until Basim shot him a look. He cleared his throat. "What possible reason could he have for that?"

"It's not a simple story." The empress paused, as if gathering her thoughts. Sunlight slanted across the courtyard, catching clouds of insects. Unseen birds rustled the branches of the trees.

"I was mistress to Michael during the time of his reign, before being given by him to Basil as wife," the empress began. Hytham noted the way her posture changed, shoulders back, body stiff as she related this information. No wonder. Hytham couldn't imagine what it would be like to be in her position, a pawn between two such powerful men. "I married him and bore him a son, as was expected," the empress went on. "Leo, though still a child, is co-emperor with Basil now and will be emperor outright after his father's death."

"Thus he also has the loyalty of the Varangian Guard," Basim interjected. "What an interesting conflict that presents." He glanced at Hytham and elaborated, "The Varangian Guard serve the *position* of emperor, offering their loyalty to that office rather than the man."

Hytham nodded in understanding. "So Thyra and the rest of the Vikings would owe equal loyalty to Basil and to Leo. If one were targeting the other for murder, it would put the Varangian Guard in an extremely difficult position."

"And so it has," Thyra said, and if her stormy expression was any indication, it was not a situation she enjoyed. The men with her kept their faces carefully blank, offering no comment.

"My husband sees no such conflict because he believes that Leo is *not* his son," the empress said. She lifted her chin in defiance. "Rumors have surrounded Leo since his birth, whispers that say he is the son of Michael, not Basil, that he will resurrect a dead man's bloodline and place it on the throne of New Rome." Her hands tightened in her lap, knuckles going white with anger. "My husband gave no credence to these rumors at first, but now things have changed. Now he can't stand to look at Leo. He says that the people whisper and laugh at him for raising a bastard son who will always stare at him with his true father's damning gaze."

Silence reigned in the courtyard in the wake of this pronouncement. Hytham glanced at Basim, but the man appeared to be in deep thought. None of them dared to ask the question he was sure had passed through everyone's mind: *was* Leo truly Michael's son?

"As you can see, the emperor has reason to want his son dead," Thyra said, giving the empress a moment to calm herself. "That is why we want you and your organization – your Hidden Ones – to take on the boy's protection. Yes, we know more of you than you think," she added when Hytham cocked his head in surprise. "Who you are and what you stand for matter less to me and mine than the fact that we share a common enemy."

"It sounds as if we do," Basim agreed, "and though I am sympathetic to your troubles, what are you offering me and my comrades for taking up your cause?"

Eudocia spoke before Thyra could answer. "The gratitude of an empress and the support of the future ruler of Constantinople." She couldn't quite summon a smile, but the amusement was back in her voice. "Surely that's a fair prize for you and your organization to claim?"

"It would be," Basim allowed, setting aside his wine, "but in your own words, you're asking us to risk much for a *future* ruler, one who may not live to ascend the throne, if what you say about Emperor Basil's hatred is true."

"If you are as good and your cause as righteous as you claim, you should have no difficulty protecting the boy," Thyra pointed out with a smile as sharp as her hand axe. "How hard can it be to guard the life of one child?"

Actually, the idea of protecting such a frail pawn in so large a game of politics was the last thing Hytham desired, but he didn't say so. He felt a brief stab of sympathy for the faceless boy whose life they discussed guarding and discarding so casually. None of this was his fault, yet he'd been marked by circumstances beyond his control.

Hytham considered Thyra's position in this game. To all appearances, she'd chosen Leo's side, and by extension the empress's, but why? The Vikings prized strength, and Leo was obviously the more vulnerable ruler. What was in this for her and her clan? And was the threat to Leo really as dire as they made it seem?

"You say that the emperor hates his son," Hytham spoke up, drawing Eudocia's gaze, "but how do you know he will resort to murder because of that hatred? Has he already made the boy a target?"

The empress sighed, and for an instant that erect posture and noble bearing slipped, and she was simply a tired mother pushed into deep waters that threatened to swallow her. "Nothing overt has happened," she said. "There have been… accidents. A few months ago, Leo fell down a steep flight of stairs. His guard had stepped away for a moment, so no one saw exactly what happened."

"Convenient," Basim observed.

"Quite," the empress said. "One of the servants who found him told me that when he first woke up, Leo said he'd been pushed. Later though, he remembered nothing about the incident, and when I went back to the servant, he said was mistaken, that the boy was just babbling nonsense because he'd struck his head on the floor. All I could do was dismiss the guard who'd left him alone and hope that was the end of it."

"But it was only the beginning?" Hytham guessed.

She nodded, a quick jerk of the head. "He was nearly trampled by a horse that had gotten loose when he went to visit the stables. His father said it was simply carelessness on the horse master's part and dismissed the woman in disgrace, though she vigorously protested her innocence."

"If the emperor *is* trying to kill the boy, he's being very subtle about it," Basim said. "It could be that he isn't involved at all. The palace is a world unto itself, and there are doubtless many people who are in a position to cause the boy harm. Are you certain you've ruled out any other potential enemies?"

Eudocia and Thyra exchanged a speaking glance. The empress shook her head at Thyra unhappily, but Thyra remained stone-faced.

"We can be certain of nothing, as you say," Thyra admitted at last. "We have no proof. But we believe the emperor is working with someone in the palace to have Leo killed. The Varangian Guard is powerful, but our movements are watched and our routines known. We're meant to be visible to deter attack. We're not used to working in secret. That's why we need you to find out who is targeting Leo and stop them."

"All of that we can do for you," Basim said, leaning forward, his hands held casually on his knees. "If the Honorable Empress can arrange a position for Hytham within the Varangian Guard, possibly as a new recruit, we can protect the boy and at the same time investigate the attempts on his life to see who is behind them."

Thyra considered the suggestion. "I could claim him to be an adopted member of the Eagle clan, someone to be trusted," she said, addressing the empress. "I would be willing to speak for him."

The empress nodded her thanks. "And I would give my approval. The emperor has many matters on his mind and would likely not pay a great deal of notice to a quiet shifting in the guards. Members do come and go, after all. It's not uncommon."

"What say you, Hytham?" Basim asked. "An infiltration mission, then?"

"Whatever is required," Hytham said.

Basim nodded. "But I say again, Honored Empress, for this service we need more than the promise of future support from your son."

"What would you ask of me then?" Eudocia said, her voice turning cold. "Jewels and riches for your Hidden Ones? My words in the emperor's ear to further your cause in the present? I can tell you I have much less sway than you even imagine."

Yet she'd managed to make a powerful ally in Thyra and the Varangian Guards, Hytham thought. Eudocia Ingerina was not to be underestimated.

"No," Basim said, glancing at Thyra. "What I want is the support of Thyra and her Eagle Clan as allies of the Hidden Ones."

Hytham kept his expression carefully neutral, but his thoughts were spinning as he glanced from Basim to Thyra. An alliance with a Viking clan, and by extension a foothold in the Varangian Guards, was an interesting request, and it would surely be to the Hidden Ones' benefit if such a thing happened – assuming Thyra and her clan were acting in good faith – but to Hytham's mind, it was beyond the scope of their mission here. Eudocia had given them the perfect opening for what they needed to accomplish. Their primary focus should be Leo and his protection, ensuring that he one day took the throne with the support of the Hidden Ones at his back. Alongside that task, they could work to root out the Order's presence in the city.

He said none of this, only waited to hear Thyra's answer.

The Viking woman was nearly as cagey as Basim, but her gaze turned calculating as she considered his proposal. She glanced at the empress, and another silent conversation seemed to take place before Thyra inclined her head.

"Should Leo be kept safe, an alliance between us would be a benefit to each," she said. "We are in agreement."

Left unspoken was what would occur should Leo *not* live to take the throne.

"Very good," Basim said. "I look forward to what we might accomplish together, Honored Empress."

"You have my gratitude," Eudocia replied, her gaze meeting Hytham's as she spoke.

They finished their wine, and soon after, the empress rose to leave, the two Vikings falling in behind her. Thyra hung back in the courtyard, waiting to speak again once the empress had departed.

"The empress and I will make the arrangements at the palace for your position as Leo's new guard," Thyra said to Hytham. "Come early tomorrow morning to the throne room for a formal audience with the empress. It will be as if we never met." She looked at Basim. "What of you?"

"Hytham has my complete confidence," Basim said, "but there are already eyes watching me. It will be better if I work from the shadows to find the person responsible for these 'accidents' while Hytham protects the boy more directly. Don't worry," he added, "I will always be close by."

"As you wish," Thyra said neutrally, and then she, too, left the courtyard.

Basim exchanged a few whispered words with Demetrios, thanking him for his hospitality and discretion, and then Basim and Hytham were suddenly alone, with only the scattered cups of wine as evidence that something momentous had occurred.

"What did you think?" Basim asked without preamble. He didn't specify which of the many revelations they'd been privy to was supposed to have caught Hytham's interest.

"I wasn't expecting to be conspiring with the empress and the Varangian Guard so soon after arriving in the city," Hytham said dryly. "You do work quickly."

"I'd hardly call it a conspiracy, my friend," Basim said, clapping him on the shoulder. "At least not yet. Basil is the one potentially trying to sabotage his own legacy in a misguided attempt to cleanse his bloodline."

"You don't believe the boy is truly Michael's son, then?" Hytham stood in the shadows of the olive trees, running his hand absently over the rough patches of bark.

"I think the emperor's word is the only thing that matters," Basim said with a shrug. "But isn't it interesting that Basil once gave no credence to these rumors of the boy's paternity?"

"Until recently," Hytham said. "Yes, I noted that. And the Order was all too ready to step in and lend their assistance again, just as they did when Basil needed Michael disposed of."

"Securing their place as the voice at the emperor's ear, poised to sway him to their will," Basim said, folding his arms and leaning against the tree opposite Hytham. "It doesn't say much for the emperor's judgment. Basil listens to whispers and lets voices that don't matter poison his thoughts. Constantinople has too many enemies for him to be focusing his rage inward this way."

Hytham couldn't help but agree. "Leo would make a better ally for the Hidden Ones," he agreed, "if he can be taught properly and protected. It's a risky plan, but the rewards are many if we succeed." He waited for Basim to mention his specific interest in allying with Thyra and her clan, but the silence stretched, and no explanation was forthcoming.

Did this have anything to do with the personal obsessions his mentor was concerned about in regard to Basim? Hytham wished again that he had more information about what Basim had been doing before they'd come together in Constantinople, but his superiors had been deliberately vague on those points.

He looked up from his inspection of the tree to find Basim watching him with a faint smile on his face. "You don't hide your worries well, Hytham," he said. "You don't like that I've chosen to trust Thyra and the empress." He shook his head. "But in fact, I've done no such thing."

"You were quick enough to make an alliance with them," Hytham pointed out, "and to create a situation where the two of us will be apart most of the time – you working in secret while I follow Leo about the palace. Under the circumstances, I can't think it's wise to divide us in such a way."

Unless you don't trust me either. He didn't say it, but the notion hung in the air between them. How would they be able to succeed at their mission if they couldn't rely on each other, and if he didn't know what Basim's true intentions were? And how would Hytham succeed in his personal mission to keep an eye on Basim if he was rarely in the man's presence?

"As I told Thyra, I have every confidence in you and your ability to protect the boy," Basim said, "and I meant what I said in that I won't ever be far away."

Hytham decided to be direct. He was tired of guessing games. "And your proposed alliance with Thyra's clan?" he asked. "What is that meant to accomplish?"

Basim shrugged. "I wanted to see what they would be

willing to give us, to weigh how desperate the situation is in their eyes. Also, I admit I am curious about the Vikings and their ways. I think that our brotherhood should know more about them and their culture. Much like the emperor, I believe they could be fierce allies if cultivated properly. I'd certainly rather we got to them first, before the Order."

Hytham couldn't argue with that. Maybe he was overthinking everything, looking for suspicious actions where there were none.

"Have you considered that there's another path the Hidden Ones could take to accomplish this mission?" Hytham asked carefully. "One that ensures Leo becomes emperor much sooner?"

"I had," Basim said simply.

Neither of them said it out loud. Even in the house of an ally, it was too risky. But they both knew that if Basil were to die in the coming days, Leo would become emperor, with the empress acting as regent until he came of age.

"It would be the quicker path," Hytham said, "but there are many risks."

"The instability it would create could throw the city into chaos," Basim agreed. "Constantinople's enemies may use the opportunity to attack, and the boy-emperor may become even more of a target than he already is." The smile he gave Hytham was rueful, teeth flashing white against his dark beard. "I think for now we must play the long game."

"I believe it would be best," Hytham said. "We should arrange to meet up regularly to share information about the palace," he said, shifting the conversation away from talk of assassination to safer subjects.

"We'll work out a system to signal each other in times of trouble as well," Basim said. "Try not to worry so much, Hytham. By this time tomorrow you're going to be a member of the Varangian Guard and have the run of the grand palace, an honor few can claim. I'm sure it will be an experience to remember."

CHAPTER SIX

Basim was right. Nothing could have prepared Hytham for seeing the palace up close the following day. Built by Constantine I, the structure had been continuously expanded by the emperors who had come after him until it was nearly a city within a city, a sprawling complex that abutted the southeastern sea walls and nestled near Hagia Sophia, creating a breathtaking collage of architecture rising above the rest of Constantinople.

Situated nearby was the great Hippodrome, where the spectacle of the chariot races took place. Four gilt-bronze horses stood in a frozen gallop in the air above the entrance, and a passage connected the palace directly to the emperor's private box. Though long past its heyday, the grand oval stadium was an impressive sight, even viewed from a distance as he and Basim observed the palace's outer walls and defenses.

"I wager you can see the entire city from up on its highest point," Basim said, following Hytham's gaze to the stadium. "A grand view. One I'd like to see someday."

"Agreed," Hytham said. He turned his attention to the palace. "What can we expect when we arrive?"

"For a start, we can expect hundreds of people coming and going daily just to keep the place running," Basim informed him as they stood in the shadow of a church, leaning casually against the building while the sounds of worship drifted out to the street. "There's a dedicated children's wing where the boy Leo will spend most of his days, although from what information we could obtain with the help of some carefully placed bribes, Leo also enjoys going exploring, and he loves visiting the Hippodrome."

"He likes the horses," Hytham murmured, remembering the incident Eudocia had related, when the boy had nearly been trampled. Impressed as he was at the sight before him, he scowled at the mighty palace. "Protecting this child will be like keeping a butterfly alive in a sandstorm."

Basim looked at him askance. "You're just now figuring that out?"

"I don't think I fully understood what we'd be walking into until I saw it for myself," Hytham admitted.

The palace was going to be just as dangerous, if not more so, than the city streets outside its walls. It was not a world Hytham was used to either. In Constantinople, though he was new to the city, Hytham felt he knew the rhythms of life and people. He knew what to expect and how to prepare for his enemies, just as he had in the marketplace. The world of palace politics, of waiting for a smiling face to offer you a knife in the back – he would have preferred a straightforward fight, or even the shadowy figures coming after them in a dirty back alley.

And at the heart of it all was a young child who had no idea how much danger he was in.

"I thought I would be a father once," he told Basim. He wasn't sure what impulse made him speak, to confide that bit of information that was surely trivial to Basim, but if the other man thought it strange, he didn't say so. Instead, he asked a question that took Hytham off guard.

"When did you realize you wouldn't walk that path?"

Hytham watched the traffic moving in and out of the towering palace gate, automatically noting how many people came and went, how many guards were stationed around the area and how closely the guards watched who was coming and going, even as he contemplated the answer.

"Probably the first time I killed a man," he said finally. "Maybe not that exact moment, but soon after. I knew that mine wasn't going to be a world fit for a child. It didn't bring me sorrow. I was at peace with the choice." He glanced at Basim thoughtfully. "When did you know your path?"

A shadow passed over Basim's expression then, something dark and distant that gave Hytham an inexplicable chill, a cold insight that Basim might once have had a family waiting for him, but no more.

"A long time before that," Basim said softly. "Yes, I found out long ago what precious things I could and could not keep."

And that was all he said.

The empress was true to her word. Hytham was summoned to the palace less than a day after he and Basim had finished their survey of it from the outside. With Hytham providing a brief distraction for the guards at the main gate, Basim also slipped inside and vanished, while Hytham was escorted into the palace and guided to one of what he learned were multiple throne rooms, this one set aside for the empress's use.

The palace was like another world. Hytham strode past glittering mosaics depicting scenes from daily life in Constantinople, his footsteps echoing on marbled floors polished to a flawless shine. The scent of fresh flowers filled the air wherever he went. The throne room itself was immaculate, with a domed ceiling situated above a mosaic in the center of the floor depicting an eagle with its talons outstretched. A gilded chair wrapped in purple silk sat on a raised dais at one end of the room.

The empress was already present and waiting for Hytham when he entered the room and bowed. Eudocia acknowledged him with a grave nod, but her expression gave away nothing, no hint that they had met the day before and plotted to protect her son from enemies who wanted him dead. Thyra was standing off to one side, alone, formally dressed this time in the scale mail of the Varangian Guard. Hytham relaxed slightly. So far, things were going well, and everyone was playing their parts to perfection.

Two other people entered the room just after Hytham, immediately drawing his attention as they came to stand at the bottom of the dais steps. The boy, he assumed, was Leo. The future emperor of Constantinople was short, skinny to the point of frailty, all bony elbows and knees – and young. Hytham hadn't expected him to be so young, though he was no great judge of children's ages. He met the boy's gaze across the room and was struck by the sharp watchfulness in his eyes, a spark of intelligence that made him suddenly seem older.

But it didn't change the fact that he was so very vulnerable, Hytham thought with a sinking weight in his gut. A frighteningly easy target for the Order of the Ancients, the boy looked as if a stiff breeze would snap him in half. Keeping him alive was going to be the biggest challenge Hytham had faced, and that was saying something, considering all that had happened to him during his time among the Hidden Ones.

Standing next to the boy was a lean man, not much past his twentieth year, in Hytham's estimation, with dark hair shorn close to his head and eyes the deep, penetrating blue of the Bosphorus. He was also dressed in the uniform of the Varangian Guard and had one hand casually braced on a short blade sheathed at his side.

For one so young, he seemed uncommonly severe in his expression, cold-eyed and suspicious as he regarded Hytham, but when the empress introduced him as Justin, the *former* head of Leo's guard detail and current subordinate to Hytham, he realized where the resentful expression came from. He'd expected to usurp someone's place in the hierarchy here – it was unavoidable, given the position he was taking on – but he hadn't expected the man to let his displeasure show so openly in front of the empress. Still, Hytham was determined to cultivate the man as an ally if he could, assuming Justin could be trusted. At this point, everyone near Leo was a suspect in Hytham's eyes.

He stepped forward and held out his hand to the man. Justin hesitated, then clasped Hytham's forearm and gave him a terse nod.

"Justin will show you the ways of the palace and go over your duties to my son," the empress said. She turned to the boy. "Leo, step forward and greet your new guardian properly."

A guardian. That was an interesting way of putting it. Hytham noted the softening of her voice, the obvious affection she had for the child.

Leo bowed to his mother, but before he moved toward Hytham, he glanced up at Justin, a hint of uncertainty in his eyes. Justin scowled down at the boy and gestured impatiently at Hytham. "We don't have time to waste, pup," he said in an undertone, the words clearly meant only for Leo, but Hytham heard them.

There was no love lost between the future emperor and this man, then. Interesting.

Reluctantly, Leo left Justin's shadow and visibly straightened up, as if he could make his bearing regal by sheer force of will. Head high, he approached Hytham, and to the boy's credit, Hytham didn't see his knees trembling until Leo stood right in front of him.

Hytham had his peaked hood thrown back, but with a day's growth of beard shadowing his cheeks and clothing so different from what the boy was probably used to seeing, he knew he looked intimidating to the child's eyes.

Smiling, he swept a graceful bow before the boy, and instead of rising, he went to one knee so the two of them could look each other in the eye. "Leo, honored son of the gracious Emperor Basil, I am glad to know you," he said. He was unsure of the proper etiquette for addressing the son of the emperor – he and Basim had not had time to go over the finer points of palace honorifics – but Eudocia appeared indifferent to his choice of words, and Thyra looked as if this were all a show that she couldn't wait to be done with.

Having overcome some of his initial fear, the boy was

regarding him with curiosity. "Guardian Hytham," he said, voice high-pitched, with only a slight wobble, "Mother says you've come here to protect my life. Does that mean you'll keep me from dying?"

The boy asked the question with all the innocence of the very young, and Hytham felt the shift in the room like a tangible thing, the tension crackling in the air. Eudocia's knuckles were white on the arms of her throne, and Justin had narrowed his eyes, looking even more resentful than before. Only Thyra seemed unfazed by the boy's unexpected pronouncement.

Hytham chose his words carefully. "As your honored mother says, I am to be your guardian. I, along with Justin and the other members of your guard, will ensure your safety at all times." He put a hand to his chest. "My life is yours, and I pledge myself to your protection."

The boy nodded solemnly and said, "I thank you." Then self-consciousness took hold of him again, and he fidgeted, blushing and looking to his mother for an indication of what to do next.

"Very good," Eudocia said. The empress rose and came down the stairs to stand at his side, and all present bowed again as she took her son's hand and led him from the room. Thyra followed behind them. Then it was just Hytham and Justin left in the throne room.

Justin's expression had lost none of its hardness as he regarded Hytham. "I'll start by showing you the children's wing," he said, all stilted politeness. He led the way out of the throne room without waiting for Hytham to agree. "There's too much to show you everything. It'll take you the first year just to keep from getting lost." His lip curled in a sneer as they turned down a wide hallway, past more sparkling mosaics and a line of graceful statues arranged like dancers at the start of a grand performance. "But don't worry. If you get turned around, just stop someone and ask directions. They'll put you right back on your way."

"I appreciate your consideration, but I think I can manage," Hytham said, smiling easily in the face of the man's patronizing tone. "You can show me as much as you like. I'm eager to learn."

There was, as it turned out, a great deal to see, and the mazelike hallways and sheer number of different rooms tested even Hytham's considerable capacity for memory.

They passed chapels where visiting monks prayed and conversed in hushed tones. Banquet halls and reception rooms were filled with a small army of servants cleaning and polishing the lavish furniture. Terraces looked out over formal gardens and peaceful courtyards thick with the sounds of birdsong and tinkling chimes. Baths and guest sleeping quarters gave way to study rooms, lecture halls, and a cavernous library that seemed capable of holding every book in the world.

Servants appeared at the top of cleverly concealed staircases bearing drinks, food, laundry, and any of the other hundreds of items required for daily living and entertaining in such a palace. They passed a guard barracks and training halls – Hytham caught glimpses of sparring matches and weapons inspections, and running throughout all the rooms and corridors was the constant sense of movement, of the place functioning like a miniature city, with people coming and going and rushing and visiting at all hours of the day.

That, added to what he'd already observed – easy access to

the open air, countless ways in and out of the palace rooms, hidden staircases, and a thousand faces that could hide an enemy.

The palace was a security nightmare.

It might have been very difficult for the common person to enter the palace without attracting the attention of several guards, but once inside, Hytham couldn't see where there were many restrictions, except when it came to the chambers of the emperor himself. That wing of the palace was quieter, and the guard presence much more keenly felt. Hytham sensed eyes upon him as he and Justin passed quickly by the emperor's chambers. Justin didn't mention stopping.

Hytham wondered what the emperor thought of the change in guard hierarchy for his son. Or were such matters truly beneath his notice at the moment, as the empress claimed? Perhaps the sheer size of the palace was how Eudocia was able to get him a place among the Varangian Guard so quickly. With so many moving parts needed to make the palace function, the hiring of one more guard, no matter his position, wasn't likely to draw much attention in the grand scheme of things. A few people shot him curious glances as he toured the palace in Justin's company, but their interest was quickly turned aside by their own duties.

Justin ended the whirlwind tour at an outdoor training yard, an open courtyard bounded by ornamental bushes and two trees whose branches met overhead to partially block the sun. A rack of weapons stood under a colonnade to his left. The training ground was deserted and looked as if it had been just recently tidied.

Hytham stepped out into the yard and turned in a slow

circle. Justin watched him, arms crossed. "You can use this area as a training ground," he said, "when you're not on duty."

Hytham realized this might be a good time to get some information, if he could. "Would you care for a match?" he invited, gesturing to the freshly cleaned yard.

Justin eyed him suspiciously, but then he shrugged and came out to stand across from Hytham. He drew his sword, finding his stance, but the tension in his shoulders was unmistakable.

Hytham drew his own sword and the two nodded to each other. "Are we going to have a problem?" Hytham asked as they came together, his sword skimming off the edge of Justin's blade.

"Why would there be a problem?" Justin lunged low, then just as quickly danced out of Hytham's reach. He was fast on his feet, always in motion, but there was an economy to his movements that Hytham admired. Justin didn't waste energy, and he wasn't letting himself be distracted by conversation or the emotions clearly simmering just beneath the surface of his carefully controlled demeanor.

"It's obvious you believe I've taken your place at Leo's side. That was not my intention. I'm only here to see to the boy's protection." Hytham blocked another strike, this time feeling more of Justin's strength behind the blow. The young man was holding back, not giving everything to the fight yet as he measured his opponent. Hytham admired that too.

"You *have* taken my place," Justin said, biting off the words, "but if you think this post will win you favor with the emperor, then I pity you."

He came in viciously then, three sharp swings that set

Hytham back on his heels, weaving as the weapon cut the air inches from his face. Hytham couldn't allow himself to become distracted either, but his words were working, getting under the younger man's skin.

"You don't think the emperor's son is worthy of protection?" Hytham asked lightly, continuing to bait the man.

Justin's expression darkened. His sword came down and Hytham ducked. Justin had almost backed him to the wall of the training yard. Good. Hytham pivoted and jumped, pushing off the wall and landing several feet away, out of Justin's immediate reach. The move also gave Justin the space to reply.

"The boy is a weakling," he said, his breath labored. "One so frail will likely not live to see manhood, let alone have the ruling of this city. You've done yourself no favors coming here."

Hytham was taken aback. To speak like that inside the palace, where anyone – namely the empress – might hear, was brazen.

Unless Justin knew it didn't matter. If he knew the extent of the father's hatred for the son, then perhaps he knew he wouldn't be reprimanded for his words.

The question was, did he know enough to conspire with the emperor to kill the boy?

But Hytham didn't press his questioning. Justin's face had closed off, and Hytham knew he'd get no more answers today. It was time to end the match.

Justin came at him again, and Hytham caught his blade and twisted it out of his hand. It clattered on the ground several feet away, and for a second, Justin stared at it lying there, glittering in the sun, as if he couldn't fathom what had happened. He glanced up at Hytham, and a brief hint of something ugly flashed in his eyes as he realized Hytham had just been toying with him.

Hytham braced himself for whatever came next. Would Justin attack him in earnest, crossing the line from sparring to true fighting?

But in the end, Justin released a long breath and relaxed his stance, bending to retrieve his sword from the dirt in an impressive show of dignity. He was certainly someone to watch here in the palace.

"You fight well," Hytham said, no lie in his words. "I wish I possessed your speed and reflexes."

Justin gave a bitter laugh. He turned his back on Hytham, putting his sword away. "Come, I'll take you to the children's wing now," he said, as if nothing had happened between them. "Your first guard shift will start soon. I'm sure you won't want to be late."

CHAPTER SEVEN

The children's wing of the palace was its own block of rooms carefully set off from the rest of the public areas, and Hytham was pleased to discover that it was almost as heavily guarded as the emperor's rooms, though there was still too much access to the servants' areas and to the outside, with a set of informal gardens for Leo to play in connected to the bedrooms.

The only thing missing from the children's wing when they arrived was Leo himself. Hytham felt a trickle of anxiety when he saw neither Thyra nor the boy where they were supposed to be, but Justin didn't seem concerned. He led Hytham down a short hall to a room that was a miniature version of the grand library they'd passed earlier. Thyra stood just inside, watching the scene taking place with a bored expression.

A long rectangular table dominated the center of the room. Leo sat behind it, surrounded by stacks of maps, a wax tablet covered in writing, and at least a dozen books, everything from grammar to arithmetic to Homer's *Iliad*. A middle-aged man stood beside Leo, a slight hunch to his stance. He had dark hair gone silver at the temples and thick brows that gave him an intent, somber look. He bent over the table, directing the boy with one thick knuckle to a certain passage in a book. The boy nodded, eyes skimming the page, reading the indicated paragraph to himself.

"Always a safe bet you'll find the boy here when you don't know where else to look," Justin said.

Leo glanced up quickly from the book, having only just noticed their entrance. He caught Justin's eye and flinched at whatever he saw in the man's expression. "I'm sorry, Justin," he said. "I only wanted to go over the agriculture lesson Theodore started this morning because I had some questions. It's really very fascinating."

The boy hefted the massive book in front of him, as if intending to show them both something written on the page, but Justin held up a hand impatiently, and the boy dropped the book with a loud thud on the table.

"I don't care about your lesson, pup," he said, again using the demeaning nickname. "I just brought your new minder. Pester him about your studies."

Hytham ground his teeth. He didn't like the way Justin stared the boy down until Leo ducked his head, flushing a deep crimson. Justin was a skilled fighter, but a man who stooped to bullying a child as small as Leo would never earn his respect.

"No matter," Hytham said easily, crossing the room until he stood on the opposite side of the table from Leo and his tutor – Theodore, the boy had called him. "I was just doing some teaching myself, taking Justin's measure in the training yard."

Out of the corner of his eye, Hytham saw Justin stiffen, anger visible in every line of his body.

Good.

"Oh, thank you for the tour and conversation, Justin," Hytham said over his shoulder, offhand, as if he'd already forgotten the man was there. "It was enlightening. I can handle things from here."

A charged silence took over the room, and for a moment Hytham didn't think Justin was going to leave. He glanced back at the man expectantly, but it was Thyra's expression that caught his attention. A smile twitched at her lips as she leaned back against the wall, clearly enjoying the little power struggle.

Thankfully, the moment passed, and whatever tension there was broke as Justin spun and marched out of the room, dragging his displeasure with him.

"Well then," Hytham said, clasping his hands together amiably, "will you show me that book of yours, Leo?" He took a risk, dropping the honorifics in addressing the boy, but he got the sense he wouldn't be corrected, at least not by anyone in this room. Throughout his exchange with Justin, Theodore had been idly paging through another book, looking utterly uninterested in the pissing contest being conducted around him.

Hytham was rewarded when Leo brightened, shifting forward eagerly in his chair. "Theodore was telling me the similarities and differences in corn varieties," he said, "before we moved on to processes for cultivating olives and making oil. It's completely fascinating." He sounded as if he meant it.

Skimming his gaze over the text Leo pointed out, Hytham would not have called it particularly "fascinating" reading.

In fact, he would have called it words to fall asleep to, but maybe the boy and his tutor saw something in the text that he didn't.

He *was* intrigued by the boy's vocabulary. Though young, he obviously read on his own and was well read at that. It was also clear he took pleasure in the act and wasn't forced to it like some children. He would be a scholarly ruler, if he made it to the throne.

The Hidden Ones could use a scholar's mind in Constantinople, with concealed blades behind it for strength. A potent combination.

"What is the lesson on farming your tutor was giving when we interrupted?" Hytham asked politely, to keep the boy talking and to put him at ease. Leo was animated and happy when he was talking about a subject he obviously enjoyed, and he was no longer flushed with embarrassment.

"Theo was teaching me what is required to feed a city," the boy said matter-of-factly, oblivious to the tutor's good-natured wince at the nickname. His brow furrowed. "There is quite a lot involved."

Hytham pursed his lips to hide his smile. "Wise of you to recognize that," he said.

The boy wore a determined look. "I've memorized the lesson, though," he said, "and the planting tables and weather guides by season. You can ask me anything," he added, in the tone of a child desperate for a chance to impress an adult.

"Very well," Hytham said, considering for a moment what he knew of farming techniques. He cocked his head. "Here is my question. How do you decide who to feed if the crops fail, and there isn't enough food for everyone?"

The boy already had his mouth open to reply when Hytham's question sank in. His eyes widened, and he fell silent. Obviously, he'd been expecting the answer to be found in his book, something he could easily recall and recite. He looked down at the text in front of him, then up at his tutor, who nodded encouragingly.

"It's a fair question," Theodore said. He glanced up at Hytham curiously, as if he'd only just realized the man was in the room and not a piece of furniture.

But Hytham wasn't worried about the tutor. He was waiting for the boy's response.

"That isn't a question about agriculture," Leo said at last, and there was a pinched, stubborn look to his face.

"But it is an important part of the question of how to feed a city," Hytham said. "Think about it. For now, you're wanted at dinner. Perhaps you can show me the way to the dining hall. I'm still learning the geography of the palace."

This wasn't true. Hytham knew exactly how far the small library was from the dining hall, and the dining hall from Leo's bedchamber. A phantom map of the palace halls appeared before his mind's eye to confirm it. But he didn't mind the people here thinking he was less competent than he actually was. He also knew it would please the boy to demonstrate his knowledge since he hadn't been able to answer Hytham's question.

Leo immediately brightened again and, with a quick glance at his tutor for permission, he jumped up and came around the table. He stopped short next to Hytham, reaching out a hand, but just as quickly he froze and checked the gesture, ducking his head and putting his hands behind his back instead.

Hytham pretended not to notice the aborted gesture and led the way out of the library.

The palace showed another face once night fell. The hustle and rush of the servants coming and going gave way to the arrival of guests and the commencement of lavish entertainments. The banquet halls filled up with revelers, and the libraries and receiving rooms were roped off for private meetings or gossip. Music swelled from several different chambers to mingle in a way that somehow managed to be harmonious, despite all the different pieces playing at once.

Hytham assumed the emperor and empress would be receiving guests in the main dining hall, but he had yet to catch a glimpse of either. Leo ate in a separate room that must have been considered sparse by palace standards but was still a more finely laid table than Hytham had ever eaten at in his entire life, and it was absurdly large for the child who currently sat under the watchful eye of his nurse.

The meal itself doubled as an education in manners and decorum. Hytham found himself bored to tears. Standing in the shadows at the back of the hall and watching a young child eat had not been in his imaginings when he'd dreamt of being a deadly Assassin fighting for a noble cause.

The only person in the room who seemed to be having less fun was Leo himself, fidgeting in his silk brocade dalmatica, sitting stiffly in his chair while the nurse paced back and forth, correcting his posture or admonishing him to keep his mouth shut while he ate.

But the nurse herself did interest Hytham. She was tall, with narrow shoulders and thick brown hair that she kept tied back and pinned. Leo had spoken of her briefly before they entered the dining hall to say that her name was Anna and that she was deaf in her right ear, so he shouldn't startle her by approaching from that side. Hytham took in the information along with the rest of what he knew about her, which wasn't much, but the most important bit, to his mind, was that she had the closest access to Leo and spent more time with him than anyone else in the palace.

Which meant she was automatically Hytham's prime suspect.

He watched her come around the table and place her hands on Leo's shoulders to get him to straighten up yet again. She must have felt his eyes on her then, because she looked up and met his gaze across the room. Her throat bobbed as she swallowed, but she didn't speak, just continued to stare with an intent expression.

Then Leo sloshed his soup on the table, stammering an apology that made Anna turn away, and the moment was broken. Hytham shifted, sliding further into the shadows.

"Frightening the servants already?"

The chuckling voice was barely a whisper, raising the hairs on the back of Hytham's neck. He didn't have to turn to know that it was Basim, hidden in the shadows somewhere behind him, his presence concealed from everyone else in the room.

And Hytham hadn't detected him either. He was that good.

Hytham felt a rush of admiration and embarrassment in equal measure. He hated to be caught off guard by anyone, even an Assassin above his rank.

"I didn't intend to frighten her," Hytham whispered back without turning. "Perhaps it's because my face is new."

"Or she has something to hide," Basim said. His voice had moved slightly to the left, probably so he could get a better view of the table. "But I was jesting. I believe she may have been looking at you with interest, my friend. Perhaps you should cultivate that interest."

It would be one way to get close to her and watch to see if she was a traitor, but Hytham thought Basim was off the mark. He thought it far more likely he'd simply startled the woman by lurking so quietly in the shadows.

"Where have you been today?" Hytham asked quietly. He was sure that whatever Basim had been doing, it had to be far more interesting than this dining lesson.

"I watched your new friend Justin for a time," Basim said, voice heavy with amusement. "You'll be shocked to learn he hates you and doesn't mind saying so to whomever will listen to him."

Hytham shrugged. "He was well on his way to hating me before we ever set foot in the training yard," he said. "I thought it might be wise to send a message early in our relationship."

"Agreed," Basim said, accepting the explanation with no further comment. Hytham had a momentary pang of guilt. Although the reasoning was sound, if he was being honest, that wasn't his true motive for calling out Justin.

He'd done it because he hadn't liked the way the man had talked to Leo in the throne room. And the way he'd spoken of the boy during their sparring match had sealed his low opinion of Justin.

Hytham told himself the motive didn't matter. He'd accomplished what he'd set out to do, and he'd accept the consequences if and when they came.

"Will you be spending the night in the palace then?" Hytham asked, and received only silence in answer. Basim had slipped away again, like a ghost.

Blessedly, the dinner and lesson seemed to be drawing to a close. One of the servants had brought out a sweet cake and some fruit, and Anna moved away from the table to let Leo eat in peace.

She was headed his way, in fact, her attention spearing him this time like a fish on a stick.

Interesting.

Hytham inclined his head at her approach. "You handle the child well," he said. "He listens to–"

She cut him off with a raised hand and a glare, looking every inch the teacher set to scold the student. "You can keep your flattery to yourself," she said, her voice low and full of anger. "I don't know what you did to get Justin replaced, but if you hurt or neglect that child, I'll see that you answer for it. Do you understand me?"

Hytham was shocked and impressed all at once. He had easily seven inches on the woman, and he knew how intimidating he looked to people who didn't know him well. Yet Anna had her finger a hair's breadth from poking him in the chest, her other hand on her hip as if all she wanted was a weapon sheathed there.

Hytham was glad she didn't have one, at least not that he could see.

At his silence, her frown deepened. "You don't have nearly as much power here as you think," she hissed. "We're none of us helpless in this place, and some of us have the ear of higher powers."

He raised his hands in a placating gesture. "Mistress, I don't know what it is I've done to earn your wrath, but you have it wrong. I intend no harm or neglect to Leo."

So Anna was also aware of the danger to the boy. That stood to reason – she was the child's nurse, and she had eyes. She'd probably been nearby for each of Leo's "accidents".

But had she helped bring them about? This could all be a very convincing act, as far as Hytham was concerned.

Anna sighed and smoothed her hands down the front of her dress. She looked up at him and shook her head helplessly. "Not like I can judge which of you is better anyway," she said, half to herself. "You're all just…" she let the thought die and started to turn away.

"Wait," Hytham said, keeping his voice low so Leo wouldn't hear. "Are you saying you have reason to distrust Justin?"

She glanced back at him, her expression guarded. "Maybe ask him where he goes some nights when he disappears after his shift," she said. "He thinks no one notices, but there are eyes all over this place."

And with that she left him, clapping her hands to get Leo's attention.

CHAPTER EIGHT

The parties lasted long into the night.

Hytham stood outside Leo's door, which was left slightly ajar so he could glance inside to see the boy sleeping safe in his bed. Thankfully, there were no windows in the boy's room, but there was another door that led down a short corridor to storage rooms and the entrance to a servants' stair. This he'd made sure was locked and rigged to make plenty of noise if it was opened in the night.

Now he stood, watching and listening to the slowly fading sounds of revelry as the palace found its way to some bit of restfulness in the quietest hours of the night. Thyra had gone to get some sleep but would be back by dawn.

Of Basim, there was no sign either, but Hytham had the strangest feeling the man was somewhere nearby, even if Hytham would never know it. In fact, he wouldn't put it past Basim to have made his way as far as the emperor's chambers just to have a look around.

A soft sound brought Hytham's hand to his sword hilt even as he readied himself to trigger his Hidden Blade. Senses straining, he listened for the sound again, something apart from the noises of the party guests.

He heard it again, and this time he was sure it came from the boy's room. Hytham pushed the door further open to slip inside.

A night candle illuminated Leo on his bed, hunched in on himself under the blankets, trembling and making small whimpering sounds. Hytham automatically scanned the room for threats, but there was no one else there.

Leo was having a nightmare. As Hytham's eyes adjusted to the dim light in the room, he saw the boy's eyes were screwed tightly shut. He was fully in the grip of whatever dream tormented him.

Now that he knew there was no danger to confront, Hytham stood there a moment, indecisive. He didn't want to frighten the boy by waking him, but nightmares were hell, and it was clear no one else was near enough to have heard Leo's distress.

He started to leave to fetch Anna – her room was at the opposite end of the hall where he'd been stationed – when he heard Leo gasp. He turned back to the bed to find the boy's eyes open wide with terror, staring at him.

"It's all right," Hytham whispered, realizing belatedly he still had his hand on his sword. He dropped both hands to his sides and cautiously went down on one knee next to the bed so the boy could see his face clearly in the candlelight. "It's only me. You were having a nightmare."

But either the words didn't reach him or the dream still held him in its grip, because the boy began to tremble. Tears welled in his eyes.

Hytham sighed and reached out to smooth sweaty strands of hair out of the boy's face, hoping the gesture would comfort and wake him more fully.

The boy surged up and locked his arms around Hytham's neck.

Hytham had been an Assassin for years now. As a consequence, he was used to keeping people a safe distance from his person most of the time, unless he explicitly allowed them close, which he rarely did. So, it took a degree of effort not to flinch and thrust the boy away when Leo grabbed him. Hytham forced his heart to calm, his tense muscles to relax. No threat, he told himself. No danger. It's all right.

Awkwardly, he patted the boy's back. "You're safe," he whispered. "It was only a dream. Nothing in a dream can harm you."

Yet something *had* hurt him deeply. Leo was crying in earnest now, but he was doing it in silence, face buried in Hytham's shoulder. Hytham had not been around many children, but he'd never seen a child Leo's age cry like this, as if he didn't dare draw attention to himself, but he just couldn't stop. The idea of it brought a twisting ache to Hytham's chest that he did not want to feel.

But neither was he made of stone.

He let Leo cry in that restrained way for as long as he wanted, keeping one eye out for any dangers, making soothing circles on Leo's back with his hand. Heaven knew the boy could probably use a friendly face in this place.

Finally, after what seemed to Hytham like hours but was

probably only a few minutes, Leo cried himself out and sat back, blinking up at Hytham in some confusion, as if he'd forgotten the man was even there and he'd been crying against a statue all this time. His face was a tapestry of red splotches and puffy skin, but he didn't seem to care.

"Do you want to tell me about your dream?" Hytham asked, because it didn't seem as if the boy was going to speak. "Sometimes talking about it can make the nightmares feel less terrifying."

Leo lifted a corner of his blanket and wiped his face. "I was in the dark," he said, his small voice raspy from sobs. "I knew I was dreaming – I always know. I tried to wake myself up. Sometimes if I scrunch my eyes shut tight and then open them wide, I can actually do it." He demonstrated for Hytham, who couldn't help but smile at the sight of the boy's comically wide eyes. Then Leo's expression twisted into misery. "When I tried this time, the voice came."

"The voice?" Hytham prompted, feeling a prickle at the back of his neck.

"It said I wasn't ever going to wake up." Leo bit his lip on a shuddering breath. "The voice said it wouldn't let me. I would be lost in the dark forever."

"A bad nightmare," Hytham agreed. Especially for one so young – too young for that dark a dream. "But you did wake up, so the voice was lying." He reached out to the bedside table and brought the night candle closer. "You found your way back to the light."

The boy stared at the flame wavering with his breath. "I did," he said, a note of wonder and pride in his voice. "You're right. The voice was lying." He shivered. "I still hate it."

Hytham nodded gravely. "I don't blame you. Do you think you can go back to sleep now?"

"Maybe." Leo looked up at Hytham curiously. "Justin never came into my room when I had a nightmare."

Hytham wasn't shocked to hear it. "You have nightmares often then?"

"Almost every night." Leo's hands fisted in his blanket. "Anna says I'll grow out of them."

"She's probably right," Hytham said, "but until you do, try to remember that I'm nearby to protect you. You're safe."

The boy looked away, frowning. "You're not a real guardian though, no matter what Mother says. You protect me because you're paid to. You don't really care if I live or die."

Hytham wasn't expecting the words or the bitter note in the boy's voice. Then he remembered the stack of books in the small library, the stories of heroes and great warriors Leo was being raised on. Perhaps Hytham had more to live up to here than he'd thought.

"It's true that I'm paid for my services," Hytham said, feeling his way through the conversation. This was as good an opportunity as any to start the boy's education in a different sort of hero and ideology. "I'm skilled with weapons, and I have speed and strength. Like any craftsmen working at their trade, I use these talents to serve others, and so I am paid just as they are." He paused and leaned forward, as if he meant to impart a secret. Despite his frown, the boy inched closer to hear it. "But I have also sworn myself to a lifelong cause, a creed that says I will protect the freedom of others, even at the cost of my life. It is a higher purpose than anything I might do for coin or other earthly rewards."

"A higher purpose?" the boy echoed, still sounding doubtful, but Hytham could tell he'd piqued his interest. "What does that mean?"

Hytham shifted so he was sitting on the edge of the bed, reaching out to tuck the blankets over Leo. "It means that even if I were not being paid, I would still protect you from the voices in the dark that threaten you," Hytham said. He pasted on a mock scowl. "And I can be very intimidating when I want to be." He replaced the candle on the bedside table. "I'll tell you more another time. You should sleep now."

When he reflected on it later, Hytham would say that it was the candlelight that saved them. The dancing flame cast long shadows on the wall and revealed a dark, sinuous shape cresting the foot of the bed. Serrated scales contrasted sharply with the pale blankets. Hytham's mind registered that it was a viper at the same instant Leo saw the creature slithering into his bed.

The boy sucked in a breath to scream, but Hytham was quicker. He leaned over and grabbed the boy, covering Leo's mouth to stifle the cry. Vipers of this type were known to be aggressive, and the sudden commotion would do nothing but provoke the creature.

"Stay still," he growled. He could feel the boy's heartbeat rabbiting in his chest, but Hytham gave no thought to comforting him at the moment.

Time slowed, but Hytham's thoughts raced – *stay still, wait it out, use the blanket as a shield if it comes close enough to strike.* A dozen different scenarios played out in his head while the snake wove uncertainly along the foot of the bed, as if it couldn't figure out where it was. As it moved, its scales made a soft hissing sound as they rubbed against each other.

Hytham felt Leo's rigid body tremble. The boy wouldn't stay calm forever. It was too unsettling, this creature out of a nightmare coming into his room in the dark.

Just wait. Just a little more.

The viper's tongue flicked out. It slowed, curling in on itself, and Hytham was silently screaming at it to move, to be gone.

His gut clenched as instead it inched its way up the bed toward the tent in the blanket where the boy's feet were.

Damn it all.

Hytham tightened his grip on Leo and began easing his way slowly to his feet. No choice but to get the boy clear. The thing was too close and too agitated. Slowly, painfully slowly, he rose to his feet with the boy dangling from his grip, easing the blanket off his body.

The snake jerked as the blanket lifted, striking at the cloth. It was a small movement, but it broke Leo's fragile calm. He thrashed in Hytham's arms, whimpering and kicking at the cloth to get free. The movement jostled the snake and it whipped around to strike at Leo.

Hytham didn't think. He pivoted and dropped the boy, pushing him into a corner of the room. Then, Hytham spun back around, snapping the blanket up to use as a shield, just as he'd hoped. He had a fleeting impression of the snake's open jaws snapping at the cloth before it and the blanket fell in a tangle on the floor.

Immediately, the snake wriggled free and snapped at Hytham's boot. He danced back, put his right hand out, and the Hidden Blade sprang free. Skidding to his knees, Hytham swept his hand across his body as the snake rose up, cutting it in half in a single swipe. He was back on his feet in an instant, kicking the severed halves of the body aside, careful to avoid the milky, venomous liquid still glistening on the fangs.

When the thing had stopped wriggling, resting in a shallow pool of blood, Hytham spun to check on Leo. He knelt next to the boy, who'd pressed himself as far into the corner of the room as he could get, knees drawn up to his chest. His face was a tight mask of fear.

"Are you hurt?" Hytham asked. Leo shook his head. Hytham checked the rest of him over quickly to make sure he hadn't been bitten by the snake.

"What is … that?" the boy asked, breathless. He was staring wide-eyed at Hytham's blade, still visible from the underside of his wrist, glistening with beads of blood. Quickly, Hytham wiped the weapon on the discarded blanket and retracted it.

"Stay there," Hytham said, rising to his feet. He went to the door and looked out in the hall, searching for more enemies. His every sense was on alert. He didn't believe for a moment that snake had gotten into the boy's bedchamber by accident. "Thyra," he barked in the direction of her bedchamber, praying the woman was a light sleeper. He didn't want to leave Leo.

There was a stirring, and Thyra's door opened. He could just see the woman's silhouette by the candlelight in the hall. "What is it?" Her voice was scratchy from sleep, but she was fully alert.

"We have a problem. Come down here and stay with the boy," Hytham said, ducking back inside the bedchamber without waiting for a reply.

Leo had gotten to his feet and was staring at the dead viper, though he'd been smart enough not to get any closer. Hytham snapped his fingers to get the boy's attention – Leo appeared dazed, as if he thought this might all turn out to be another nightmare.

"Stay with Thyra," Hytham told him, just as the woman pushed open the door. She was fully dressed, though she had no armor. She took in the room and the dead snake, her eyes narrowing.

She reached out to the boy, who came immediately and pressed himself against her hip. "It's all right," she said roughly. "We'll get rid of it."

Hytham was already across the room, unlocking the rigged door to the servant's hallway. Someone releasing the viper would have done it out here where it could easily slip under the door into Leo's room.

The hall outside was dark. Some of the candles had been extinguished. Hytham crept out, sword ready, looking for anyone lurking nearby. He moved quickly down the hall, rounding a corner to see a dark shadow crouched at the top of the servant's stair. He braced himself for an attack, but the figure didn't move. When he approached, he realized it was an older woman, her long gray hair coming loose from its pins. She was slumped against the wall. Hytham edged closer, still braced for an attack, but as he crouched beside her, he realized she no longer breathed, though he could see no visible marks on her. No blood either.

Reaching out, he took hold of her shoulder and turned her gently toward him.

The second viper was still latched onto the hollow of her throat, its jaw distended, fangs jerking in her flesh as twin blood trails rolled down her chest.

Hytham reared back as the snake, jostled by the movement, instinctively released and struck at him, but it was caught, tangled in a cord around the woman's neck. A carved wooden crucifix dangled from the end of the cord, pressed tight against the snake's body. The woman's face was frozen in a death mask of terror, lips pulled back from her teeth, hands clenched into claw-like curls at her sides. She'd likely either died by the snake's venom or by some kind of heart failure brought on by it.

Hytham cursed. He sat back on his heels, out of reach of the thrashing creature, tasting bile in his throat. Two venomous snakes. How many more of them were there?

"Everything all right?" Thyra said from down the hall. Leo peeked out the door around her to see what was happening.

"Keep the boy back!" Hytham snarled, positioning his body to block the horrible scene. "Take him with you and wake the rest of the guards. We need more lights and searchers for the rest of this area. Now!"

He heard Thyra murmur something to the boy, and the door closed behind them. Hytham flexed his fingers around his sword hilt, moving back in toward the dead woman and the snake. He took a deep breath, willing his nerves to settle. Reaching out with the sword, he swiftly cut the pendant's cord from around the woman's neck. The snake wriggled free, slithering over the woman's body toward the stairs.

"I'm sorry," he muttered, bringing the sword down to kill the second snake. "This wasn't your fault."

But someone was going to answer for what had happened tonight. Hytham started to reach for the dead snake when he heard footsteps pounding up the nearby stairs.

Acting purely on instinct, Hytham swung toward the

sound, and the shadow of the figure coming up toward him flinched. Hytham had his hand outstretched, ready to trigger the Hidden Blade, when the shadow leaned out into the sparse light, illuminating Justin's pale, shocked face.

Hytham only just managed to check the strike when he saw the young man was obviously not intent on violence. He dropped his arm to his side, and the two of them stared at each other, frozen. Justin had not yet come to the top of the stairs, so Hytham was standing slightly above him. The young man didn't move, though his gaze flicked to Hytham's right arm. He'd obviously seen Hytham's aborted move for the weapon, even if he hadn't glimpsed the blade itself.

"What are you doing out here?" Hytham demanded. "It's not your shift tonight. You shouldn't be here." He didn't bother to hide the accusation in his tone.

Justin's eyes narrowed. "I heard you shouting at Thyra to wake everyone," he said. "Is Leo all right?"

"Leo", not "pup" tonight. Yes, he was wise not to use the word in front of Hytham, especially considering the mood Hytham was in right now.

"He's fine," Hytham said. "He–"

But Justin had glanced around Hytham, and his gaze fell on the old woman's body and the dead snake. He sucked in a breath. "I see. There could be more of them. I'll get Leo out of here."

The corridor was narrow. Justin moved passed Hytham, attempting to shoulder him out of the way.

Hytham's arm shot out, snagging Justin by his tunic like a commander grabbing a new recruit. He yanked him back and put his other hand to Justin's chest, pinning him to the wall.

Fury sparked in the young man's eyes, and he tensed to strike back.

But then he glimpsed Hytham's expression, face close to his in the dark. Hytham had three inches on Justin, but that wasn't what made the young man hesitate. For all that Hytham could be a gentle man – cruelty was counter to his nature – he knew how to project the cold detachment of the Assassin looming over his target, how to make his enemy understand that he would not survive the encounter. It could make the difference in a close fight, by making your opponent believe their defeat was inevitable. Battles were won and lost in the mind as often as with a blade.

He used a bit of that lethal expression on Justin now, here in the dark, where there was no one else for him to bully. He used it to let the young man know that if he attacked, the outcome would not be pleasant for him.

"Stay here," was all Hytham said to him in the end. He stepped back, releasing Justin, and gestured down at the dead woman. "Keep this area clear of anyone but guards. *I'll* see to Leo."

Then he walked away.

CHAPTER NINE

The next few hours before dawn were a strange mix of activity. As word about what happened spread among the servants and aristocrats alike, the remaining strains of music and revelry died, and guests were ushered quickly out of the palace with apologies and in some cases lavish gifts to ensure there was as little gossip accompanying them as possible. Most of them were tired, drunk, or both, and happy enough to go home to their own beds without asking too many questions.

Meanwhile, the servants moved like ghosts through the palace halls, removing the body of the servant woman – a candle lighter who came through the halls at night to check the tapers and tidy up wax spills. The other servants cleaned up after the body was gone and removed the dead snake from the hall and the one from Leo's room. The boy stayed with Thyra through this while Hytham waited for Basim to find him. He didn't want to risk signaling the man with the night bird's call they'd agreed on to find each other around the palace. He didn't want to draw any undue attention to either of them right now.

When Basim found him at last, Hytham was in the children's garden, checking the shrubs and flowers for signs of vipers, though he didn't expect to find any at this point. The servants and guards had mounted an effective search, and no other snakes had been found loose in the palace. The old woman had been the only victim.

"Hardly an auspicious start to your duties as guardian," Basim said. Hood up, he leaned against the high garden wall, where ivy clung and trumpet-shaped flowers snaked across the cool stone. Hytham stood beside him, watching the palace and listening to the sounds of muted footsteps moving through the halls.

"If the boy hadn't had that nightmare, he'd probably be dead now," Hytham said.

Basim cocked his head. "If the boy hadn't been thrashing around and whimpering, maybe the snake wouldn't have become so agitated," he said. "It's the whims of fate, my friend. You were there when you were needed. That's all that matters."

"Do you think the emperor will try to pass this off as another unfortunate accident?" Hytham asked. Word had spread among the servants that the emperor and empress were aware of the situation, but no one had seen them outside their rooms yet.

"He probably will, but if I were in the emperor's place, I would be getting impatient," Basim said. "These attempts to kill the boy strike me as being clumsy, relying too much on luck. They're certainly the work of a palace insider hired by the Order to do their bidding, not the Order of the Ancients themselves."

Hytham went still, considering. "You believe, with the emperor facing yet another failure, he might be looking for more direct intervention in his problems?"

"Perhaps, which may in turn strengthen the Order of the Ancients' involvement in the conspiracy. They'll want to keep the emperor happy if they hope to retain him as an ally. I'm sure your presence and your actions have also complicated things." Basim sighed. "I predict you'll be summoned to receive the emperor's thanks at dawn."

Hytham glanced at him in surprise. "You've heard this? You might have mentioned it before."

Basim shook his head. "A fortune teller's prediction, nothing more. But I imagine the emperor will want to take your measure, just as you tested Justin. By now he's heard some embellished version of your heroics from the servants. They'll call you Slayer of Serpents, or something like that. In any event, the emperor will want to know what kind of enemy he has in you. It's what I would do, in his place."

Hytham felt a surge of alarm. He'd hoped to keep a low profile as Leo's guardian, not attract attention to himself or his skills. That element of secrecy was lost now. He'd inadvertently walked right into the emperor's view, which was the last place he wanted to be. "Should we alter the mission?" he asked. "I can leave the Varangian Guard and take to the shadows with you to find the assassin. Our identities will be safer that way."

"I believe it's too late for that," Basim said ruefully. "The best thing we can do is take advantage of the protection your new reputation offers."

"It feels like a fragile protection," Hytham said, "especially when the emperor can simply dismiss me from the Varangian Guard whenever he wishes."

"If he does that, he'll look the fool by dismissing the man who saved his son – or worse, arouse suspicion," Basim said. "Despite his efforts to keep this quiet, word will spread beyond the palace of what you've done. Even if they don't know your name, people will be talking of you, so the emperor won't risk dismissing you. No, I imagine instead he'll lavish you with praise, with some threats buried in there somewhere." Basim smiled faintly. "Again, it's what I'd do."

Wonderful, Hytham thought. A long night with no sleep, and a meeting at dawn with the emperor, who sounded much like a viper himself – aggressive, lying in wait for his chance to strike at his enemies. He'd have to stay sharp. But he had to admit he was also curious to meet the infamous Basil, if for no other reason than to get a true reading on the man, unfiltered through anyone else's views and expectations.

He couldn't possibly be any more difficult to pin down than the man standing next to Hytham now.

"I had a brief but interesting conversation with Anna at dinner after you left," Hytham said, and filled Basim in on the warning Anna had given him and her comments about Justin.

Basim made a thoughtful noise. "So, dear Anna would give her life for a child not her own, and she's been watching Justin – and probably the rest of Leo's guards – very closely. Interesting. Perhaps we should be recruiting her."

"You'll keep an eye on Justin then?" Hytham asked. He had to get back soon to check on Leo, then maybe try to get an hour's sleep before sunrise.

"Among others," Basim said cryptically. He looked at Hytham more closely, making Hytham shift in discomfort. "Are you truly all right?" he asked, something like concern in his voice. "It was a job well done, though I imagine an unsettling piece of work."

"I'm fine, though I vastly prefer a straightforward fight with a human opponent," Hytham said.

And one that he could easily identify. He was the one who was meant to sneak up on his enemy in the shadows, to get the jump on them and end their lives before they ever knew he was there. But here in this place, all the enemies were shadows, everyone a suspect, and he wasn't even sure where he stood with Basim.

It was a lonely feeling.

"Leo said he dreams about a voice in the dark, taunting him," Hytham said quietly. "That's what he told me, right before the snake came into his room."

"The voice of a jinn," Basim murmured, and there was a strange, haunted look in his eyes.

Hytham shook his head in some confusion. "The boy was not so specific. He simply described it as a voice. Why do you call it—"

"It's nothing," Basim said, cutting him off. "Just a flight of fancy."

"I see." Hytham almost stopped the conversation there, but then he added, "I find myself sympathizing. Ever since I set foot in this place, I feel like I'm being taunted by that same voice, something inside that tells me I will fail."

Basim put a hand on Hytham's shoulder and squeezed briefly before letting go. He still had that haunted look in his eyes. "We're all victims of that voice, my friend. Every one of us. The trick is not to let it gain power over you."

Basim's prediction turned out to be correct, of course. Hytham received the summons from two of the emperor's guards a little after sunrise. He followed the pair down the winding hallways to an even more ornate throne room than the one where he'd met Leo, the throne itself a more imposing seat.

Hytham had heard rumors that at least one of the emperor's grand thrones had a mechanism inside it that allowed the seat to soar high up in the air, causing the emperor to tower intimidatingly over his subjects. It was said that he saved the novelty for particular guests he wanted to impress or to frighten subjects who had displeased him. Hytham had also heard tell of rulers past who'd had golden lions placed beside their thrones that could be made to roar, and golden birds with jeweled eyes that could be heard to sing. Hytham wondered if there was any truth to the rumors, or if these were just fantastical stories of the palace told by those who could only dream of the opulent life led by those within.

As Hytham stood before the emperor, offering a deep, albeit brief bow, he took a moment to study the man he'd heard so much about. Basil was handsome, broad and burly, just as Hytham had heard him described, but he could also see the softening around the man's edges, where a lifetime of labor had begun to turn to fat with age and a much easier lifestyle. His skin was sun-weathered and creased, but his eyes were sharp, watchful as he took in Hytham.

What feelings had caused the previous emperor to elevate this man to be his equal? Hytham found himself wondering.

Michael had all but given away his own family legacy, put his trust in a man who had betrayed and murdered him in the end. What bond had been between them before that tragic ending, and how had it all gone so wrong?

The emperor cleared his throat. "I'm told I owe you thanks," he said, leaning back with his elbows braced on the arms of the gilded throne. "You saved my son's life last night."

He was a very good politician, Hytham noted. The softening of his face, just the right note of emotion creeping into his voice when speaking of his son – it was a calculated and skillful performance. Raised in common poverty Basil might have been, but he'd learned much since those humble beginnings. Hytham almost believed he was sincere when he spoke.

But the eyes didn't lie. Basil's gaze was flat, looking right through Hytham. He may as well have been getting a crop report from his agricultural advisors.

"I did my duty as commanded in your service, Honored Emperor," Hytham said, executing another graceful bow. The words were cloying in his mouth. A straightforward fight, he'd told Basim. Not politics or flowery platitudes that meant nothing, especially when they came from the tongue of someone who'd murder a child.

"And I honor you for that duty," the emperor said, oblivious to Hytham's internal struggle. "You are new to the palace, yes? I don't remember seeing your face before."

Hytham felt the weight of the emperor's attention, heard the subtle accusation in his tone. "I was recruited recently by Thyra from among the Eagle clan," he confirmed. "It is an honor to serve in the palace and guard the emperor's family and legacy."

"And serve us you have," the emperor said. "Yes, we're very pleased to have your loyalty." The door to the throne room opened, drawing both men's attention. "Ah, very good, he's here."

Basil's gaze strayed over Hytham's shoulder, at the same time Hytham heard footsteps approaching. He turned, and his brows lifted in surprise when Thyra and Leo entered the throne room. They approached the throne, bowed, and then stood next to Hytham. The emperor regarded the three of them with an unreadable expression, but the tension in the room was unmistakable. Hytham wondered what the emperor was doing. Was this part of the threat Basim had mentioned?

The emperor waved Thyra away with an imperious gesture, so she bowed again and left the room. Hytham glanced at Leo, but the boy had fixed his gaze on the floor, his posture stiff and shoulders hunched up to his ears. If the boy had been an animal, he'd have crawled to the back of his den by now, burrowed halfway into the earth.

"My son," the emperor said, addressing the boy in a gentle voice that still managed to make Hytham's skin crawl, "you owe this man thanks for saving your life. Pay him the respect he's due."

Leo took a steadying breath and turned, staring at Hytham's belt as he spoke. "Th- thank you for my l- life, Guardian Hytham," he said in the barest whisper.

"Louder," the emperor snapped, and Leo flinched.

"Thank you, Guardian Hytham, for saving me," the boy said, voice thin, but this time he spoke clearly and met Hytham's eyes. Surely that would satisfy the emperor.

"Now the rest," Basil said, in a tone of smug satisfaction.

He leaned forward, expectant gaze pinning Leo in place like an insect under a cruel child's thumb. Hytham's presence had ceased to be relevant. He might as well have been a piece of furniture in the room.

"I'm s- sorry," the boy said, voice dropping, stumbling over his words again, even as Hytham's thoughts reeled in confusion.

"Sorry for what?" Hytham asked, letting his bewilderment show. He knew it was a mistake as soon as he saw the gleam of triumph in the emperor's eyes. Basil stood and came sedately down from his throne to stand just behind Leo, an immense shadow looming over him.

In an instant the boy went from looking like a hunted animal to a statue. He just went blank, the color draining from his face as he awaited whatever was about to happen.

Hytham summoned all of his training and his considerable sense of self-control to keep from stepping forward to put his body between the emperor and Leo. He held himself rigid as Basil laid a big hand on the boy's shoulder and gripped hard.

"You hear that, Leo?" he said, and the boy gave a pained whimper. "Your guardian doesn't know the shameful thing you've done. Tell Hytham what it is you're sorry for."

"I'm sorry I accidentally left the outside door open so the snakes could get in," Leo said in a rush, and just like that, the emperor lifted his hand away. The boy's expression crumpled. He started to reach up to touch his shoulder but checked the move and dropped his hand to his side.

"You accidentally left the door open," Hytham repeated, but his eyes were on the emperor, "and that's how the snakes got inside?"

"He confessed it to me just a few hours ago," the emperor said, looking for all the world like an exasperated father forced to clean up a spill. "A careless mistake, but now the boy has seen what can happen when vermin are allowed to work their way into the palace." He gave Leo and Hytham a significant look. "People can die."

The boy hugged himself and stared at the floor, nothing but misery on his face. Hytham took a calming breath. So this was how the emperor was going to explain away the presence of the snakes, just like he'd found ready scapegoats for all the other "accidents" that had befallen Leo.

And there too was the threat Basim had predicted. The emperor wanted Hytham gone, and if he didn't leave of his own volition, he was likely to become a target as well.

"We've taken up enough of your time, Honored Emperor," Hytham said with another bow. When Basil dismissed them, Hytham swept out a hand and smoothly tugged the boy out of reach of his father, guiding him by his uninjured shoulder toward the door.

"Keep up your fine work, Guardian Hytham," the emperor called out mockingly as they left the throne room. "Never doubt that it's being noted by more eyes than mine."

CHAPTER TEN

To his credit, the boy stayed on his feet as Hytham guided him out of the throne room, but he wouldn't respond to any of Hytham's attempts at conversation. He just stared blankly ahead as they made their way down the hall. Hytham had the feeling he could have led the boy all the way to the Sea of Marmara, and he wouldn't have noticed the journey.

Fresh air was the only immediate comfort Hytham could think to give the boy, so he steered him outside into the training yard where he and Justin had sparred. Luckily the area was empty. Weak early morning sunlight filtered down between the trees, and the soft breeze held a slight chill that would soon be burned off by the heat of the day, but after the stifling tension in the throne room, it felt like a cool caress against Hytham's skin.

He sat Leo down on a bench near an empty weapon rack and crouched in front of him. "Are you all right?"

The boy's eyes were red-rimmed and glassy, and he still

wouldn't look at Hytham. But Hytham was a patient man, and he was willing to wait for Leo to come out of whatever place he'd crawled into in his mind, whatever space made him feel safe from his father.

Finally, Leo took a hitching breath, wiped his face and looked up at Hytham with a miserable expression. "I killed Drina," he said. "It was my fault."

Drina. He meant the old woman Hytham had found in the hall. Hytham hadn't learned her name in the chaos of the night's events. "You did no such thing," he said calmly.

But the boy was shaking his head, pulling his knees up protectively to his chest. He winced in pain and rubbed his shoulder. "I left the door open," he said. "I let the snakes in. That's what my father said. Because I left the door open, I killed her."

The way he said it was just like a command. Because the emperor decreed it, it must be so. And no one called the emperor a liar, least of all his son.

Based on the books he'd been reading, Hytham thought the boy appreciated knowledge and learning, logic and reason. He decided to try using those tools in this situation. "You left the door to the servant's hall open? You, the emperor's son and heir, are in charge of such things? Is that true?"

The boy hesitated, looking up at Hytham with a wary expression, as if he were afraid Hytham was setting a trap for him. "No, I'm not in charge of that," he said slowly, "but–"

"And were you anywhere near the servant's hall last night, Leo?" Hytham cut him off gently. "Were you anywhere near the door you supposedly left open?"

Mute, the boy shook his head.

"No, of course you weren't, because myself or Thyra were with you all night, and we both know you never went near that door," Hytham said. He leaned forward, putting a light hand on the boy's arm. The last thing he wanted, after that scene in the throne room, was for Leo to feel threatened by his presence. "You aren't responsible for what happened last night, no matter what anyone tells you."

"But my father–"

"Was mistaken," Hytham said. He couldn't quite bring himself to call the man a liar, not when he wasn't sure what ears might be listening. What he wanted to say was, *your father is the emperor, but he is not the Almighty, and he will not control you forever.*

"But he said it so many times – that it was my fault. He was so sure. I thought it must be true." Leo looked helpless, as if desperate to believe Hytham but unable to shake the memory of the hand that had gripped his shoulder hard enough to bruise.

"It doesn't matter how many times he says it. He's still wrong."

Over Leo's shoulder, Hytham caught movement in the far corner of the training yard. Basim stepped out from behind one of the trees and strode leisurely toward them, slipping easily from the role of one skulking in the shadows to a person who looked as if he belonged there in the training yard, had lived there all his life. Hytham again had that strange sense of time being irrelevant when it came to Basim. He shook away the feeling and turned back to the boy.

"Leo," Hytham said, sitting back and gesturing at Basim so the boy wouldn't be startled by his silent approach. "I'd like to introduce you to a friend of mine." He wondered how Basim was going to play this scene. He was surprised the Assassin had chosen to show himself to the boy at all, but he kept his expression in a neutral mask.

Leo looked up at Basim, his eyes wide. "Wh- where did you come from?" he asked, looking around the training yard as if he'd only just realized they were outside.

"I've been here all along," Basim said, sketching a half bow to the boy that seemed more for his own amusement than out of any sense of deference. "I can choose to walk very quietly when I wish." He grinned, a charming smile that tended to disarm everyone he met.

Leo wasn't immune either. He returned Basim's grin with a tentative one of his own. "Who are you?" he asked, taking in his peaked hood and scimitar.

"Basim Ibn Ishaq, at your service." He reached into a small pouch at his waist and pulled out a jar that was filled with some healing salve. Hytham remembered Basim offering him some after a particularly intense training session that had left his calves burning and cramping. "I noticed you favoring that shoulder," he said, nodding to Leo. "Try some of this. It will make you feel better."

Leo took the salve gingerly and removed the lid, sniffing and wrinkling his nose. "It smells bad."

"That's how you know it will work," Basim said with a wink.

Hytham motioned to Basim while the boy was distracted rubbing the salve on his shoulder beneath his undershirt. They drifted away from the bench and Basim said quietly, "I take it your audience with the emperor didn't go well?"

"As you see," Hytham said. He tried to keep the emotion

out of his voice, but he must have done a poor job because Basim glanced at him with a concerned frown.

"You didn't do anything rash, I hope?"

"I wanted to, but no." Hytham snorted. "You'll be pleased to know I bowed and simpered and held my tongue, like a good servant of the emperor."

"All the while imagining how easy it would be to step forward and bury your Hidden Blade in his heart the next time he so much as touched the child." Basim kept his tone light, his face expressionless. But his eyes were on Leo, rubbing the salve over his skin, and there was a peculiar light in them, something Hytham had never seen before.

"It was a bit like that, yes," Hytham admitted. He wanted to ask what had possessed Basim to show himself like this to the boy, but Leo had finished applying the salve and hopped down from the bench to come over to them. He held the jar out to Basim with a serious expression.

"Thank you," he said, rolling his shoulder gingerly. "It does feel better, even if it smells."

"You're welcome," Basim said, putting the salve away. "Now, boy, would you like to see a magic trick?"

Leo's eyes lit up, but he bit his lip at the same time. "Magic isn't real," he said.

Basim laughed, his eyes sparkling with mischief. "Ah, you're too young to be so cynical." He bent down so he was at eye level with the boy. "I've seen wonders in this world that would make you a believer. Come, close your eyes now, and I'll prove to you that magic exists."

Leo still looked skeptical, but he obediently closed his eyes. Hytham stood watching him in amusement for a few seconds, until Leo started fidgeting and said, "What's going to happen?"

"You can open your eyes now," Hytham said, and chuckled when Leo opened them to find Basim had disappeared from the training yard.

Leo's mouth fell open, the remnants of fear and pain chased from his eyes by this wondrous distraction. "Where did he go? I didn't hear him move!"

"Perhaps he was never here at all," Hytham said cryptically, smiling at the boy. Then he sobered. "Perhaps it's best that he be a secret between the two of us. Think of him as simply another guardian watching over you. Can you do that?"

Leo must have sensed the gravity of the situation, because he nodded solemnly. "I won't tell anyone."

"Good."

Hytham gestured for Leo to go back inside. He would be expected at his lessons soon, and both of them would have their work cut out for them to stay awake after the events of the night before.

Walking beside him, Leo was looking up at Hytham thoughtfully, and his gaze kept straying to Hytham's right arm. It took him a moment, but then Hytham remembered that the boy had seen him use the Hidden Blade on the snake the night before. He wasn't sure the boy would remember, but the event had obviously left an impression. Leo was staring at his arm in fascination.

They got a few more steps before Leo could restrain himself no longer. "Does your friend have a weapon like you do?" he asked.

"Maybe," Hytham said, and the boy made a sound of

frustrated excitement. Hytham much preferred this version of Leo to the cowed, terrified child in the throne room.

The one he couldn't protect.

He glanced down at Leo. "Perhaps we should keep that a secret between us too."

It was a great many secrets for one so young, but Hytham suspected Leo might be more trustworthy than other children of his age. One had to grow up quickly in the palace.

"But will you show it to me?" Leo begged. He had to double his short stride to keep up with Hytham, and he was practically skipping now. "I want to see how it works. How does it spring out so fast? Who made it for you? Why do you carry a sword as well?"

"So many questions," Hytham said patiently. They'd reached the small library by this time. The door was closed, and the smell of dust was strong when they entered the room. Leo's tutor had yet to make an appearance, but the boy didn't seem concerned. He trotted over to the shelves and began searching the titles on the book spines as if looking for one in particular.

"Theo gave me a book on weaponry a few months ago," the boy said, finding and tugging a small volume free. He flipped through it quickly, brow furrowed in concentration, but when he looked up at Hytham again, he was even more excited. "I knew it! There's nothing in here about such a blade."

"Not all the answers to life's questions are found in books," Hytham said, taking a seat at the long table. He glanced at the door. He'd left it half closed, and the hall outside was quiet. They were as alone as they were going to get until Theodore arrived. Laying his hand palm up on the table, he revealed the Hidden Blade for Leo's inspection.

The boy gasped and scrambled over to examine the blade and its attendant mechanism. To his credit, he didn't try to touch it, and he kept his fingers away from the lethal edge.

"This weapon and others like it are made specially for people like Basim and myself," Hytham said. "Do you remember last night when I told you about the cause I serve?"

With an effort, Leo tore his gaze away from his fascinated study of the blade and nodded. "You fight to protect people."

"That's right," Hytham said. "That fight is often a brutal one, and so it requires tools like this that allow us to strike quickly from the safety of the shadows. We work in the dark to serve the light." He removed his arm from the table, hiding the blade once again.

"I would like a weapon like that," Leo said, with all the seriousness of his age. "With a blade like that, I could protect myself." He seemed to catch himself and looked at Hytham, flushing red.

Hytham nodded gravely. "But you would have to learn how to use it properly," he said, "and you're still a bit young for that. You should keep practicing with the tools you have here in this room." He nodded to the books. "If you're going to be a ruler in charge of feeding a city one day, you'll need all the knowledge these tools have to give you."

The boy stared down at the table, his expression darkening. "I won't become a ruler," he said quietly. "I'll be dead long before then."

Hytham's breath caught, but otherwise he didn't react. "What makes you say such a thing?"

Leo frowned at Hytham as if *he* were the child. "My father hates me," he said flatly. "You saw it. People say he wants to kill me because he thinks I'm not his son. Everyone thinks I don't know it, but I'm not stupid."

"No, you're not," Hytham agreed. Many people had underestimated this boy, himself included. He'd thought Leo was ignorant of his father's intentions, but obviously that wasn't the case. Hytham told himself he wouldn't make that same mistake twice. "But I'm here to make sure that doesn't happen," he reminded Leo.

"You're only one man," the boy said, and he sounded much older in that moment. "You can't be with me all the time. I want... I want to learn to protect *myself*. I hate feeling like this!"

The boy's hands clenched into fists. Helpless, Hytham realized. That's what Leo was trying to say. He didn't want to feel helpless, blown about by fate and the whims of men who had all the power over him. Hytham could sympathize.

He sat back in his chair, musing on an idea, wondering if it had merit or if he was going soft. Probably both. "There are things I could teach you," he said slowly, and raised a hand when the boy lit up like a candle. "I'm not teaching you the ways of the Hidden Blade. You're too young, as I said, and that weapon must be earned through years of dedication and training."

"But I've used weapons before," Leo protested. "Justin taught me archery, or he started to, but then–" the boy cut himself off abruptly.

"What happened?" Hytham asked. He'd never heard the boy mention archery lessons.

Leo shook his head. "Nothing, it just didn't go well," he said. "Never mind."

Hytham could easily fill in the missing parts of the story. A bully like Justin was the last teacher Hytham would have chosen for the boy.

"How about this," Hytham said, wanting to rekindle the boy's excitement, which had diminished significantly. "Eventually, you can work with a practice sword made of wood, but I'll start by teaching you a bit of how people like Basim and I move so quietly, how we can hide in the shadows. These skills will be easier to master because you're so small and slight."

The boy looked intrigued but also indignant. "I'm not small," he argued.

Hytham chuckled but didn't relent. "You *are*," he said, "but so was I, at your age. You must learn to take what you're given and use it to your advantage. That's what I can teach you." He raised an eyebrow. "Are you interested or not?"

The boy thought about it for a moment and, just as Hytham hoped, his excitement grew. He practically bounced on the balls of his feet. "Yes!" he said. "I want to learn, Hytham. Please teach me."

Heaven help him against Leo's obvious joy and enthusiasm. He'd forgotten all about the pain in his shoulder in his excitement, and he stared at Hytham as if he'd singlehandedly remade the world.

Was this what it felt like to be a father?

The thought drifted through Hytham's mind as he helped Leo select more books from the shelves for his morning lesson, with Theodore eventually coming in to help. It was vaguely alarming, this thought, but he banished it quickly from his mind.

He wasn't interested in being a father to the boy. He was simply trying to keep Leo alive, and to educate him about the ways of the Hidden Ones, so he could be an ally and a force for their cause when he came of age.

That's all it was.

CHAPTER ELEVEN

Hytham had hoped that Leo would get some measure of peace and time to recover from his ordeal with the viper and the confrontation with his father that had followed the incident. So, when Leo announced that he had a riding lesson in one of the paddocks next to the Hippodrome the following day, Hytham was cheered by the thought of the boy getting out into the open air and away from the stifling intrigues and rules of the palace.

But the riding lesson itself was a problem.

Leo dreaded the proclamation. Hytham remembered the boy had suffered one of his "accidents" while near the stables, when he'd nearly been trampled. Naturally, he'd be fearful of getting near the horses again. But the lesson was part of his education, so Leo had no choice but to go.

Things became even more complicated when they entered the stables to find Justin watching the stablemaster saddle a small chestnut mare. Hytham and Leo both stiffened in what would have been a comical move, were Hytham in a joking mood.

He'd expected Thyra to be there to relieve him for the riding lesson, and his surprise and displeasure must have shown on his face, because Justin gave a soft laugh with no humor in it.

"Thyra was called away to meet with the Honored Empress," Justin explained. "I was summoned to duty in her stead."

Hytham nodded unhappily. Thyra could hardly refuse a summons from the empress, but now Hytham was faced with the prospect of leaving Leo to Justin's mercy, something he had no wish to do. He had no good excuse to stay, but he wouldn't let that stop him.

"I'm sure Thyra appreciates your commitment to your duties," Hytham said neutrally. "Leo has just been telling me all about the emperor's grand stable of horses."

At the moment, Leo was standing silent and rigid, watching Justin like a mouse trying to decide if the hawk has seen it from the sky.

Hytham put his hand on the boy's shoulder. "I was hoping to stay and watch the lesson, as I'm fond of horses myself. I assume you don't mind." He smiled to soften the fact that he was clearly not asking permission.

Justin didn't seem to be in the mood for an argument today. He only shrugged and said, "Suit yourself. I'll wait outside for you."

After the young man had gone, Hytham gently prodded Leo to introduce him to the mare. The boy was distracted at first, but he relaxed a little when the horse bent its head and nudged Leo, searching for food. When the stablemaster stepped away for a moment, Leo confided to Hytham, "I call her Sky because the white patch on her neck reminds me of a cloud," he said.

Hytham nodded. "I believe the name suits her," he said, reaching up to stroke Sky's neck. "I think she likes it as well."

At that, Leo frowned. "She doesn't care what we call her. She's a horse."

"You're right," Hytham said, biting back a smile, "but it's still a good name. Are you nervous about Justin being present for the riding lesson?" he asked.

Leo's face clouded, but he shook his head. "It will be all right," he said, in the tone of someone who knew for a fact that it would not be all right at all.

The stablemaster led the horse out to the fenced paddock, with Hytham and Leo trailing behind. Hytham had watched the man saddle the mare, looking for any sign that he might tamper with the riding gear or do anything else to agitate the animal, but he hadn't seen anything out of the ordinary.

Justin was waiting for them by the gate. He swung it open to let the stablemaster and the horse into the paddock. Then he motioned to Leo.

"Go on," he said gruffly. "Your guardian and I will be just on the other side of the fence."

Reluctantly, Leo followed the stablemaster into the paddock, and Justin swung the gate shut behind them and latched it. Hytham draped his arms over the fence to watch. He thought that Justin had very deliberately angled to keep both him and Hytham outside the fence. Interesting. Was it because he wanted to separate Hytham from the boy?

If that was the case, Hytham wasn't particularly worried. With his training, strength, and reflexes, the fence might as well not have existed as a barrier separating him from Leo if things went awry.

The lesson started uneventfully. The stablemaster took pains to instruct Leo on everything from how to approach the horse, to identifying each piece of tack and how it was used. This led to a discussion of the horses that ran in the chariot races, and Leo had all kinds of questions about the history of the races, the teams, and the rules. He seemed to forget his earlier anxiety as he talked, and the stablemaster, obviously interested in the same subjects, was only too happy to give him lengthy answers.

Through it all, Justin looked bored, but his gaze was still watchful as he eyed the horse and tracked Leo's movements around it, as if to make sure the boy didn't accidentally step into harm's way.

Was he misjudging Justin's intentions here? Hytham wondered. The young man was difficult to read, but just because he didn't care for Leo or was angry at his perceived demotion in rank, it didn't mean he wanted the boy dead. Hytham reminded himself that he needed to stay objective in this investigation.

Hytham walked casually along the fence, coming to stand next to the young man. "I feel as if we had a bad start when we first met," he said. He still had his suspicions, but he was determined to give Justin the benefit of the doubt. He wasn't going to dismiss any potential allies to be found in the palace. "I wonder if you and I could begin again?"

Justin shot him a wary glance. When he spoke, it was with an edge of mockery. "I wonder that you took the time to notice any of the rest of us. You're the hero of the palace, after all. You don't need to make friends with anyone."

"Whether we become friends or not, we can surely still

work together with civility," Hytham said, keeping his tone neutral. "It would be easier for us both, don't you think?"

At that, Justin laughed, and it was a harsh, bitter sound, very much at odds with what Hytham had thought was a simple conversation. "You want civility from me, do you?" he asked, an unpleasant twist to his lips. "Civility in the palace of vipers – I truly can't tell whether you're naïve or just very skilled at playing the fool."

"Educate me then," Hytham said, and this time he couldn't keep the edge out of his voice. His patience with this boy and the chip on his shoulder was wearing thin.

But Justin appeared to be done talking. He stepped on the bottom rung of the fence and vaulted over into the paddock. "Let's get on with this," he called out to the stablemaster. "We don't have all day."

He stopped dead, as Hytham was suddenly standing in front of him.

Justin's eyes widened, and he glanced back at the fence, as if unsure how Hytham had managed to get over it so fast and put his body in front of Justin's.

"Actually," Hytham said lightly, "we do have all the time in the world." He glanced at the stablemaster. "Don't mind us. Continue with the lesson."

Justin held his gaze for a second, and again, Hytham wondered what he was going to do. But in the end, Justin backed toward the fence, leaning against it with his arms crossed. Hytham gave him space and stood a few feet away.

At last, it was time for Leo to mount his horse, and Hytham could already see trouble brewing. As soon as Leo walked up to the beast, the boy's nervousness took over, and he froze, unwilling to put his foot in the stirrup, even when the stablemaster held out a hand to coax him.

Leo glanced over his shoulder, giving Hytham and Justin a pained expression, as if caught between the desire to ask for help or to try to escape. Hytham stepped forward, but Justin called out, "An emperor's son who can't ride a horse isn't fit to rule anything. Get on the damn beast."

Hytham clenched a fist at his side and took a deep, calming breath to keep from turning and punching Justin in the face.

And his words had the worst effect possible. Leo ducked his head, but then, in a desperate burst of courage, he turned and flung himself at the horse before the stablemaster was ready. He got himself halfway up the horse's flank before his foot slipped from the stirrup. Leo cried out and clutched at the horse's neck and mane, startling the beast. It snorted and shied to the left. Leo lost his grip and fell.

Hytham reached him before he could hit the ground between the restless horse's legs. He plucked Leo up in one arm and grabbed the loose reins in the other, calming the horse with some soothing words until the stablemaster could reclaim the beast.

"I think that's enough for today," Hytham said decisively when the man started to ask if Leo wanted to try again. The stablemaster nodded and led the horse away.

Ignoring Justin, who still stood near the fence, Hytham put Leo down and knelt so he could whisper in the boy's ear. "Go with the stablemaster," he said. "Give Sky a treat to show there's no hard feelings. You'll get along better next time, when there are fewer eyes watching."

Leo nodded. His face was flushed red, twin spots of color

high on his cheeks. He trailed after the stablemaster and Sky. Hytham kept them both in sight, positioning himself so he could see into the stables and down the row of stalls, just in case there was any further trouble.

Then he turned to Justin.

"Did you accomplish what you set out to do here?" Hytham said, keeping his voice soft and controlled. "Did it give you pleasure?"

Justin's posture was stiff, his jaw tight, just as he'd been that day in the training yard. His eyes blazed as he regarded Hytham.

"You don't know anything," he said. "Stop coddling the boy. It'll go better for the both of you if you do."

"What does that mean?" Hytham asked. What was the man playing at? Was he warning Hytham, or threatening him?

But Justin just shook his head and turned, vaulting over the fence. He stomped off, muttering to himself, but Hytham couldn't hear what he was saying.

Once again, Hytham was left with more questions than answers. He stood alone in the paddock, the shadow of the palace and the Hippodrome looming over him, and contemplated his place in all of this, and whether he was doing more harm than good.

Chapter Twelve

Hytham had been inside the palace walls for nearly two weeks before he got the chance to be back on the streets of Constantinople, and the respite came not a moment too soon. Large as it was, the palace was starting to feel like a cage, with eyes always watching his and Leo's movements. It felt exhilarating to fade into the crowds of the markets again and simply be an anonymous presence. The hunter instead of the hunted.

Today, he'd left Leo and his parents sitting in the formal gardens having their likenesses sculpted by a visiting artist who'd gained Basil's favor. Thyra was watching over the boy in his absence, but Hytham didn't think it likely the emperor would orchestrate an assassination attempt on the palace lawn in full daylight with the rest of his family present, so he felt relatively safe leaving for the afternoon to accompany Basim on this investigation.

The past two weeks had turned up frustratingly little in the way of evidence as to who in the palace was conspiring with the emperor to murder Leo. And since Basil had managed to convincingly blame the incident with the snakes on his son, no formal investigation into that attack had been encouraged. So, Hytham and Basim had been on their own.

There were many suspects in the palace, but three were strong contenders simply by virtue of their proximity to Leo on a daily basis.

Justin was the frontrunner, in Hytham's mind, though Basim didn't seem convinced. Then again, Basim hadn't witnessed Justin's disdain for the boy the way Hytham had. But Hytham couldn't discount the other two suspects either.

There was Anna – to all appearances the devoted servant and second mother to Leo. She'd certainly been suspicious of Hytham's intentions that first night at dinner, but that didn't make her innocent.

Then there was Theodore, the tutor who seemed to Hytham to have little personality or passion for his job as chief educator of the emperor's son. He was quiet and non-threatening, which made him a favorite of Leo's and also exactly the sort of unassuming man the Order of the Ancients might recruit, someone who could blend in, make friends with anyone, stand out to no one, and essentially be invisible while going about the business of spying and murder.

Today it was Anna he and Basim followed through the market, keeping a respectable distance so as not to lose her in the crowd, but they also didn't want to chance being seen. The woman did seem inordinately suspicious. She kept looking behind her, scanning the market as if worried she was being followed, though she hadn't noticed Hytham or Basim's presence.

"She seems very worried about discovery," Hytham remarked as they faded into the crowd yet again while Anna slowed and glanced over her shoulder. It must have been the fifth or sixth time she'd done it since they'd reached the market.

"Perhaps fortune will favor us and she'll lead us right to an Order stronghold," Basim remarked.

"Let's see how outnumbered we are before we count that outcome a victory," Hytham said, and Basim laughed.

Finally, Anna slowed, and with one last furtive glance at her surroundings, she ducked inside a squat brick building near the end of the street. A crude, weathered sign above the rickety door indicated it was a fortune teller's house.

Hytham and Basim exchanged a glance.

"Well, I was right about the fortune part," Basim said.

"It's possible she's simply embarrassed at having anyone find out she visits a fortune teller," Hytham said.

"If that's the case, we'll simply listen in and see what fate has in store for her," Basim said with a thoughtful look at the building. "I'll circle around the back and search for another entrance."

"I'll go in the front as another paying customer," Hytham said.

They split up, Hytham approaching the door. He opened it a crack, just far enough to see Anna passing through an interior doorway curtained in dirty cloth. The smell of incense was thick in the air. Hytham waited a beat and then stepped inside.

The cramped front room held a small table where a girl of about thirteen sat with a box of coins. She was just putting away whatever amount of money Anna had given for her reading when she looked up and saw Hytham. Her eyes widened, and she put the money box out of sight in her lap.

"Ursina is busy," she said, picking nervously at the dirt under her fingernails. "Come back in an hour."

"My wife went in to have her fortune told by Ursina," Hytham said quietly, improvising the story as he went. "She won't let me hear the outcome, but I'd very much like to listen in." He pulled out a generous handful of coin, likely more than Ursina or the girl had seen in a month, and held it up.

The girl's mouth dropped open, and she sprang up to snatch the money from his hand before he could change his mind. While she busied herself hiding the coins on her person and not in the coin box – apparently her loyalty to Ursina only extended so far – Hytham crept up to the curtains. Beyond them a narrow hall wound to the back of the house. The incense couldn't quite cover the scent of sweat and dust lingering in the air. He followed the short passage until he came to another door, this one left slightly ajar. Soft voices drifted from within.

Hytham took up a position to one side of the door, keeping an eye on the curtains at the opposite end of the hall in case the girl in front came looking for him. Inside the room it was very dark, with only the light of a single candle set on a low table. Two women sat opposite each other, and the one with her back to Hytham was definitely Anna. The tiny space reeked of candle smoke and incense, making his eyes water. There was no sign of Basim, but then Hytham hadn't expected to see the other Assassin.

The fortune teller was speaking. "Isaac requests an offering," she said, and Anna shifted, rummaging in some kind of bag she carried with her.

"How do I know that you truly speak for him?" Anna asked uncertainly as she drew the object out. Hytham leaned in, squinting to see what it was – a jeweled hair comb, grander than anything a servant of her station would wear, even if she did care for the emperor's child. Had she stolen it from the empress?

"You will ask no questions," the fortune teller admonished Anna. She pocketed the comb and folded her hands on the table. "I will take your offering to Isaac. You'll have your answer soon."

"I want you to give him a message as well," Anna insisted, leaning forward. "Tell him there's more where that came from – whatever he wants."

"I'll tell him. You must go now." The fortune teller blew out the candle on the table and retreated into the shadows.

Brief and cryptic, but Hytham noted the name and retraced his steps to the outer room. It was empty. No sign of the girl who'd taken his bribe. Quietly, Hytham slipped out to the street.

And froze.

Theodore the tutor was coming down the street toward the fortune teller's house.

"Well, well. What a popular place this is on a busy market day."

Basim's voice came from above him. Hytham looked up to see the Assassin perched on the edge of the roof, his hand extended to Hytham. Hytham took it, using the wall for leverage as he scrambled up the side of the building to join Basim. Crouching so they were out of sight, they heard

Theodore's footsteps approach the door, and then the sound of Anna leaving the house.

"Oh!" Anna said, at the same time Theodore gasped. Hytham couldn't risk looking over the side of the roof to get a glimpse of their faces, but their mutual surprise was evident. Neither one had expected to meet the other. Interesting.

"Anna, what are you doing here?" Theodore demanded, and there was more of an edge to his normally flat voice than Hytham had ever heard. "Have you been following me?"

"No!" But there was a hint of guilt in her voice. "I'm just taking care of some things. Don't worry. No one saw me leave the palace."

"That you know of." Theodore cursed. "Anna, you need to leave here and don't come back. It's dangerous."

"I know what I'm doing," Anna insisted. "Everything's going to be all right. I promise."

There the conversation ended, but there were other sounds coming from below that suggested neither Anna nor Theodore had left yet. Hytham had come upon his share of secret trysts while sneaking around in dark alleys to know what it sounded like when two people were kissing enthusiastically.

"Let's get out of here," Theodore said after a moment, his voice husky. "I'll escort you back to the palace."

Hytham and Basim looked over the edge of the roof in time to see the two of them heading off together, back into the thick of the market.

"Well, that was an interesting revelation." Basim leaned back against the slanted roof tiles. "I suppose you won't be cultivating a relationship with the lovely Anna after all. I hope you're not too disappointed."

"Should we follow them?" Hytham asked, annoyed that Basim was jesting rather than planning their next move. "What if they stop somewhere on their way back to the palace?"

"Oh, I don't think dear Theodore will risk that," Basim said. "He seemed quite shaken to see his beloved here – or whatever she is to him. No, I'm more interested in who Isaac might be and who he represents."

"By the sound of it, he's someone who accepts offerings in exchange for solving problems," Hytham said, unsurprised that Basim had also overheard Anna's conversation, though Hytham had never detected his presence. "You think it's the Order of the Ancients?"

"It's possible," Basim said. His hood was up, so it was difficult to read his expression, but Hytham noted the edge of excitement in his voice. "The question is, do Theodore and Anna know that it's the Order? And if it is, how far up the chain of command is Isaac placed here in Constantinople? There are many tantalizing mysteries afoot."

"I suppose I know what you'll be doing for the next few days," Hytham said.

Basim's smile was downright gleeful. "You do indeed."

CHAPTER THIRTEEN

Hytham half figured Leo, being a child with a child's attention span, would have forgotten about his desire to learn the ways of the Hidden Ones and that he would have turned his interests to something else within a week.

As with many things concerning Leo, Hytham turned out to have underestimated the boy yet again.

"You promised to teach me, and I want to start today," Leo insisted, standing in the training yard with his arms crossed, a stubborn set to his jaw that reminded Hytham unsettlingly of the emperor. Perhaps Basil shouldn't have been so quick to question his parentage, at least without taking a good long look at the boy. By Hytham's judgment, Leo also had Basil's eyes, and they were currently spearing Hytham with a child's single-minded determination.

He held up his hands in smiling surrender. "I haven't forgotten my promise," he said. "We can start whenever you like." He'd already been thinking about how he wanted to go about this, in case the boy didn't lose his nerve. He couldn't teach him real swordplay, not yet, at least not until he managed to lay his hands on some wooden practice swords, but even then, he wasn't certain the boy was quite ready for that. The empress might not thank him either. But there were plenty of other useful skills he could learn, and ones that might serve him well in the immediate future.

So, before Leo could gaze too longingly at the weapon rack in the training yard, Hytham steered him indoors and down the endless, mazelike corridors of the palace.

"Where are we going?" Leo asked, though he didn't sound disappointed, only curious. And trusting. Ever since the night Hytham had killed the snake, he'd earned Leo's unswerving loyalty, and the boy seemed completely comfortable in Hytham's presence. Hytham was glad of that, even if he couldn't banish the terror Leo held for his father or the tension that gripped him whenever Justin was nearby.

"We're going someplace where I can best show you what you need to know," Hytham said. He led Leo down the twisting hallways, past the mural of an eagle with its talons extended to strike, to a set of double doors that opened into one of the cavernous libraries and study rooms scattered throughout the palace. Light from the high windows cast pools of gold on the marble floor. A cluster of heavy wood tables had been arranged in the center of the room, with the bookshelves spread out around these. It was quiet and deserted this time of day. Hytham had made sure of that before he chose the room. He wasn't particularly eager for anyone to know what he was teaching the boy.

They stood near the largest table, and Hytham gestured

to an open space of floor in front of Leo. "Show me how you think you should move in order not to be heard," he said.

Leo nodded and, very carefully, he began to walk on tiptoe across the floor. He walked all the way to the nearest bookshelf, turned and came back. He was frowning when he reached Hytham.

"You hear yourself moving, don't you?" Hytham said.

Leo nodded. "It's because the room is so quiet." His voice echoed off the walls. "My feet sound very loud."

Hytham pointed to the boy's bell-sleeved dalmatica, the fabric falling nearly to his knees. "What you're wearing is part of the problem too. It's made with silk, which is good, but it's also very loose on your body, which is bad. See how the sleeves flare out at the wrist? You can hear the rustle of the fabric every time you move. Take it off and try again."

The boy did as he was told, draping the heavier garment over the back of a nearby chair, leaving him in his undertunic and trousers. He hesitated, then slipped off his sandals as well, looking to Hytham for confirmation that this was the right approach. Hytham nodded.

This time when the boy began to move, he was much quieter. Hytham walked alongside him and stopped him after a few steps.

"Crouch lower, like this," he said, and demonstrated, waiting for Leo to match his pose. "Feel the weight of your body pressing down into your feet, connecting you to the floor. Now, before you take each step, look at the terrain in front of you. Watch for anything that might slip or crack or creak beneath your feet."

"But the floor is clean here in the palace," Leo said, putting one foot gingerly in front of the other. "Why do we have to be so careful? We're not sneaking through a forest."

"Someday you might be," Hytham said. "Best be prepared for anything. And it's true, there are no dry twigs to snap or leaves to crunch beneath your feet here, but what about the hidden perils? The stairs that creak in the middle of the night? The rug that trips you because you forgot it was there in the dark? You must always test the area in front of you, unless you've walked it so many times that you know it by heart."

He demonstrated again, bringing his foot down toes first, feeling his way, gradually letting his weight rest on the floor without a sound. Leo tried to imitate him, but Hytham could tell he was restless.

"It's too slow," the boy complained, standing up straight. "If someone is chasing me, they'll catch me before I ever manage to hide."

"We're talking of two different things," Hytham said patiently. "Sometimes your only choice is to run, and if I ever tell you to do that, you shouldn't hesitate or try to be quiet. Your only task then is to get away. But no one can run forever, so when you have the chance to disappear and be silent and hidden, you take that as well."

"When do I fight?" Leo pressed, his gaze straying to the Hidden Blade that would be a Hidden Blade no longer if he kept openly staring at it all the time. Hytham suppressed a sigh.

"We'll cover fighting another day," he said firmly. "Today is about patience and stealth. You said you wanted to learn my ways. Did you mean it or not?"

Leo fidgeted, but in the end he nodded. "I do," he said. "I'm sorry. Let me try again."

They returned to the center of the room. Then, barefoot, Leo crept across the floor on his own, doing a fair imitation of moving his feet as Hytham had shown him. He was a quick learner when he wanted to be.

"Very good," Hytham said as Leo turned and crept back to the table in the center of the room. "This next part will probably be a bit more fun. I'm going to teach you to hide."

The boy laughed, his eyes dancing with amusement. "Oh, I already know about that," he said. "I used to hide from Anna, until she threatened to box my ears. I know all the best places in this part of the palace." There was no mistaking the pride in his voice.

"I see," Hytham said, crossing his arms. "Why don't you show me then? We can start in here."

"In the library?" Leo shook his head, his grin turning wicked. "You'll never find me in here."

"Try me. I'll give you to the count of twenty."

Hytham closed his eyes and heard the boy scamper off with another laugh. He couldn't help sparing a moment to marvel at the fact that he was in the imperial palace of one of the most powerful cities in the world, playing hide and seek with its future emperor. No doubt Basim would be just as amused if he could see Hytham right now.

He finished counting and opened his eyes. The room was silent. Dust motes caught in the sunbeams, and the silent library almost felt like a church in that moment, a holy place for scholars. Hytham stood, listening, gradually picking up the faint sounds of servants moving in the corridors outside, their voices muted by the heavy wood doors. Still he didn't move, just listened for the sounds of anything out of place in the cavernous library.

There. The slightest creak of wood, followed by a quiet gasp. He strode forward, three shelves deep, turned right and walked to the end of the row of books, glancing up to meet Leo's gaze where he was perched on top of the shelf next to a ladder.

Leo stared at him in wonder. "How did you find me so fast?" he demanded, scrambling down the ladder. "Did you cheat?"

Hytham laughed at the accusatory note in the boy's voice. "I *heard* you, little mouse," he said. "Remember what I told you about being aware of your surroundings?" He reached up and flexed his fingers against one of the bookshelves. It creaked softly under the weight of his hand. "Sometimes this is all it takes to give you away."

He'd expected the boy to be frustrated, but instead Leo clapped his hands excitedly. "It was such a soft sound, and you still heard it! You're amazing, Hytham!"

The flattery of a child should not have affected him. Hytham was a hardened warrior, an Assassin, a killer when he needed to be. Yet the smile on Leo's face was enough to make him feel like a hero in a story. He was definitely going soft.

"All right," Hytham said, clearing his throat. "Let's try again. Then we'll go around to some of the other rooms and find you some good hiding places." He turned serious. "I want you to remember these if it becomes necessary. If you are in danger someday and you manage to hide yourself somewhere safe, I want you to stay there until I come for you. Do you understand?"

The boy nodded, though he wore a pained expression now. "What if something happens to you?"

Hytham put a reassuring hand on the boy's shoulder as they

walked back to the tables in the center of the room. "Nothing is going to happen to me," he said.

The words had come to his lips without his even considering them. In that moment, Hytham thought he understood a little bit more about the relationship between parents and children, and why adults often lied to them. *There are no monsters in the dark. Nothing can hurt you. I will always be here to save you.*

He wished all these things would stay true for Leo forever. But that was not the way the world worked, and he was a poor teacher if he let the boy believe that, especially with the destiny that lay ahead of him.

"If something does happen to me," he amended gently, "there will be others to stand at your side. That's the strength of the brotherhood to which I belong – there are many of us, and when one falls, there are always more to take our place, to honor our sacrifice and continue the work we start in our lifetimes." He hesitated. "It's not unlike the task you will have in ruling this city one day and forging your own legacy."

The boy stared down at his hands, clasped tightly in front of him. He looked nervous, unsure. "Father talks about that sometimes," he said. "The legacy he will leave behind when he dies. He talks to other people, but he doesn't tell *me* anything."

The implication of that lay heavily between them. Basil would have no desire to prepare a boy he thought would not live to take the throne. Again, Hytham wondered how he could have ever thought Leo was ignorant of his father's feelings toward him.

Leo looked up at Hytham, his expression open and trusting, so much so that it made Hytham shift uncomfortably. "How will I know what to do when it's my time?" Leo asked in a small voice. "Everything here," he gestured, and his skinny arms seemed to encompass the whole of the palace, "is bigger and louder and stronger than I could ever be. I don't know what to do to rule." The last words were barely above a whisper, as if he feared who might hear him.

Hytham guided Leo to a seat at one of the long tables. He pulled out a chair and sat down across from him. "No one who is wise rules alone," he said. "When you come to power, you would do well to surround yourself with people who are smarter than you, who have strengths that you lack, and views you may disagree with."

Leo's forehead scrunched in the same way it had that day Hytham had questioned him about how to feed a city. "Why would I want to be talked to by people who disagree with me? I heard Father say people like that will be chains weighing you down."

Hytham wasn't surprised to hear that coming from the emperor. "Some people are threatened by those who think differently, look and act differently from them. It challenges them to see the world with a deeper gaze, and not everyone is strong enough to do that. They would rather hide their eyes and keep everything the same forever." He leaned forward. "But that is not the way you have to live and rule, Leo. You can make a different choice, and even if I'm not around to see it, if you make the right choice, you will always have allies to support you and help you be a great ruler."

The boy sat silently, absorbing Hytham's words. Finally, he nodded and stood up, shoulders thrown back, once again assuming that pose he used to show his confidence. "Let's try again," he said, then faltered, as if a thought had just occurred to him. "Isn't it wrong for an emperor to hide?"

Hytham stood up too. "Hide in the shadows now," he said, "and one day, we'll see to it that you never have to hide again."

Chapter Fourteen

They worked the rest of the day, and in the evening after their training session concluded, Hytham saw Leo safely back to his room – the boy was asleep almost as soon as his head hit his pillow – before turning his shift over to Thyra. He had not had the opportunity to speak to the woman in private since that day at Demetrios's house, and neither had the woman sought him out. His curiosity about her had only intensified over the weeks he'd been here, so he took the moment to pull her aside in the shadows outside Leo's door.

"You and the members of your clan in the Varangian Guard risked a great deal allying yourself with the empress," he commented.

The integrity of the Varangian Guard itself, in fact. If Basil was behind the attacks on Leo, and if he discovered that elements of the Viking presence he'd come to trust as his personal guard contingent were secretly working against him, it would be catastrophic for all of them.

If Thyra was surprised by his directness, she didn't say so.

Her expression gave little away. "We continue to fulfill our oath to serve the emperor," she said. "It was Basil who forced an impossible choice on us. As I see it, we simply made our choice."

"In doing so, you're both honoring and defying the purpose of the Varangian Guard." It was, now that Hytham considered it, very much like his own relationship with the Hidden Ones and Basim. He'd given his loyalty to the Hidden Ones' cause, but that same oath had put him in the position of having to spy on one of his brothers. "It's a complicated burden you've taken on," he said quietly.

"Such is life," Thyra said, shrugging. "The way forward may not always be clear, but the choice I made is one I'm content to live with, no matter what comes."

Hytham knew she was right, yet he envied such certainty. This mission, Leo, and Basim were challenging him in ways he'd never anticipated, teaching him uncomfortable but necessary truths about himself and the world.

"I understand having to make a difficult choice," he said, "but I still wonder why you chose Leo?"

"You mean because the boy is soft and weak?" Thyra asked, her gaze narrowing on him.

"I believe he is neither," Hytham said. "I'm simply trying to see him through your clan's eyes. Surely, you prize strength above all?"

The Viking woman chuckled. "Leo wasn't born to our clan," she said. "If he had been, his upbringing would have been very different." She gave him a shrewd look. "But if you think we don't recognize and acknowledge different forms of strength, then you know hardly anything of our people."

"That's a certainty," Hytham said, "and I mean no offense. I would welcome the chance to know more about you and your people."

"Ah, but I'm curious about you as well, Hytham, since clearly, I'm not the only one taking a risk being here." Thyra regarded him coolly. "You are all alone in a palace full of unseen enemies, drawing the attention of the emperor, and not in any way that will bring you glory. Of the two of us, you seem to me to be more vulnerable by far."

Hytham was hardly alone here, and they both knew it, but she had a point. He and Basim were only two men, and at times he felt very disconnected from his brotherhood here, as if aid were far away.

"The risk is part of my oath as well," Hytham said. "I'm here for Leo, to protect him and to guard what he could become, the good he could do in the world if given the chance."

He knew he should remain neutral, but Hytham couldn't help the swell of pride in his voice. Had he given away too much to the Viking leader in sharing his thoughts?

For her part, Thyra remained frustratingly inscrutable. "The boy does like you," she said, with a glance at the door to Leo's room. "He seems more a person when you're around and less a quavering shadow."

"He's also alone here," Hytham said, "and the danger he faces from enemies disguised as friends would make anyone a shadow of themselves." He glanced around the hall again, constantly seeking listening ears or the lingering footsteps of servants passing by. "Speaking of that, Basim and I overheard an interesting conversation between Theodore and Anna at a fortune teller's house recently."

Thyra raised an eyebrow. "They were together?"

"I don't believe they intended to meet each other there, but it was clear from their interaction that they are involved somehow." Hytham shrugged. "We're not sure what it means yet. Basim is looking into it."

"Very inquisitive, that one."

The cryptic words caught Hytham's attention. "You've spoken with him?"

"He sought me out," Thyra said. "He wanted to know more about the members of my clan and what other clans we had relations with."

"I see," Hytham murmured. "Did he say why he was asking such questions?"

"He didn't, but it sounded to me like he was looking for someone," Thyra said.

Looking for someone. A suspect, someone conspiring against Leo? But Basim had shown a keen interest in the Vikings even before they'd learned of the assassination plot against the boy.

Who was Basim looking for, and why?

Thyra said, "I know what you're thinking, but you won't get answers from that one. He's slippery as a fish. Seek out your bed, Hytham. Your shift starts again early in the morning."

Hytham suppressed a sigh as he bid her good night and slipped away to his room in the barracks. Was this what his mentor had warned him to watch out for when he'd told Hytham to watch Basim? Were his inquiries to Thyra serving some private cause of Basim's, something that went counter to the Hidden Ones' mission? So many questions, and he felt he was no closer to getting satisfactory answers.

For now, Thyra was right. He was tired, and it was late. He would speak to Basim in the morning. Perhaps the cagey man would be more forthcoming if Hytham pressed the issue.

Though he doubted it.

Hytham knew something was wrong before he awoke.

In his dreams, he was falling, plunging down the shaft of a dark well, fingers clawing at the slimy stones on either side of him. In the way of dreams, time skipped, and the next moment he was sinking, pulled beneath the water into the dark. He tried to swim, but his arms were weighted, and he could only watch the small point of light that marked the water's surface get dimmer and dimmer. His chest drew tight, and he convulsed, slowly suffocating in the cold darkness.

Then he was no longer in a dream.

But he was still suffocating.

He was awake, and his blanket was pressed flush against his face, a punishing weight sealing it over his nose and mouth. There was no air, and he could see nothing through the thick fabric.

Hytham thrashed and roared, but the sound of his scream was muffled, and he discovered there was another weight pressing down on his legs, holding him to his bed. What felt like a leg was situated crosswise over his arms and stomach, bearing down to keep him still. He heard the grunts and whispers of what sounded like two different men.

Two killers coming for him in the dark.

He forced himself to calm. There were only seconds before he would lose too much air to think clearly, becoming a mindless animal just trying to survive. No. He was not an animal in a trap, and he was not helpless.

Hytham let his body go limp, in the hopes they'd believe he'd passed out. He waited a beat, but the pressure on his body didn't relent. No amateur killers these. They were trained, sent by the Order to eliminate him.

Where was Leo?

At that thought, new strength surged into Hytham's limbs, and he focused, drawing on all of his training and all of his anger. Anger could be useful in times like these. It could be harnessed for something great and terrible and necessary.

Hytham, for all his gentleness, had anger in him too, and he used it all now as he thought of Leo lying helpless in his bed while Hytham was being murdered in his.

He screamed, and surged upward, throwing both men off his body and off the bed with a tremendous crash. He rolled to the floor, tearing the suffocating blanket from his face. He sucked in a relieved breath. The stale air of the barracks was blissfully cool on his flushed skin, but he had no time to savor it. In the darkness, a shape came at him, large and indistinct.

Hytham swept his attacker's legs out from under him. The man stumbled with a grunt and fell. Hytham rolled, brought his arm up and released the Hidden Blade just in time for the man to impale himself on it as he fell. There was a wet choking sound, but Hytham didn't pause to relish that victory either. He pushed the body aside, shaking it viciously off the blade.

There had been two men holding him. One was dead, and the other had fled the room.

He needed to find Leo.

No candles burned in the small space. Only the meager light from the hall spilling into the room offered any illumination. How many other men had been in the barracks when he'd come in to sleep? At least three – he remembered marking each one when he'd arrived. They had all been Varangians, but he couldn't remember if they were all from Thyra's clan. He crouched by the body, rolling it to get a look at the man's face by the light from the hall.

Yes, he had been one of the three. Hytham didn't know the man's name, but Thyra would.

Silently, he crept into the hall, moving as quickly as he could to Leo's chamber. He felt a small surge of relief when he saw Thyra stationed outside the boy's door, with the calm, slightly bored look of the night guard on a long, uneventful watch.

Then he noticed Basim standing in the shadows next to Thyra. Obviously, they'd been talking, or they'd been about to talk, but they looked up at once when they saw him.

"Check on the boy, leave your most trusted guard with him, then come to us in the barracks," Hytham told Thyra curtly, and turned his attention to Basim, who was looking at him in concern. "We have a new problem."

Hytham filled them in on what had happened as they returned to the barracks. The body of the Varangian was still there, empty eyes staring at the ceiling in the darkness. The blanket that had nearly suffocated Hytham lay nearby. He tried not to think about how very close the men had come to killing him.

Thyra crouched by the body. "Steros," she said, shaking her head. "He's young and quiet. Not one I would have expected to be involved in this."

"Does he know about your alliance with us and with the empress?" Basim asked.

"No," Thyra said, to Hytham's relief. "There are only a small number of the Varangians, members of my own clan, that I would trust with that knowledge. The rest of them, we must now assume, are ready and willing to kill you at the emperor's word," she added, looking to Hytham.

"If the emperor wanted me out of the way, he could easily have found an excuse to dismiss me," Hytham said. "Why do this?"

"Because this method of removal poses the least risk to himself or his reputation," Basim said. He was standing in the doorway acting as a lookout. "You've become an obstacle in Basil's path, so he called upon the Order to remove the obstacle." He glanced at the twisted blanket on the floor. "They likely intended to dispose of your body over the sea wall and claim you'd abandoned your post in disgrace. Quiet and easy, no blood to clean. Dismiss you, especially after your heroics saving young Leo from the viper, and people might start to whisper about why. They might question the emperor's judgment. The last thing the emperor wants is to draw attention to himself or his plot." His expression darkened. "Except now, after another failure and a dead Varangian, I suspect he'll be more dangerous than ever."

"That won't be good for us," Thyra said. She looked at the two of them. "There will be another shift change soon, with new guards coming here to sleep."

Basim checked the empty hall. He was wearing his mischievous smile again, which was a bit unsettling considering the circumstances. "Let's dispose of the body and claim he abandoned his post in disgrace," Basim said.

Thyra shrugged. "If it's a good enough story for the emperor, it works for me," she said.

Hytham glanced at the bloodstain under the body. "What about that?"

Basim and Thyra exchanged a glance. "An injury," Thyra said. "One of my men will take up the story, and we'll get a servant to clean it up."

"Let's move, then," Basim said, and they went to work.

With Thyra serving as guide and lookout, Hytham helped Basim spirit his attacker's body away into the depths of the palace, emerging into the night and down a steep, rocky hill to throw the body over the sea wall. Hytham did his best not to dwell on the fact that this had nearly been his own fate, but the weight of the dead man in his arms and the chill of the night air crawling over his skin were difficult to ignore.

He did not watch the dark sea swallow the body.

Afterward, Thyra left them to arrange for the barracks to be cleaned, and Hytham and Basim stood a moment beside the wall in the darkness.

Hytham laid his hands against the cool stones, feeling salt spray on his lips, gazing out at the vast stretch of black water scrolling away to the horizon.

"I've heard the sea at night can be terrifying to new sailors unused to being on the water," Basim said.

Hytham glanced at him. "I've always found it comforting," he said, "that there's something out there in the world so much bigger and grander than myself." He smiled ruefully. "Even if it seems infinite and likely to swallow me whole."

Perhaps his voice caught a bit, or his hands moved restlessly over the stones, for Basim turned toward him. "I regret not being there when you were attacked," he said, his voice low.

Hytham was shaking his head before he got the sentence out. "You aren't my keeper," he said. "It isn't your job to save me from my own mistakes."

"Mistakes?" Basim seemed genuinely confused. "How have you erred?"

"I should have seen the attack coming," Hytham said, picking at the loose rock, scraping it absently with his finger-nails. "I missed a sign somewhere, something that should have told me what they were up to. Most people don't get a second chance after an error like that."

Basim was quiet for a moment, looking out to the vast darkness. "It's true," he said. "But you won't waste that chance. You will learn from this. And you were right to be uneasy at the beginning of this mission. We are apart more often than not and unable to watch each other's backs. I made a mistake as well, and I will be more careful about that in the future."

Hytham hadn't expected to hear what sounded like genuine regret in Basim's voice. He'd thought it suspicious that Basim had engineered a situation where Hytham wouldn't be able to watch him or to see to it that he stayed on task in their mission. But maybe he'd been mistaken about Basim's motives.

Still, he remembered what Thyra had said earlier, remembered the conversation between her and Basim he'd interrupted just now, and a niggling suspicion remained.

Could he really trust Basim to have his back when Hytham needed him?

"We should return to the palace," Hytham said, pushing off the wall. "Thyra may be looking for us."

They picked their way carefully over the rocky ground and back up the hill. At night, the structure was like a hulking beast crouched on the edge of the sea. Hytham no longer felt awed in its presence. Tonight in particular, he felt as if it were nothing more than a particularly large eyesore on the side of a hill.

They'd been walking in silence for a moment when Basim said, unexpectedly, "You've been training the boy in our ways."

It wasn't a question, and of course Hytham should have expected that Basim would find out. He seemed to be everywhere in the palace, though Hytham never saw a trace of him unless Basim wished it.

"He saw the Hidden Blade the night I killed the viper," Hytham explained. "Ever since then he's been curious, so I worked a bit of stealth training into his general education about our brotherhood and what we stand for. He's committed to it fiercely for one so young, and it's helped him appreciate what we are, by seeing it in action."

Basim didn't comment, and Hytham wondered if he'd erred again somehow. "Do you disapprove?" he pressed. For some reason, in that moment, he felt a bit like Leo trying to impress his elders, and he didn't like the feeling.

Basim stopped on a low rise, looking out again to the dark sea. "No, I think your reasoning is sound, perhaps even inspired," he said, and Hytham was appeased. But then Basim went on, "It's simply that I worry about how close the two of you are becoming." He looked at Hytham, his eyes glittering in the pale moonlight. "Forming an attachment to someone can cause unexpected complications."

Hytham waved it away. "The boy is young," he said, "and lonely. He favors me because I've shown him attention where others haven't, especially his father. If anything, gaining his trust will be a benefit to us."

"It will be, yes, but I was referring to *your* attachment to the boy, my friend."

"Mine?" Instantly, Hytham was defensive. "Maybe it appears that way from the outside, but I've been assigned a mission to protect him, and I take that seriously. Anything more—"

Basim raised his hands for peace. "I'm not reprimanding you, Hytham," he said. "You've done everything you've been asked to do and protected the boy admirably, and your plan to educate him in our ways can only be to his and our cause's benefit. I worry only about your emotions becoming involved in this. It's obvious to me – and to Thyra – that you care for the boy, but let me remind you that he's a pawn in a very long game we're playing. When you care about someone, it can be hard to see them used in such a way." He stared at Hytham intently. "I just want you to keep a clear head during this mission."

He resumed walking, and Hytham had no choice but to follow, picking his footing carefully as they made their way up the hill. His thoughts were in turmoil, a mix of confusion and anger coursing through him.

Had Basim really accused him of not keeping focus on their mission? He, who was under scrutiny by the Hidden Ones for that very indulgence? Was Basim mocking him?

Of course Hytham had become close to the boy. If he was

going to protect Leo effectively, he had to have the boy's trust. More than that, Leo had precious few people in the palace that held his best interests at heart. And if Leo came to embrace their brotherhood's cause the way that Hytham and Basim had, so much the better. He would be a powerful ally in the years to come. All of this was to the good, in Hytham's mind.

"Is that what you and Thyra were discussing earlier, when I interrupted you?" he demanded. "My relationship with Leo?"

The words were out of Hytham's mouth before he'd given them much consideration, driven by frustration and impatience. He was tired of Basim's cagey nature. If Basim was going to demand accountability from him, Hytham would do the same.

Basim paused, the sharp points of a crescent moon shining over his shoulder as he turned and looked down at Hytham from a few paces up the hill. "We did discuss it briefly," he admitted. "You'll be gratified to know that Thyra sees no harm in your bond with the boy. Since you insist on the same, I'll let the matter drop in favor of more pressing concerns." Before Hytham could interject, Basim continued. "Thyra and I also spoke of Anna, and her and Theodore's trip to the fortune teller. I wanted to know if she thought Anna could be a traitor."

Now Hytham felt the fool. What had he expected? That he'd confront Basim, and the man would confess to plotting some secret conspiracy with Thyra outside the Hidden Ones' purview? No, he simply swept along and dodged any attempt Hytham made to probe beneath the surface of his plans and intentions.

"What did Thyra say?" Hytham asked. Whatever his

feelings, he would not let Basim accuse him of improper focus on their mission.

When Basim spoke, Hytham heard the frustration in his voice. "She said if Anna was a traitor, the boy would be dead already. She's as close to him as the boy's mother."

Hytham sighed. "That doesn't help us explain what she was doing speaking to the fortune teller. What of Isaac?" he asked. Perhaps Basim's contacts had turned up some more information.

"Now that's where things get more promising," Basim said. "Up until now, we haven't been able to get much information on the leadership of the Order of the Ancients here. But this man who calls himself Isaac seems to be the head of the Order in Constantinople. He will be the one working with Basil, strengthening their alliance by agreeing to assassinate Leo." A flash of teeth as Basim smiled, a tiger's grin. "And he will be equally frustrated that we continue to thwart his efforts."

That was promising, though Hytham wondered how Basim had obtained this information. Then again, he'd disappeared for long stretches while Hytham guarded Leo at the palace. Obviously, Basim hadn't been idle during that time, and his talent for uncovering secrets continued to impress Hytham in spite of himself.

"Is Isaac our target as well then?" Hytham asked.

"If we can find him, yes," Basim confirmed. "Striking such a blow to the Order will help keep them from getting a hold on the city, and it may even be enough to discourage the emperor from putting his faith in them."

But would it be enough to cause Basil to abandon his plot to kill Leo? Hytham wasn't so sure, not after tonight. "We need to find the traitor and remove them as well," Hytham said. "That may help discourage anyone else in the palace from targeting Leo."

They crested the hill, and, stepping out from the shadow of the palace, Hytham could see the lights of Constantinople spread out tapestry-like before them, and the dome of Hagia Sophia, like an oasis of peace looming out of the dark. It represented people, and life, and faith, and it was a much more peaceful sight than the monstrosity of the palace, a reminder to Hytham that the world was much bigger than this narrow sphere he'd embroiled himself in. This mission would not last forever.

Assuming he survived it.

"I'm going to keep an eye on Justin," Hytham said, pushing those darker thoughts aside. They'd neglected the young man in recent days in pursuit of Anna and Theodore, but Justin was at the top of Hytham's list of suspects, and he was more determined than ever to know where the man's loyalties truly lay.

He needed to know if one of the men holding him down and suffocating him had been Justin. If so, there would be a reckoning.

Basim nodded. "We're making progress," he said. "In the meantime, go and get some rest. Remember, I'll be watching your back. Your sleep can be peaceful, my friend."

Hytham's sleep wouldn't be peaceful. He knew that much. Not until he'd left this place far behind him.

Chapter Fifteen

As it turned out, Hytham didn't have to seek out Justin the following day. The young man found him in the gardens at sunset while Hytham was watching Anna and Leo conducting what appeared to be some kind of nature lesson that included collecting several beetles and spiders, but really seemed like a thinly veiled excuse to be out of doors on a fine evening. Not that Hytham was complaining. The sun had reached that pivotal moment where it turned the city of Constantinople to gold, lighting up the harbor and the palace grounds with that calming, radiant light.

Anna and Leo had been tucked away in the shade of a group of tall, flowering shrubs for the past hour, and all was quiet and secure. The garden walls were at their backs, and Hytham could easily hear anyone coming, so he was able to watch Justin's approach from some distance, his eyes half closed by the angle of the setting sun.

He seemed agitated, Hytham noted, though he suspected

the stiff posture and sullen expression were probably always a part of Justin's demeanor.

"You're not scheduled to relieve me for another hour," Hytham commented when Justin came to stand next to him but did not immediately speak.

"I'm not here to relieve you." The man eyed him sidelong, mouth twisting as if he'd swallowed something sour. "Steros left last night," he said, naming the man Hytham had killed.

"Oh?" Hytham said neutrally. "Was he a friend of yours? I haven't had a chance to get to know everyone in the Varangian Guard, I'm afraid."

"Not a friend, no, but we knew each other. It's not like him to leave so suddenly." Hytham could feel the younger man's eyes boring into him, but Hytham simply stood serenely watching his charge dig in the dirt with his nurse.

His thoughts were racing. Had Justin been with the other man attacking him? Had the two of them planned it together, only for Justin to abandon his partner in the middle of the fight?

To his surprise, Justin took a step closer to him. Hytham shifted, subtly firming his stance in case Justin tried to attack him. It would be folly to do so out here in the garden, but Hytham wasn't taking chances anymore.

"You have a wound on your neck," Justin commented.

Hytham reached up and touched the abraded skin where the blanket had dug into his flesh. "I took a fall during a training session," he said. "Nothing to be concerned about."

As lies went, it wasn't a very good one, but Hytham didn't care. The young man knew something had happened last night. The only question was how much, and did he have that knowledge because he was present?

And was he threatening Hytham now by calling attention to the injury?

During his time with the Hidden Ones, Hytham had learned hard lessons about trusting his instincts, and his gut told him Justin was guilty. His behavior was more than that of a sullen man who'd had his place usurped by an outsider. He was hiding something. All Hytham needed was for the young man to make a mistake, to give him the evidence he needed to prove his guilt.

"Was there something else you wanted, Justin?" Hytham asked when the man didn't leave.

Justin stepped back, glancing over at Leo when the boy let out a peal of laughter. He ignored Hytham's question and turned, shook himself, and left the garden.

Hytham watched the man walk away from him, and he suddenly felt a strong pull inside him, a prickle of awareness that told him he should follow Justin, that there were answers here if he was willing to look for them.

Following those instincts that he could not quite explain but which had rarely steered him wrong, he crossed the garden and passed through the same archway Justin had taken, following the man at a discreet distance. He found Thyra coming toward him from the opposite direction.

"Can you relieve me for a time?" Hytham asked, giving her a meaningful look as he strode past her.

Thyra nodded, asking no questions. She broke stride and immediately went out into the garden to where Leo and Anna were crouched, leaving Hytham free to follow his target.

Yes, as an Assassin, he viewed Justin as a target, one he was fully prepared to eliminate if it became necessary. He'd felt that way since the night Hytham had found the snake attached to the old woman's body and Justin had emerged from the stairway directly after, determined to get to Leo. Hytham had been prepared to kill him then if he proved to be a threat.

But even before that, hadn't he felt animosity toward the young man? That day in the throne room, when Justin had made Leo shrink into himself by calling him a pup…

No.

This wasn't personal, Hytham told himself. Personal grudges had no place here.

He dipped into the shadows as he tailed Justin down the nearest set of servants' stairs. There were more people here, so it was harder to stay hidden, but Hytham knew how to use people to his advantage, to make himself smaller, to fade into the normal bustle of the work day.

Justin paused in the doorway to a large kitchen. Hytham could feel the heat from the cooking fires even back where he stood in shadow. A man had called out to Justin. He must have been a servant, but Hytham didn't recognize him. The noisy kitchen made eavesdropping difficult, but Hytham heard the man say something about a message. Justin scowled as the man handed him a folded scrap of parchment and walked away.

Hytham watched as Justin stood in the kitchen doorway for several minutes, looking down at the message in his hand as if it were one of the vipers Hytham had dispatched. His fingers clenched around the parchment, and Hytham thought for a second that Justin was going to crumple the message and throw it in the fire.

But in the end, his fingers loosened, and he unfolded the message and read it. Hytham watched his expression, but though the young man was quick to show his emotions to Hytham – he could never seem to hide them at all, in fact, when the two of them were together – he gave nothing away of how he was feeling as he turned and strode from the kitchen.

Hytham followed, and it soon became clear that Justin was leaving the palace, though not by the main gate with its steady flow of traffic. Hytham paused for a moment in the shadow of an archway, and used the call of the night bird he and Basim had agreed upon to signal each other.

Assuming the other Assassin was nearby.

It turned out, he didn't have to worry. Less than a minute after Hytham issued his call, Basim was there at his elbow, moving through the shadows with him as they followed Justin out of the palace and through one of the secondary gates, back into the city as dusk was turning into full dark. Candles, house fires, and lanterns illuminated the night, permeating the air with a rich, smoky scent. Above them, the sliver of moon shone pale silver on the rooftops, but there were clouds gathering in the east, promising a night storm.

"Here," Basim said simply, handing Hytham his Assassin garments. "You're not part of the Varangian Guard right now."

He was right. Hytham's easily recognizable scale chainmail would draw too much attention. He slipped the robes on over it and pulled the peaked hood up to conceal his features.

As they moved through the streets, Hytham filled Basim in on his encounter with Justin and everything he'd observed of the young man afterward.

"I believe he's going to meet someone," Hytham said in a soft whisper. Through open windows around him, he could hear the clink of dishes and soft conversations as people prepared their evening meal or spoke to each other by their fires.

"Wherever he's going, it's a place he knows well," Basim said, gesturing to the way the young man turned unerringly down street after street, barely glancing at his surroundings. "You feel strongly about this?" he asked, casting Hytham a sidelong glance.

"I do," Hytham said. "I've felt strongly from the start that the man is suspicious, and before we arrived, he was the member of the Varangian Guard with the most direct access to Leo. Why shouldn't we investigate him?"

"I'm not doubting you," Basim said, holding up his hand in a conciliatory gesture. "I simply want to make sure you're thinking this through."

"I am," Hytham insisted, "and it doesn't matter if you doubt me or not. I have my own doubts and uncertainties – about you and this mission – but one way or another, I'm going to see this through and find out if Justin is a traitor or not."

He'd not meant the words to come out with such vehemence, but he couldn't take them back now, and Hytham couldn't honestly say he regretted them.

Basim hesitated, and for the first time since they'd met, Hytham thought he might've truly surprised the man. "Very well," he said. "Lead on."

Going by their surroundings, they were entering the city's poorer districts. The streets were narrower and dirtier, less well-lit than the main thoroughfares. The buildings were tall and sagging against one another, with many apartments clustered together under one roof. The smells of waste grew thicker, the air hazy with poorly ventilated smoke.

They were well removed from the world of the palace now. It struck Hytham that they hadn't had to travel very far to see the gap between the immense wealth and poverty in Constantinople, but having been on both sides of the divide now, he realized he'd never truly appreciated how enormous that gap was.

Justin turned down a dark alley, and for a moment Hytham feared they would lose him as he quickened his step.

"Look," Basim said softly, laying a hand on Hytham's arm.

Hytham looked where he indicated, and at the other end of the alley, he glimpsed a figure in a dark cloak and hood step out of the shadows to intercept Justin. The young man tensed, but then relaxed, seeming to recognize him.

Hytham and Basim pressed their bodies to the alley wall and crept closer. The men were speaking in low voices now, and Hytham desperately wanted to hear what they were saying, but other voices and drunken laughter from the tenements above drifted down, making it impossible to hear. He glanced at Basim, who gave a nod, and they crouched low and moved nearer, using ssome broken crates and piles of trash stacked along the wall as cover. It was a risk, but Hytham was willing to take it.

He was rewarded when he could finally make out Justin's voice, low and angry, scant feet away from where they hid.

"... gave you my answer," he was saying tersely. "You won't get more than this meeting from me."

"The blow doesn't have to come from you directly, if that's what troubles you," the other man said, and reached out as if to lay a hand on Justin's shoulder. Justin's body went rigid, and the glower he sent the man caused him to retract his hand. "All you have to do is make sure he's in the place we tell you to put him. Others will do the rest, but I promise you, you'll reap the largest of the rewards. The emperor will see to it. He's calling on your loyalty, Justin, the vow you swore to your master."

Justin shifted, turning slightly away from them, so Hytham couldn't see his face, but he read the young man's body language clearly enough. He watched Justin fight the instinct to recoil, fists clenched at his sides.

When he didn't immediately reply, the man leaned in closer, being careful not to touch him. "You know where we are," he said. "We know there are things here that are precious to you. This is a chance to protect and provide for the people you care about. Think hard before you throw that away. This is the last time we're going to ask."

A soft rain was beginning to fall, clicking off the tiled roofs and running in small rivulets down Hytham's covered neck. He hadn't noticed the way the clouds had scudded in to cover the moon, so fixated was he on the conversation unfolding in the alley.

After a moment, Justin nodded slowly. "I understand," he said. "You've been patient. I'll give you my answer now."

The man was still standing very close to him. Justin pivoted, and Hytham saw the flash of the knife blade as Justin brought it up, stabbing the man in the armpit. Hytham's breath caught in shock as the man grunted, but he didn't fall to the ground. Instead he grabbed Justin and threw him against the wall opposite where Hytham and Basim were hiding. Justin's head hit the bricks with a dull, sickening thud, and his attacker staggered back, reaching beneath his cloak for a weapon, his movements clumsy as blood ran down his flank.

Justin went for his sword, and the blades clanged off each other in the narrow space, quick, dirty slashes that had little finesse. Both men were injured, but it was clear the one losing blood was also losing the upper hand. Justin drove him deeper into the alley, feet slipping on the trash and wet stones. The rain was coming harder now, affecting visibility as the water splashed up from the ground, and the sound of the roaring downpour helped cover the clash of weapons.

Hytham moved instinctively to intervene, but Basim put a restraining hand on his arm. Hytham wanted to shrug it off, but he knew what Basim must be thinking. If they distracted Justin by showing themselves now, his opponent could take advantage and land a killing blow. Fortunately, Justin seemed to have the fight in hand. He continued to herd the man toward a deserted street at the other end of the alley. Hytham and Basim followed, both tensed to spring.

But just as the man reached the mouth of the alley, he tripped over some broken stones, feet sliding in muck and animal dung, and Justin had his opening. He ran the man through with his sword, hand over his mouth to muffle the cry of pain. Then Justin pulled him back into the darkness and dumped his body behind a pile of trash. He wiped his sword and dagger clean and put them away, breathing hard.

Hytham watched him for a second, waiting for the haze of battle to fade from him so that they could reveal themselves without startling him into an attack.

Basim put a hand on Hytham's shoulder. "Be ready," he whispered.

Hytham's head whipped around, and then he saw them. Two more figures approached Justin from behind, a man and woman, cloaked and armed, their swords out. Justin must have heard them, for he spun, sword hissing out of its scabbard again. He stood with his shoulders thrown back defiantly, but Hytham knew he was tired and probably still reeling from the head wound he'd taken against the alley wall. He couldn't fight both of these enemies and win.

Justin gave a hollow laugh as the man and woman advanced, walking right past Basim and Hytham where they hid in the shadows.

"At least you can say it took three of you," Justin said. He spat on the ground.

And then Basim stepped away from the alley wall, Hytham at his side.

They had maneuvered themselves behind their targets. The rain hid any sound their footfalls might have made, and they moved through water as effortlessly as air. The shadows held them safely, concealing them from the rest of the world. Because the shadows were their home, that liminal space where they could hide and observe.

Or hunt.

They moved as one, their Hidden Blades flashing silver in the rain, and just like that, it was over. Justin's attackers were dead before they realized they were in danger. They made very little sound as they fell, their blood already washing away under the assault of the rain.

Justin's breath caught when he realized what had happened to his attackers, his sword still raised defensively. "Who are you?" he demanded of Hytham and Basim. "Show yourselves."

Hytham stepped further into the light, letting his hood drop. "It's me," he said.

Justin's eyes widened in recognition, but he didn't lower his sword. His brow furrowed, as if he didn't know whether Hytham's appearance was a blessing or a danger. Hytham felt a pang of shame at that, that Justin thought him a person who'd stab him in the back in a dark alley.

The downpour had slackened but rain continued to fall steadily. Justin's hair was soaked, and the water had washed away the blood from a cut on his cheek. "You followed me," he said to Hytham, unnecessarily.

"We thought we were following a traitor," Basim said. He sheathed his sword and brushed some of the water from his robes. "But I suppose in a way you are a traitor, aren't you, Justin? You just defied your emperor, after all."

Justin stood straighter. "Does that make you my executioners?"

At that, Basim laughed. "I like him, Hytham," he said, clapping Hytham on the shoulder. "He reminds me a bit of you. Perhaps that's why the two of you clash so perfectly."

"I'm glad you're finding humor in this," Hytham said. He turned to Justin. "We followed you because we thought you were being paid to assassinate Leo." He nodded to the dead man in the trash heap. "That is what he wanted from you, yes?"

Justin nodded. "It's not the first time they've tried to recruit me," he said, and huffed a laugh that had no humor in it. "I don't even know who 'they' are, just that they work for the emperor." He took in Hytham and Basim's clothing, the peaked hood and robes, wet with rain but still impressive and distinctive for all that. "Who are you?" he repeated. "You don't work for the emperor, but you're not truly one of the Varangian Guard either."

"We've been hired independently to see to Leo's safety and the future prosperity of Constantinople," Basim said. "You say this isn't the first time you've been asked to join the conspiracy against Leo. I assume this is the first time you've answered with violence?"

Justin nodded. "They gave me no choice when they asked to meet me in this neighborhood," he said, his expression hardening. "Someone I care for lives here, and they found out about it. Bringing me here was a threat, so I knew I either had to join their cause or give them my answer once and for all."

Hytham tried to reconcile the picture he'd been building of Justin in his mind with what was confronting him here. Everything he thought he'd known had been upended. "What about your friend?" he asked. "They'll be in danger now."

Justin gave Hytham a flat look. "I take care of my own," he said. "I'll make sure they get somewhere safe and that they aren't found again."

"I don't understand," Hytham said, letting some of his frustration show. "You hate the boy. You hated *me* for taking your place in the Varangian Guard hierarchy. If you'd taken their offer, you'd have had everything you wanted and the emperor's favor on top of it."

Justin's expression turned to disgust. "And that's enough to make me a child murderer, is it?"

Next to Hytham, Basim shrugged. "For some men, it takes much less," he said. "You were near the top of our list of suspects."

"You didn't do yourself any favors with how you treated Leo," Hytham said.

"How I treated…" With jerky movements, Justin sheathed

his sword, then took a moment to gather himself before glaring at Hytham. "You have no idea what you're talking about. You show up at the palace out of nowhere, stay for a few weeks to play hero, and you think you know what that boy's life is like and what he needs. You don't know anything."

Hytham crossed his arms. The hostility was back, flaring in the young man's gaze, and they were in familiar territory again. "You're a bully. If you'd shown him a degree of kindness, then maybe–"

Justin laughed, the harsh sound echoing off the alley walls. "You think I wasn't kind to him?" He took a step toward Hytham, fists clenched. Beside him, Basim tensed, but Hytham glanced at him and shook his head slightly. "Leo was like a younger brother to me when I first came to the palace," Justin said, voice tight with anger. "I was just like you. I saw how lonely he was, that he needed a friend." He looked away, scrubbing the rain off his face. "I thought I was helping him, but then the emperor noticed how happy Leo was, and it didn't take long for him to figure out that I was to blame."

Hytham was shaken. He searched Justin's face, looking for a lie, but he couldn't see any deception there. "What happened?" he asked. His throat felt constricted.

"Nothing," Justin said bitterly. "He never reprimanded me or confronted me about it. He sent all his messages through Leo. I tried to train him, just like you," he said to Hytham. Hytham's surprise must have shown on his face, because Justin just laughed again. "I saw Leo practicing. It made me realize what you must have been doing, and you were right to keep it a secret." His expression twisted briefly with guilt. "I should have thought to do that."

Hytham forced himself to speak, recalling a conversation he'd had with the boy. "Leo said you started to teach him archery, but something happened. He wouldn't say what."

"He tried to show his father that he could hit a target," Justin said. "He thought it would make the emperor *proud*, that if he showed some strength, maybe his father wouldn't hate him so much. Can you imagine?" He shook his head. "The emperor broke his arm. It took months before he was able to hold a bow again, and by that time, he didn't want to go near one again."

A sickening sensation tightened Hytham's stomach. "So every time you showed Leo kindness, the emperor punished the boy," he said.

Justin nodded. "I was afraid he would dismiss me outright, so I went back to being indifferent, thinking that was what it would take, but it wasn't enough. I had to pretend to despise him before the emperor was satisfied. He wanted nothing less than for Leo's trust in me to be shattered." He looked at Hytham. "He'll do the same to you. He'll wait until he knows how much you care about him, and then he'll take it all away."

Justin fell silent as Hytham's thoughts reeled with these revelations. The rain continued to fall in icy needles against his skin, but he barely noticed it.

Justin had never hated Leo. In fact, he had cared for him so much that he was willing to destroy the relationship he'd built with the boy in order to save him from his father's wrath.

And he'd refused to conspire with the emperor to kill the boy, even though it might end up destroying his own life.

Hytham was at a loss for words as everything he'd thought he knew about Justin realigned in the space of a few moments.

He knew it was possible the man was lying, of course, and they would have to try to verify his story to be sure. But staring at the young man's defiant face in the alley with the three bodies lying nearby, Hytham knew deep in his gut that it was all true. His view of Justin had been wrong, based on assumptions that he'd made by looking at the surface of things. He'd made no attempt to dig deeper.

He could feel Basim's gaze on him, and Hytham tried to pull his thoughts together. "If you aren't the traitor," he said, addressing Justin, "then it must be Theodore or Anna. Do you have any idea which of them it might be?"

Justin scoffed. "Don't you see? The emperor could be making offers like the one he made to me to both of them, to *anyone* in the palace." His voice rose with anger and frustration as he spoke. "I don't know who you are or who you represent in this city, and I'm grateful you want to protect the boy, believe me. For a while, I was certain you were the one who was going to kill him." He shook his head, and his expression took on an edge of despair. "But I have to accept that Leo's going to die. It's only a matter of time. We can't protect him from the might of the emperor forever."

At that, Basim stirred, and there was that predatory smile again, the one Hytham was used to seeing when the man was presented with an impossible challenge. "Given time enough," he said, "we may surprise you."

Bold words, but Hytham didn't contradict him. A terrible suspicion had taken hold of him based on what Justin had said.

It's only a matter of time.

Maybe his attackers had just been waiting for a way to engineer that moment.

"They lured you away from the palace," Hytham said. "No matter what answer you gave, you're away from Leo right now." He looked at Basim and immediately saw understanding in his gaze. "And in following him, they've lured us away too."

Justin cursed, but Basim grabbed his arm before he could move. "See to your friend," he said. "Make sure they're safe, and then come to the palace as quickly as you can."

Chapter Sixteen

Hytham and Basim raced through the city streets. Rain had soaked the world and cast everything in pale, liquid silver. The weather had driven many people inside, so they moved unimpeded, but it still seemed to Hytham that the palace was a hundred miles away and that they couldn't possibly reach Leo in time.

The sense of dread Hytham had been feeling since talking to Justin only grew. If he was wrong about him, what else had Hytham missed?

"Now's not the time to doubt yourself," Basim said from beside him, as if he could read Hytham's thoughts. Perhaps he could. The man was supernatural. How many things about *Basim* had Hytham misjudged in all this?

"If the boy dies because I read Justin's motives wrong, then–"

"If the boy dies, it will be because his father had him murdered," Basim snapped. "You or Justin will have had no hand in that. But we're going to do everything we can to prevent that from happening. Focus, Hytham," he said, as they climbed the hill toward the palace. "Remember the mission. You're serving a higher purpose here. It isn't just about Leo. There is so much at stake beyond him. Don't lose sight of that."

No, he wouldn't, but that didn't mean Leo wasn't important. Hytham cared for the boy, but it was more than that, he told himself. Basil was twisted. He would drag the city down in his sadistic games and machinations. He would let the Order run rampant in Constantinople, digging themselves in deeper and deeper until there was no way to root them all out. For generations they'd be trying to clean up the damage that Basil had caused because he could never see beyond a personal grudge against a dead man. People like that were prime targets for the Order to control and manipulate.

Leo would be different. Leo deserved better, and Hytham would make sure he lived and thrived and became the leader Hytham knew he could be.

They reached the palace gates. Basim disappeared, and Hytham had shed his robes in favor of the uniform of the Varangian Guard, so he was let through with haste. When he told the guards at the gate that he suspected an attack was about to happen, they came on full alert.

None of this would mean anything if the assassins were already inside.

Hytham stopped briefly at another guard checkpoint once they were inside, while Basim melted into the shadows and continued on to find Thyra and Leo. He questioned the woman on duty to ask if she'd seen anything suspicious, but there had been nothing. It had been quiet, and Hytham felt a quick jolt of relief. Maybe he was imagining things, enemies around every corner. Maybe nothing was planned for tonight.

"It's the quietest night we've had in some time," the woman said, sounding pleased. "For once there's no parties and no guests staying the night. Makes for a pleasant change if you ask me."

No parties. No guests of the emperor tonight. Hytham's dread came rushing back.

No witnesses.

"Gather anyone else who's on duty and send them to search the premises," he told her, and ran, not bothering to wait to see if she complied.

He knew something was wrong as soon as he reached the hallway leading to the children's wing. The candles lining the halls had all been snuffed out. He could smell the remnants of smoke in the air.

And then, a distant scream, quickly cut off. Hytham plunged into the darkness toward the sound, drawing his sword as he went.

The door to Anna's room was ajar. Moonlight from the windows beyond illuminated blood pooling on the marble floor around the door. Hytham shoved it open the rest of the way with his blade.

The room had been torn to pieces. The body of a male servant – one of the cooks, Hytham thought – lay just inside the room. His throat had been slashed. Beside him, a chair and wardrobe had been overturned, and there was more blood on the walls. That was all Hytham could take in before that choked scream came again.

On the opposite side of the room, near the bed, Anna

struggled on the floor with a cloaked and hooded man. He had his arm around her throat, trying to choke her. With one hand, she tried to free herself. In the other she held what looked like a small paring knife, good for slicing fruit. She stabbed her attacker in the soft flesh of his forearm once, twice. He roared in pain, and his grip on her slackened but didn't break.

She was defending Leo. Otherwise the assassin wouldn't have bothered to target her. The boy must be hiding somewhere in the room. Hytham stepped over the body of the cook and crossed the room in three quick strides. The man looked up, his eyes widening as he beheld Hytham. Hytham lifted his sword, but the man had the presence of mind to wrench Anna's body around, using it as a shield between himself and Hytham's blade.

Cursing, Hytham reached down and grabbed the man by the hair, slamming his head into the wall. The man howled and retaliated by thrusting Anna at him with all his strength. Hytham only just got his sword out of the way before the weight of Anna's body knocked him to the floor. Anna's temple struck the marble, and she gave a broken cry of pain.

Hytham rolled her off him, trying not to hurt her, but it cost him speed. The man slammed into him, and Hytham's sword went skittering across the floor. He landed on his back with his attacker straddling him. Shards of broken glass and other debris littered the floor, digging into Hytham's back. His attacker had no knife or other ready weapon, but he went for Hytham's throat with his large hands. Hytham grabbed the man's wrists before he could get a grip on hm.

His attacker was strong, the weight on him substantial, and it reminded Hytham sickeningly of the night he'd almost been suffocated in his bed. This time he was ready and shoved back hard, pushing up to a sitting position, grabbing for the man's face. He'd just gotten a leg under him to stand when the man changed tactics and seized Hytham by the waist, shoving him into the wall. Hytham felt the breath leave him, but he brought his right hand up as the man slammed him into the wall again, aiming the Hidden Blade to slide between his ribs.

The man saw the gesture, and his gaze darkened. He came in fast and drove his fist into Hytham's ribs. Hytham gasped, his arm going slack at the explosion of pain in his abdomen. He managed to recover, and the Hidden Blade sprang free. Hytham stabbed at his attacker, but the man was fast, and Hytham's strikes were clumsy with pain. The man dodged them, scrambling away across the room. Hytham pursued, and barely had time to get out of the way when his attacker grabbed a small statue that had fallen and cracked on the floor, throwing it at Hytham.

He didn't have time for this. He needed to find Leo, Basim, and the others. He needed to finish this.

His attacker turned, and must have seen something of Hytham's thoughts in his expression, because he lunged desperately for Hytham's sword where it lay on the floor near the door. Anna, lying nearby, recovering from the blow she'd taken to the head, reached out and wrapped both her arms around the man's ankles and pulled viciously. He swayed, off balance, and Hytham took advantage of the distraction to retrieve his sword before the man could grab it.

The man kicked Anna viciously in the chest. She groaned in pain but clung to him, her face twisted in rage. "You… won't… have him," she snarled.

He kicked her off him and dropped, dodging Hytham's lunge, but he caught a slash on his arm, sleeve tearing and bright blood trailing after. He backed away, grabbed a wooden serving tray to use as a shield. Hytham stalked him, calmer now. He had the Hidden Blade and his sword, and there was no place for the man to run.

Still, the assassin was good. He blocked Hytham's sword strikes, using his weight to keep Hytham off balance and prevent him from driving him into a corner. But his shield was flimsy, and Hytham's patience was at an end. He feinted, then brought his leg up, aiming a kick right at the man's shield. The tray snapped in half, and Hytham pivoted, burying the Hidden Blade in the man's chest. The man looked down at the weapon, and though he surely knew that he was dead, still he grabbed at Hytham. He snatched at clothing, skin, hair, even as his strength drained away and his knees gave out. Hytham let him drop to the floor. He stepped back, waiting a beat to make sure the man was dead before he turned and went to check on Anna.

She was curled into herself on the floor, clutching her chest. Blood ran down one side of her face, but her eyes were alert, and her gaze fastened on him like a hawk as he knelt beside her.

"Where's Leo?" Hytham demanded. "Is he in here hiding?"

"No." She grabbed a fistful of his uniform, blunt nails digging into the cloth, using it to pull herself to a sitting position. Her other hand fastened on his arm. "I looked for him, but he wasn't in his room. You have to find him. They're all over the children's wing. They came for him."

And for her. Hytham had thought the boy had been hiding

in here, making Anna a target when she tried to protect him, but that obviously wasn't the case. That meant one of the assassins had come into her room, targeting her specifically. The poor cook must have tried to help and paid the price. Hytham put that knowledge away for now. They'd address Anna's role in all this later, if everyone lived through the night.

"Get yourself somewhere safe," Hytham said, helping the nurse to her feet. "Find the other servants. Barricade yourselves in a room and don't open the door until this is over."

For a second it looked as if she would argue, but whatever she saw in Hytham's expression stopped her, and she gave a nod. "Go," she said.

He went out into the hall first, blade leading, covering her as she ran toward the nearest servant stairs. Hytham watched her go, then headed down the hall toward Leo's room. Anna had said Leo wasn't there, but maybe he would see Basim or Thyra.

Leo. Had they taken him? Or had he managed to hide, just as Hytham had taught him? A surge of painful hope went through him at the thought.

He crooked an arm over his ribs as he moved down the hall. Breathing was difficult. He must have cracked one or two in the fight. He put the pain out of his mind and listened. Sounds of fighting drifted down the hall to him, and he quickened his step.

A door to his right burst open, and another cloaked figure came charging out. He didn't see Hytham but called out to someone down the hall. "He's not here. Check the next one."

He also didn't see Hytham glide swiftly up behind him. Hytham covered his mouth as he stabbed him at the base of his spine. Shifting his weight, Hytham dumped his body back into the room the man had come from and continued on without breaking stride.

The sounds of fighting grew louder the closer he got to Leo's room. He rounded a corner and nearly stumbled over the bodies of two of the Varangian Guards. They'd fallen at an intersection, and there were three cloaked figures dead around them. They'd died slowing the attacking force down. How many were left?

Beyond the bodies, outside Leo's door, Hytham found Thyra and Basim fighting two more assassins. Thyra's face was covered in sweat, her arms trembling, as if she'd been fighting for some time, and her hand axes showed the proof of it. She swung again with a howling cry, teeth bared. It made her attacker draw back, and that was all the opening she needed to slash him in the arm, opening a deep wound and leaving the appendage dangling limp at the man's side.

Basim was fighting in a corner, driven there by a man Hytham recognized. He still wore the livery of the Varangian Guards, but he was obviously no longer an ally. He shoved Basim against the wall, at the same time grabbing a dagger from his belt and hurling it at Thyra. The weapon missed her, but not by much. The fighting was close here, and dirty, and with so many bodies to trip over, one slip could mean death. Hytham couldn't wade in to help them without risking doing more harm than good. He had to find Leo.

Hytham turned his attention to Leo's room. Like Anna's, it was as if a storm had blown through. The bedclothes were torn and scattered over the floor, and the bed itself had been yanked away from the wall and overturned. The chest by the foot of the bed had had its lid torn off, the lock broken, its contents emptied.

As if they were searching for him. Again, Hytham felt that quick pull of hope inside him. He may have gotten away. He may have hidden.

"Leo!" he called, just in case. He kicked aside the chest and checked behind the overturned bed, but there was no sign of the boy.

Hytham went back out into the hall. He caught Basim's eye even in the midst of battle. Basim gave him a quick nod and a hint of that dangerous smile. *Find the boy*, the look said. *I'm just having a bit of fun.*

Hytham knew the situation was far more serious than that, and he did not want to leave Basim or Thyra, but he knew his mission, and Basim and Thyra expected him to carry it out.

He took off down the hallway, deeper into the palace. Mentally, he ran through the different hiding places he'd shown to Leo that day they'd trained together. He started in the sitting rooms just past the children's wing, but the rooms were silent, undisturbed, and a quick check found them empty. Hytham pressed on to the library. Surely here, Leo would feel comfortable. It was where they'd spent the most time.

He checked the bookshelf with the creaking board, but it was empty. He stopped, listening for signs of breathing or other hints as to a presence in the room. The silence was complete, oppressive. Hytham could hear only the distant sounds of the fighting in the children's wing.

Back in the hall, he went left, in the general direction of the empress's rooms. Maybe Leo had panicked and run to his mother.

He stopped short when he caught sight of a small pair of sandals discarded near the wall. He picked one up, but he knew before he touched them that they were Leo's. At least he knew he was going in the right direction. Hytham looked around, but a sudden inspiration made him double back to a small arched doorway that led out to one of the many private gardens in this section of the palace.

Moonlight cast the trees and walkways in stark silver glows, raindrops still glistening on the leaves, though the rain had finally stopped. Like many of the formal gardens, its centerpiece was a large stone fountain, water pouring in three wide curtains from the mouths of three stone lions into a shallow basin. Benches surrounded the fountain, flanked by potted lemon trees and flowers brought in from all over the world. It wasn't a place where Leo was usually allowed to play, but they'd trained here too, and Hytham remembered Leo had been particularly pleased with his choice of hiding place out here.

First Hytham paced the garden, searching among the trees and flower beds for hidden enemies, but all was quiet, no sounds but the night insects humming and the gentle fall of water.

He approached the fountain cautiously, dropping to one knee while keeping an eye on the arched doorway. The faintest bit of movement behind the curtain of water told him his instincts had been right, and Hytham clenched his fist at the unexpected swell of relief in his chest.

"It's me," he said, though he wasn't sure his voice carried above the fall of water. He reached into the curtain of water with his right hand, palm up, so Leo would see the Hidden Blade.

There was a small, choked cry, and then cold, wet hands grabbed onto him. Hytham hauled Leo out of the fountain like a struggling fish. He was drenched, clothes sticking to his skin, shivering all over, though that might have been more from shock and fear than the cold. Hytham wished he had a blanket with him.

"It's all right," he murmured when Leo clung to him. Even shaking and afraid, the boy stayed quiet. He knew that the danger hadn't passed.

That same instinct made Hytham look up just as two cloaked men came into the garden, the grays and blacks they wore blending them so thoroughly with their surroundings that Hytham almost thought they were from the brotherhood. But no, when they saw Hytham, the taller one drew a pair of curved knives, and the shorter a sword. They separated, intending to come at him from either side of the fountain.

"Leo," Hytham said, his face close to the boy's ear. "Can you climb trees?"

He kept his eyes trained on the approaching assassins, but he felt the boy nod against his chest. Hytham stood up, pushing the boy behind him, in the direction of a small grove near the back garden wall. The trees there were more mature, and they stretched all the way up to a seven-foot stone wall. He didn't know if he could take both his attackers, but if Leo could climb one of the trees and get to the wall, he could cross the garden and get back to the palace.

Hytham would at least ensure he provided that escape.

He drew his sword and came around the side of the fountain, keeping it for the moment between him and the approaching men. He gauged the distance in his mind, muscles loose, feet pressing firmly to the ground to center himself. He took a deep breath, and heard the sounds of distant night birds and gulls hovering over the sea.

Then he exploded into motion, leaping up onto the lip of the fountain, launching himself into the air, over the cascading water and the lions' mouths. The Hidden Blade flashed in the moonlight as he came down on the taller man. The assassin tried to dodge, but Hytham impaled his shoulder with his blade. The man cried out and staggered back. He brought his knives up in defense, but his left arm was slower, weaker from the wound, which gave Hytham time to bring his sword up to block one blade even as he dodged the other.

Out of the corner of his eye, he saw Leo climbing the tallest tree in the grove with surprising speed. But the shorter man was crossing the garden toward him, determined to catch him before he climbed too high.

Hytham tried to pivot around his opponent and took a knife slash in the arm. Hytham grabbed the man's wrist and came in close, using his wounded shoulder to shove him off balance. The backs of his knees hit the rim of the fountain, and he dropped one of his knives into the water as he scrambled for balance. Hytham wanted to push further, to try to finish him off, but he had to intercept the other man before he got to Leo.

He danced back, leaving his opponent to scramble for his weapon while Hytham ran across the courtyard. The shorter man was at the base of the tree, reaching up to grab Leo's ankle. The boy let out a frightened shout, losing his grip on a branch. Somehow, he held on with one hand, struggling frantically.

Hytham came in behind him, but the man saw him and at

the last second released Leo and spun. Their sword clash rang out in the garden. Over the man's shoulder, Hytham saw Leo recover and scramble up into the safety of the upper boughs of the tree.

But the man with the knives had recovered too, and he was coming for Hytham.

Hytham feinted and backed up, retreating until the ivy-covered garden wall loomed at his back. He didn't like giving ground, but he couldn't risk any other enemies coming out into the garden where he couldn't see them.

Next to his feet was a line of clay pots filled with colorful flowers. Not quite as good as a knife or a bow, but they'd do. He scooped two of them up and threw them at the man with the knives. He dodged one but the other caught him in the chest, and he staggered long enough for Hytham to engage the shorter man again. He kept moving as they fought, leading his opponent so he was between Hytham and the knife wielder. The breath was starting to burn in his lungs, and his arms were on fire. He couldn't keep this up forever, but he couldn't risk looking for Leo again to see if he'd escaped.

A knife whistled past his head, nicking his right ear in a bright flash of pain.

He could almost hear Basim's voice in his head. *Don't let your mind wander.*

Blood dripped down Hytham's neck, and sweat drenched his skin. His breath sounded loud in his ears as he fought, using speed to keep the swordsman at bay, and occasionally hurling potted missiles at the knife-wielder, who seemed content to keep his distance and look for an opening to throw his other weapon.

Because they know I'm tiring. They know it's only a matter of waiting until I make a mistake.

Anger gave Hytham renewed energy. He would not be an exhausted horse waiting to drop. He'd take at least one of them with him.

He drove harder, teeth gritted, letting his fury show. His sword arm trembled as he caught the other blade at the hilt. A few feet away, the knife wielder became impatient and came at his exposed flank. Hytham went to pull back, but the sword wielder grabbed him and tried to pull him in instead. Hytham wrenched free and dodged, but the knife wielder's attack had been a feint. He kicked out, connecting solidly with Hytham's knee.

An explosion of pain threatened to drop him. Hytham only remained standing by grabbing onto the swordsman. They were tangled together, blades between them, breathing fast and harsh, neither giving ground.

The man with the knife laughed and spun his blade in his hand. "You held out longer than I thought you would," he said.

Hytham braced for the attack that would end him, but it didn't come.

The man stiffened, dropping his knife as he coughed.

"What are you doing?" the swordsman demanded.

Then Hytham saw it, the red stain spreading from the man's torso and the blade protruding from his skin. He crumpled, and Basim stood up from where he'd been crouched behind the man, utterly silent for the kill.

The wave of relief that swept through Hytham almost caused him to drop his guard. The swordsman, suddenly outnumbered himself, ripped his sword free from Hytham's grip and turned to run, vaulting over the fountain and scaling the garden wall. He was fast. Hytham tried to limp after him, but his knee was on fire, harsh waves of pain radiating through his body.

Basim caught and steadied him before he fell. "Let him go," he said. "He won't get far. Every guard in the palace is alerted."

It reassured Hytham, but only a little. He lowered himself to sit on the lip of the fountain to take some weight off his knee. Across the garden, Leo was climbing down from the tree. He jumped the last few feet and came running across the courtyard, throwing himself at Hytham. Hytham caught him, wrapping an arm around his shoulders.

"You're going to push us both into the water," he said dryly.

"I thought they were going to kill you!" Leo's voice trembled. He looked up at Basim with wide eyes. "You came back."

"I never left," Basim said with a wink. "You did a fine job hiding, little one."

Still clinging to Hytham, Leo swelled with the praise.

"How many of them were there?" Hytham asked, his gaze straying to the garden wall again, where the assassin had fled. There was blood dripping from the ivy, black in the sallow moonlight. He'd not realized the swordsman was hurt so badly. He must have been injured sometime during his assault on the children's wing. The wounds would slow him down, but would it be enough for the guards to corner him? These assassins had been well trained, vicious and skillful. The average palace guard wouldn't stand a chance.

"Nine that we counted," Basim said, answering Hytham's question. "Seven are dead, and two escaped."

No one alive to interrogate. Hytham closed his eyes against the hot anger that burned in his chest.

"We have to find them," Hytham said, appealing to Basim. "They came too close tonight." His grip on Leo unconsciously tightened. Basim tracked the movement and his eyes narrowed. Hytham knew the man would think he was overstepping, that this was personal.

And it was. Tonight, it was. Hytham didn't bother to deny it anymore. The anger burned too bright. He and Leo had both come close to death. He wanted to take the fight to his enemies instead of waiting within the palace walls for a knife in the dark.

Before Basim could reply to his request, they heard the sound of footsteps approaching. Hytham tensed, but it was only Thyra. She still held her hand axes, and blood soaked the front of her uniform.

When Thyra's gaze fell on Leo, some of the tension around her mouth and eyes eased. It was the only visible change in her demeanor. "The children's wing is secure," she told them. "Justin has returned as well and demanded to know where Leo was." The curl of Thyra's lip told Hytham exactly what she thought of Justin's demands.

But Hytham felt an uncomfortable mixture of relief and shame to hear of Justin's concern for Leo. They would still have to verify the story he'd told them, but Hytham was now convinced of the man's innocence. He'd been made a pawn, just like Leo, in a game the emperor had initiated with the power of the Order behind him.

"Leo," Hytham said, "go back inside with Thyra. It'll be safer there." They'd find another room for him tonight since his own had been destroyed.

Thyra held out her hand, and Leo reluctantly peeled himself from Hytham's side to join her. When they'd gone, Hytham stood up, testing his weight on his injured knee. There was still the throbbing pain, but it was starting to fade, and he could walk well enough. Maybe even run, if he had to.

He glanced again at the garden wall.

Basim was scrutinizing him. "You fought well," he said, his expression unreadable. "There was a moment when I first came into the garden that I thought they would overwhelm you."

"So did I," Hytham said. "And they would have, were it not for your intervention." He nodded toward the palace. "One of the assassins was targeting Anna."

Basim cocked his head. "Targeting her directly? Are you sure? Maybe she just got in his way while he was headed for Leo's room."

It would be like her, with her devotion to the boy, but Hytham shook his head. "He was in her room. He killed another servant who was in there too, probably come to help her. There were no signs of a struggle in the hallway, but her room was torn apart like Leo's. I believe she was also a target this time." Had the assassin succeeded, it would have been easy enough to make it look like she was simply collateral damage afterward, dying while shielding Leo.

"The fortune teller," Basim said, meeting Hytham's gaze. "And Isaac."

Hytham nodded. Anna was involved in something she didn't understand, and Hytham was beginning to put the pieces together where her role was concerned, but he needed to talk to Anna to confirm his theory.

"I'm going to make sure there are no other assassins lying in wait," Basim said, pulling up his hood. "I'll shadow Anna as well and make sure she doesn't leave the palace. Stay with Leo for now."

"But we should go after the assassin who escaped," Hytham insisted. "There's still time to track him."

"No," Basim said, his voice stern. "Keep your focus on the mission, Hytham. Don't make this more personal than you already have."

Hytham's patience snapped.

"You would truly stand there and lecture me about not focusing on the mission?" he burst out. "*I'm* not the one who's lost sight of our purpose."

The sudden tension in the air was palpable. Basim took a step toward Hytham. "Do you want to go down this road, my friend?" he asked softly. "Do you finally want to admit that you've been spying on one of your brothers all this time?"

Hytham recoiled. "You knew all along, didn't you? How?"

Basim laughed. "Of course, I knew. Ah, Hytham, if you could only see how painfully transparent you are. You're going to have to learn to curb your emotions and reactions if you want to survive in the Hidden Ones' ranks."

Hytham felt his cheeks flush with anger. "Why didn't you say anything?" he demanded. "You could have confronted me."

Basim lifted his shoulders with a mocking smile. "If I had, the Hidden Ones might have sent someone more competent to watch me. I preferred this arrangement."

And then he slipped into the shadows and was gone before Hytham could reply.

For a moment, Hytham stood in the dark, hands fisted at his sides as the anger and humiliation roiled through him. Well, at least he knew where he stood with Basim now. He'd pitied Leo in the beginning for being an unwitting pawn in a bigger game than the boy could comprehend.

But Hytham had also been a pawn of Basim's, and he'd never known it either.

He'd been given his orders. Hytham knew what Basim expected of him. Basim was the Master Assassin, and Hytham was the Acolyte. All that was left was to do what he was told.

Not this time.

Let Basim play his games and toy with people. Hytham would see the mission through, with or without him.

He tested his weight on his knee again and winced. Good enough. He could handle the pain. He went to the garden wall and, being careful to avoid the blood, climbed up and over to pick up the trail of the assassin.

The anger burned hot and bright inside of him, spurring him on. If the guards at the palace hadn't caught the man, Hytham would. He had been in this city long enough to know its streets, its colors, its vibrancy, and its people. And he'd been trained to track his enemies, to hunt them, graceful and silent like a raptor gliding over a winter field.

He could track an injured man, and he would find the nest where he went to ground. It was time to take the fight to their enemies, and maybe even to this mysterious Isaac. Hytham was more than ready for that confrontation.

CHAPTER SEVENTEEN

It was getting late, an hour of the night when the traffic on the streets was sparse, but Hytham could hear the distant, raucous cries of revelers, the shouts of drunken arguments. He glimpsed the shadows of figures slipping off into alleys for secret dealings or trysts.

Hytham was making no attempt to hide himself yet. He needed to move quickly. The enemy he tracked already had a good lead on him, even if he was injured. Hytham had followed a steady blood trail out of the palace gate, but he'd stopped long enough to question the guards there about how an injured man could slip past them. The guards apologized profusely for their lapse, but Hytham privately suspected that money had changed hands, though he had no proof.

Once back on the city streets, he'd stopped a few people stumbling back to their homes, most too bleary from drinking to be of much help, but two young men swore they saw an injured man in a cloak leaning against a building to catch his breath before moving on south. When Hytham went to examine the bricks where they pointed, he found more blood, still fresh. It spurred him on, hopeful that he might catch up before the man disappeared into the depths of the city.

He rounded a corner, and the street he was following emptied into an open square. Here the city was awake and at play, even late at night. Dancers in colorful costume spun before a small fire, lifting their hands and moving their hips in time to a pair of musicians gathered off to one side. Others simply watched or stomped their feet in time to the music, sitting just out of the firelight, or leaning out the windows of the surrounding buildings.

It was the moods and flavors of the city, Hytham thought, as he wove unnoticed through the energetic crowd, that allowed a person to turn from one dark street and discover these pockets of light and laughter. He had a fleeting pang that he couldn't join them, couldn't sit in the firelight and watch the dancers and lose himself in simple joys, and not worry about what lay in front of him or what waited for him back at the palace.

Basim would be angry when he realized that Hytham had run off on his own. Leo would be frightened. He'd nearly lost his life again, and now he knew there was no safe place in the palace. Anyone could come for him in the dark. That voice would be back in his nightmares, telling him that he would never wake up. That was what drove Hytham on, out of the square of revelry and back into the shadows.

He wanted to ensure that one day, Leo could sleep peacefully again. He was willing to risk Basim's disappointment – or worse – in order to bring that about.

Just outside the square, Hytham encountered another

group of people, but these were not revelers, or at least they had removed themselves from the party. There were four of them, clustered around a young woman who was dressed like the other dancers, barefooted, with a fresh bruise rising on her face and an angry red scrape running down her arm.

"I was only asking him if he needed help," she was saying to a man standing next to her. "He was bleeding, and he breathed like he was fighting for it."

"He didn't say anything, just pushed her into the wall and limped off," said an older man with a creased face and a gap where his front teeth should be.

"Which way did he go?" Hytham asked, interrupting their speculation about how far the man would get before he collapsed.

The group turned in surprise at his sudden appearance. The older man nudged the injured woman gently and pointed to the uniform Hytham wore.

"He's from the palace," he said in a low voice.

This didn't set the group at ease, but the woman cautiously stepped forward, lifted her chin, and pointed down the street behind her. "He went off that way and turned left," she said. "You might catch him if you hurry."

Hytham thanked them and passed by, ignoring their whispers and questions about what the man had done. He spared a thought for how much of the news of the palace was reaching the general public. These people had no idea that nine assassins had attacked the palace tonight, seeking to kill the emperor's son. Would word have spread by morning of the attack? Or would the emperor suppress the knowledge and downplay the incident, as he'd tried to do after each of Leo's "accidents"? How long did he possibly think he could keep up such secrecy?

Hytham pushed those thoughts aside. He was getting close. A trail of blood stained the street before him, and he didn't need to examine it to know it was fresh. Unless he was a poor judge of wounds, the man he tracked was losing too much blood and was going to die soon. Hytham needed to get to him before that happened.

He took the left the woman had pointed him to, and there, at the end of the street, was his target. He was leaning against a door, fumbling to get it open. He stumbled inside and shut it behind him.

Hytham approached cautiously, crouching low and circling the building, surveying the entrances and exits. It was a two-story building, one of many in the city where a shop occupied the ground floor and living space dominated the upper story. There were only two grimy windows, and a front and back exit, but the back door was nearly concealed by several large crates. He wasn't getting in or out that way without making some noise.

Finding handholds in the pitted gray bricks along the back of the building, Hytham pulled himself up toward one of the second story windows. The opening was narrow, and with only the moonlight to guide him, he moved very slowly. Once he was inside, he maneuvered around a small bed and table, heading for a door which led to a set of stairs going down. He listened, and there came the sound of harsh breathing and dragging footsteps from below.

Hytham pressed himself against the wall and slowly made his way down, testing the stairs carefully with each step, listening for betraying creaks, just as he'd warned Leo. At the bottom of the stairs there was a small anteroom for storage and then the shopfront beyond.

No, not a shop, Hytham realized, but a small tavern, long closed by the looks of it, with grimy glasses and plates still stacked on dust-caked shelves along one wall. Several tables and chairs were stacked in haphazard piles throughout the room.

His quarry had righted a chair and was sitting in the middle of the room, sword on a table nearby. He peeled off his cloak and shirt to examine the wound that ran from his armpit to his hip. Hytham hadn't dealt him that blow, but he suspected Thyra had, judging by the ragged shape of the wound. It looked like the slash of an axe.

The wound was deep. Hytham saw that knowledge register on the man's face. A kind of resigned, dazed look came across his face, and he leaned back in his chair with his arm dangling by his side, while the blood dripped silently in a small puddle on the floor.

"I know you're there," the man said. "You can show yourself now."

A chill crept across Hytham's skin. He had not been seen. He'd been careful. And yet…

Was the man bluffing, testing to see if someone had followed him? It didn't matter, Hytham realized. The man was no longer a threat to him.

He stepped out of the shadows and into the room. The man rolled his head to look at Hytham through squinted eyes, as if it was difficult to focus. "You," he said, sounding almost disappointed. "I'd hoped it would be the other one."

Basim. Hytham's disquiet deepened. "What do you want with him?"

The man shook his head, dropping his chin to his chest. "Not me. Someone else wants him."

"Who? Isaac? Where is he?"

The man smiled, and there was blood on his teeth. "You'll get nothing more from me. You shouldn't have come to this city. It's already claimed. All that's left is for you to scratch for crumbs."

He lunged at Hytham, knocking back his chair with the sudden, violent movement. There was no grace in the attack, only a kind of wild desperation. The man hadn't even bothered to pick up his sword.

Hytham caught him and stabbed him with the Hidden Blade, giving him the quick death he'd been looking for, a release from the agony of the axe wound. He felt a brief stab of regret at not being able to interrogate the man further, but he suspected he'd obtained all the information he could.

When it was done, Hytham guided the man's body gently to the floor, searched him quickly, and then turned his attention to the tavern around him.

The man had used all of his strength to get back here, though he knew his wound was likely fatal. What task did he come here for, and had he completed it before Hytham arrived?

He began a methodical search of the room, moving furniture, searching on shelves and cabinets, tapping the walls and floor. This place could have many hidden nooks where things might be concealed. Hytham wasn't sure exactly what he was looking for, but he thought he would know it when he saw it.

He moved through the rest of the building room by room, but when he finally found what he was looking for, it was behind a loose stone in the firepit in the building's rear courtyard, where more tables had been abandoned to gather dirt and bird droppings. Hytham pulled the stone free and reached his hand in the dark space revealed. He pulled out a folded piece of parchment.

His heart sped up as he unfolded the message. He recognized the handwriting at once. He'd seen the meticulous lettering all over the tables in Leo's study room.

Theodore, the tutor.

The message bore today's date, and described the time of night when the assassination should take place. Theodore went on to say that he would poison the guards at the south entrance to the children's wing to clear the way. The letter was unsigned, of course, but it was damning enough without a signature.

Hytham refolded the parchment and started to put it inside his uniform, when he thought he heard a soft sound. He froze, listening, but there was only silence and the faint whistling of the wind through the courtyard, stirring dead leaves into piles around the faded chairs and benches.

But Hytham knew what he'd heard. It was the sound that might be made when the front door to the tavern opened and shut, letting in a soft gust of wind that barely rattled the glasses on their shelves.

It was as he'd told Leo. Sometimes the littlest things could give you away.

And now Hytham knew why the man had prolonged his agony to get back here. It hadn't been to destroy the message and protect Theodore. The Order cared nothing for him. They had only wanted to lure an Assassin here – Basim, apparently.

Hytham didn't know how many there were, but he knew he had only seconds to act. He ran to the low wall bounding the courtyard on three sides. He looked beyond it to the street to see if there was a path to freedom, but his heart sank when he saw several shadows converging on the building from that direction, hemming him in.

He'd have to fight his way out. But if he was taken, he needed to leave the letter someplace Basim might find it later. It was a slim hope, but if anyone could follow this twisted trail, it was the Master Assassin.

Hytham crouched by the wall. It was crumbling in places, piles of loose stone everywhere. He stuffed the letter into one of these, stacking the stones on top so the letter wouldn't blow away. It wasn't much of a hiding place, but it would have to do.

When he was finished, Hytham stood and went to the center of the courtyard. It was as good a place as any to make his stand.

Two men stepped out of the rear entrance to the tavern, armed with swords. Hytham glanced over his shoulder and saw three more enemies converging on him from the street – two women and another man.

"Only five of you?" he said, feeling an echo of the bravado of the man he'd just killed. He gave a half-hearted salute with his sword, defiance in his smile.

There was still the low wall between himself and the three attackers behind him. In a burst of movement, Hytham grabbed two of the crumbling stones at the base of the wall and threw them at the men in front of him. One stone missed entirely, but the other caught one of the men in the side of the head. He staggered back and dropped to one knee, cursing.

Hytham had no time to celebrate the small victory. He swung round as the first woman was leaping over the wall. He caught her with an arm crosswise at her chest, planting her on her back on the hard stone of the courtyard. The air whooshed out of her lungs and she lay stunned.

The other woman stayed on her side of the wall. "Put him down," she growled at the others.

"We're supposed to take him alive," the man who'd been hit with the stone snapped at her.

"Doesn't mean he can't be in pain," the woman said. She drew a knife and flicked it at Hytham. He batted it out of the air with his sword at the same time the other man in the courtyard came at him. Hytham turned to block his strike, but at the last second the man checked his sword swing and landed a kick to Hytham's injured knee.

There was no question of staying on his feet. Hytham's leg buckled, and he went down with a curse and cry of pain. The woman he'd knocked prone took advantage of his position to get behind him, putting a knife against his throat.

"Move and I'll cut you open," she said.

Hytham laughed. He had no desire to be taken alive.

He reached up, sliding his hand between the knife and his neck. The blade bit deep into his palm, but Hytham gritted his teeth and wrenched it aside.

It wouldn't be enough. The men were behind him now too. They seized his arms, yanking them behind his back. His shoulders burned, and his knee was a ball of agony, but still Hytham struggled. He struggled until he felt a blow at the back of his head. The moonlight seemed to brighten for an instant, then everything went black.

Chapter Eighteen

Hytham came to consciousness slowly, in shards of pain lancing through his skull, flickering lights at the edge of his vision, and voices whispering, but he couldn't make out what they were saying. He tried to claw his way up out of the darkness, to force his eyes open, but it was too difficult, and the blackness swallowed him again.

When next he woke, he was more alert, but it didn't matter. Wherever he was, it was pitch black in the room. He was lying on his side on a dirt floor with his wrists shackled behind him. He shifted, rolling to his back to take some of the pressure off his right shoulder. Pain shot up his leg, and Hytham bit back a groan. His mouth was bone dry, and it hurt to breathe, as if someone had kicked him in his already bruised ribs.

Good a time as any to assess his injuries, he supposed.

Carefully, he bent his knees, drawing them up toward his body. This time the pain made gold spots dance across Hytham's vision, and he realized he was panting, cold sweat dripping down his neck. Possibly a broken knee then, or at least one that was severely bruised. Hard to say until the swelling went down. He could be certain he wouldn't be running long distances anytime soon. That was probably why his captors hadn't bothered to tie him at the ankles.

He flexed the fingers of the hand that had taken the knife slash. He felt the stiff cloth of a bandage wrapped around his palm. Of course. His captors hadn't wanted him to leave a blood trail for someone to track him to wherever they'd brought him.

Lying on his back, he listened for sounds of anyone moving nearby. The darkness was absolute, but distantly, he heard the whistle of the wind outside, the night insects chirruping. He hadn't been unconscious very long, assuming this was still the same night he'd gone chasing after the assassin that had attacked Leo.

Leo. Hytham let out a breath and allowed himself to feel how thoroughly he'd failed the boy, leaving him alone to chase after a target that had led him straight into a trap.

And Basim. By now, he would have noticed Hytham's absence, but would he be able to find him? Would he even try? Hytham couldn't help entertaining the latter thought. Hytham had run off, against Basim's orders, and been captured. It would be well within Basim's authority to cut Hytham loose and focus on Leo's protection. It was the right thing to do.

Basim would no longer have to worry about Hytham watching him either, spying on him for the Hidden Ones.

What Hytham had done couldn't be changed, and it did him no good to dwell on it. Escape was what he needed to focus on now, and to do that, he'd need to learn more about his captors.

Hytham listened again, lying still in the darkness, keeping weight off his injured knee. Finally, after about an hour or so of nothing, he heard a door open and close somewhere outside the room, and two people's voices – a man and woman – drifted to him through the thin walls. He thought he recognized the woman from the fight in the courtyard.

The voices stopped outside the room, and finally, Hytham could make out what they were saying.

"We'll get what we can out of this one until Isaac arrives," the woman was saying. "Are you ready, Arman?"

The man, Arman, answered in a honeyed voice that made Hytham's skin crawl. "I'm always ready to serve. How coherent would you like him to be for Isaac's questioning?"

Sweat broke out on Hytham's forehead, his heartbeat loud in his ears, but he forced the fear aside. There was no point in being afraid, he told himself. Whatever was going to happen to him in the next few hours was going to happen. He'd brought this fate on himself.

He focused instead on the name – Isaac. The leader of the Order of the Ancients in Constantinople. He was coming here to interrogate Hytham, but why? His captors had made it clear that they were only interested in Basim. Either they were hoping Hytham had his confidence, or they hoped to use him as bait to draw Basim in.

They would be disappointed in either case.

Hytham lay back on the hard dirt floor, staring up into endless darkness. This was not going to be easy.

He remembered that day he and Basim had sparred in the olive grove. He remembered the mist clinging to his skin, wavering like sea foam around his waist. The thrill of sparring with a worthy opponent. He could have learned much from Basim, if he hadn't been so suspicious of the man.

The door opened. Candlelight poured into the room, and though it was sparse light, it still made Hytham's eyes sting after the total darkness. The woman and his assumed torturer, Arman, walked in. She was the woman from the courtyard. She was tall, her long dark hair swept back from her face, her expression all business as she regarded him.

"Let's get him up into a chair," she said, and Arman nodded and left the room, leaving them briefly alone. She folded her arms, and something like disappointment flashed over her face. "You fell into a trap that wasn't meant for you," she said, half accusingly. "Now we're going to have to make the best of it."

He lifted his shoulders as best he could while tied. "Life doesn't always give us the choices or situations we might desire," he said in a hoarse voice.

"Would you like some water?" she asked. "I'd be happy to get you some."

"Will you untie me so I may drink it?"

She smiled and shook her head.

"Then I thank you, but no," he said.

Hytham knew the kindness and civility was a facade, all part of the game of interrogation. He was supposed to think kindly toward this woman, to think that she was not responsible for whatever came next and would help him if she could.

His task was not to believe it.

Arman came back with two chairs and set them roughly three feet apart in the center of the room. Now that Hytham could look around the space by candlelight, he saw it was much smaller than he'd thought. A few empty shelves lined the walls, but the rest of the space had been cleared, though there were indentations left on the dirt floor where heavier objects or furniture had once rested. There were no windows, and the smell of damp earth was strong in his nostrils. Hytham concluded they must be underground. He had no way of knowing if they were still in the city, but he suspected they were. The Order would not risk taking him far. Or maybe that was just a fragile hope on his part.

Arman and the woman came around behind him and lifted him by the armpits, depositing him in the chair with as much courtesy as one could when dealing with a bound man. Hytham carefully bent his injured knee, trying not to draw attention to the fact that it pained him. The woman was still standing behind him, and he felt her uncurl his fingers to get a look at the bandage on his hand.

"This will have to be changed soon," she said, making a noise of concern that almost caused Hytham to smile. She was very good at playing her part. "I'll see to it." She left the room as if to do just that, shutting the door behind her.

Without the light spilling in from the door, the room was now lit only by a pair of candles that Arman had placed on the floor nearby. They were out of Hytham's reach at the moment, but if he could get free, they would make decent weapons.

Arman sat back in his chair, watching him. He had a dark, well-kept beard and brown eyes, though the right eye was filled with red, and there was a bruise on his temple as if he'd been in a fight recently, though Hytham didn't remember seeing him at the courtyard. Had he been one of the assassins that had escaped the palace?

Arman caught him staring at the wound. "A small injury.

Nothing to worry about," he said. "I was hunting the boy, but he slipped away from me." He sounded impressed. "That's never happened before. Under other circumstances, it would have been a novelty." He regarded Hytham with interest, the way one would a particularly colorful insect. "Was that your doing? Were you grooming the boy to make him one of yours? Is that your intention?"

Hytham bristled, but he kept his mouth shut. The man's words were designed to provoke, nothing more.

Arman nodded, as if he hadn't really expected an answer. "Well, if that is your goal, you're doing a fine job. If the boy lives, he'll know nothing but your way of life, and the lessons that you've taught him will become sacred. You're very good at what you do, Hytham."

Hytham inclined his head at the compliment. Arman smiled, leaving the rest of his thoughts unspoken but clear: *I am also good at what I do.*

"How is your knee?" Arman asked, and Hytham's breath caught, just slightly. Still, he didn't answer.

The blow, when it came, was so quick Hytham couldn't track it. There was a blur of movement and then white-hot pain. Hytham curled in on himself instinctively, seeking to protect the injury, but Arman grabbed both his legs and forced them back to the floor. Hytham grunted but refused to cry out.

"In these situations, it's almost not worth going after the injured limb," Arman said conversationally. "At least not too much. If I overdo these things, eventually, you'll come to expect the pain, and so it won't mean anything to you." He shifted in his seat, turning to Hytham's uninjured knee. "On the other hand, if you threaten what's perfectly healthy, dangle the possibility of making you lame, then we may get somewhere."

He rested his hand lightly on Hytham's good knee.

The blood roared in Hytham's ears, and he fought to control his breathing. The weight of the man's hand on him may as well have been an anvil. But he forced himself to meet the man's gaze, putting all the coldness of his training into his expression. A mantle of calm settled over him. It didn't matter what this man did to him. This man was nothing compared to the people he called brothers. He wouldn't betray them. He wouldn't betray Basim.

"Answer a question for me, if you wouldn't mind," Arman said, tapping Hytham's good knee with his index finger. "Why did Basim put you in the palace with the boy? Why did he not go himself?"

Hytham hesitated, licking dry, cracked lips as he pretended to contemplate the question.

Arman smiled encouragingly. "This bit of information isn't a betrayal, Hytham," he said. "It's more a matter of opinion than anything else. Give me your opinion about Basim, and afterward we'll have some water. I can see that you're thirsty."

Still that hand resting lightly on his uninjured knee. Not a threat now, but a reassurance. Everything is going to be fine.

Hytham leaned forward slightly as if to speak. Arman waited expectantly.

"Only an opinion," Hytham said thoughtfully, and then he brought his knees together as hard as he could, crushing Arman's fingers between them.

It wasn't as devastating a blow as Hytham would have liked.

He didn't have the leverage from his seated position, so there wasn't enough strength to break bones, but Arman felt it.

Oh yes, he felt it.

Arman let out an involuntary cry of pain and tried to snatch his hand back. Hytham planted his feet on the floor and sprang up, dragging the chair with him as he plowed into the man and knocked them both to the floor. Hytham landed on his side, and a fresh wave of pain went from knee to shoulder.

It was not a very elegant showing, but it was all he could manage, and he had the satisfaction of hearing Arman, his cool façade shattered, cursing and yelling as he got back to his feet, cradling his injured fingers and staring down at Hytham with the disbelief of a child stung by a wasp.

Hytham stared back at him.

You thought I wasn't dangerous. Now you've learned better.

The door opened, and the woman strode back into the room. She took in the scene with a brisk glance, but if she was surprised to see Hytham lying prone on the floor, still tied to his chair, she didn't show it.

Instead she looked at Arman. "Are they broken?" she asked, indicating his fingers.

He glared at her. "I don't think so, but–"

"Then if you're not going to be useful, go and guard the door," she said, cutting him off.

He drew himself up, his gaze darkening, but before he could speak, she took a single step toward him. That was all. Her expression never changed, but he wilted before it. He jerked his head in a nod and left the room, slamming the door behind him in a last show of temper.

When they were alone, she looked down at him impassively. "You would have been better off answering a few of his questions before trying something like this," she said. "You might have caused us to lower our guards and given you an opening to escape." She tilted her head. "But you're too angry for that, aren't you?" She went down on one knee so they were closer to eye level. "This is personal to you, isn't it?" She spoke half to herself. "That's the missing piece we failed to consider here."

Hytham's gut clenched. All his training, and he hadn't realized it was possible to give away so much vital information without ever speaking a word. Yet he felt that was exactly what he'd done, and the shame of it unfurled inside him like a poison flower.

The woman stood up, brushing dirt off the cloak she wore. She came around behind him and grabbed the back of his chair, hauling him upright with less effort than he would have expected for her slender frame. "Isaac will be very happy with how you've cooperated so far," she said.

A red film of rage descended over Hytham. As soon as he was upright, he shoved backward with all his strength. But his injured knee betrayed him, and there was little force behind the movement. The woman caught the back of his chair with one hand and wrapped the other around his throat, yanking his head back so he was looking up at her.

"You're just making it worse," she whispered, running her fingernail down his stubbled cheek. "You're giving us everything we need. Your masters didn't train you very well. They never prepared you for this, did they?" The false sympathy in her voice burned inside him, but this time he couldn't fight back. She was slowly squeezing his windpipe. Dark spots grew in his peripheral vision, but all Hytham could do was squirm and thrash in his chair.

"Rest for now," the woman's voice whispered in his ear as his consciousness faded. "It's going to be a lot harder after this."

Chapter Nineteen

The next time he woke he was on his feet. Well, that was being generous. In fact, he was hanging from his arms, which were tied so far above his head he was nearly on his toes, and he'd obviously been unconscious in that position for some time, because the burning pain of cramping muscles was what woke him.

Wrenched arms, wounded knee, gash on the hand, ribs still on fire. He catalogued the hurts in his mind as he struggled to see his surroundings, but it was pitch black again, the darkness and silence absolute. That darkness clawed at the edges of his mind, unsettling him, but his more pressing problem was that he was so thirsty it felt like his throat was coated in flame.

He wondered how long it had been this time, how long he'd slept while the world went on without him outside this moldy hole in the ground. Of all the ways Hytham thought he might end this mission, he had not expected it to be beneath the earth, so far from the light.

But you *should* have expected it, Hytham chided himself, his thoughts fraying and scattering as he tried to put more weight on his feet to take the pressure off his arms and shoulders. His life belonged to the shadows. He worked in the dark to serve the light. This was precisely the kind of death he was trained to expect, and he wasn't afraid to face it.

Yet he'd also stood in the olive grove of the golden city, sparring with a Master Assassin. In those moments he'd been young and powerful, feeling the taste of immortality. This was a harder death to accept than the greater glory of dying with a sword in his hand and allies at his back.

Basim would agree. Hytham felt sure of it.

The door opened, spilling golden light into the room. It reminded Hytham of the sunrise on the harbor, the fractured light dancing on the waves and casting the city in its finest aspect for the glory of the artists.

He blinked, and the dark-haired woman was standing in front of him, haloed by the light. She was speaking to him, but he was having trouble understanding her. Then she was holding something to his mouth, and Hytham's body recognized it as water and was drinking, gulping it down before his mind could catch up to what was happening, but even when it did, he found he couldn't stop. Eventually, she pulled the cup away from his lips and threw the rest of the water in his face. The cold slap made him suck in a breath, and suddenly the world sharpened around him.

"Are you back with us now?" the woman asked. "I'd hoped we didn't push you too far. We need you to be able to speak."

He didn't speak, just watched her warily as she took the cup away and left. When she returned, she brought a single chair and placed it in the middle of the room. While she did this,

Hytham took the opportunity to study his surroundings again. He was in the same room as before. That was no surprise. It smelled the same, after all. His hands were tied to a beam above his head. Pulling on the ropes made the beam creak and groan, but it felt secure. Hytham didn't think he would be able to break it, not in his current condition.

The woman came back to stand in front of him, just out of reach of his legs. "Isaac is here," she said. "He wants to speak to you."

The leader of the Order of the Ancients in Constantinople, come to speak with him. If Hytham hadn't already been certain they meant to kill him, he had no more doubts now. Even Basim had been having a difficult time obtaining information about the Order's leader, the man in charge of taking control of the city. Isaac had hidden himself too well, but now Hytham was going to meet him.

They would not let him live after seeing the man's face.

The woman seemed to be waiting for him to answer. Hytham gave a nod of acknowledgment. "Let's get it over with, then," he said. His voice still sounded strange. Hoarse and pained.

The woman went to the door, glancing back at him. "Goodbye, Hytham," she said. "You fought well. I was… impressed."

Then she was gone. Hytham waited, but it was several minutes still before he heard footsteps approaching. He wasn't sure what he'd been expecting of the man who entered the room, but he was not prepared to *recognize* him. The familiarity was brief but sure. He had met this man before, but where?

There was nothing terribly remarkable about him. He was

tall and reed slender, a bit broader through the shoulders, his arms well muscled and darkened by the sun. His head was clean-shaven, his eyes the pewter stillness of the sea on a cloudy day.

His identity hit Hytham with the taste of figs and honey, as clear on his tongue as if he'd just washed them down with cool water.

"It's a fine day to sit idle and watch the people pass by."

The server at the wine bar. The man who'd brought them water. He'd sought them out from the first. He could have poisoned their drinks, and they never would have known it. But no, that would have accomplished nothing in the grand scheme of things. The Hidden Ones would have simply sent someone else to Constantinople, and this way, Isaac had the chance to know who he was up against. He had wanted to meet his enemies and take their measure. Their conversation, the chase and battle on the rooftop and in the alley, had been exactly that.

A way to take *Basim's* measure, Hytham corrected, reminding himself that it was his superior the Order wanted. They were presumably interested in him for the same reasons the Hidden Ones were. Reasons Hytham had yet to learn.

Perhaps silence was not what was called for here then. Perhaps Hytham needed to dredge up the strength to play the game, though he might be hopelessly outmatched.

"Hello again," Hytham said, glancing down at Isaac's empty hands. "No water? No figs and honey this time?"

The man smiled, pleased to be recognized. "No wine either, I'm afraid." He sank into the chair with the grace of a dancer, but he reminded Hytham of a snake at rest, sinuously coiled but always prepared to strike. "You're not looking as fresh as you were that day, newly arrived to the city with ambitions to overthrow an emperor."

"You're mistaken," Hytham said. "Ensuring the line of succession is an honorable goal, is it not?"

Isaac lifted his shoulders. "Assuming the correct bloodline endures, of course."

"Why should it not," Hytham countered, "when the emperor himself declared Leo his successor? What greater proof of blood than that the father claims his son and names him to be the next emperor?"

"Is that you talking," Isaac said, still smiling, "or are these your superior's words?"

"We're of a mind on this," Hytham said, "but if you'd like to speak of Basim, all you had to do was say so."

"So, you're going to cooperate with us?" Isaac leaned back in his chair. "Somehow I had my doubts after speaking to Arman. He indicated that you'd been less than forthcoming about your activities in the city."

Hytham might have shrugged, but the gesture would have looked ridiculous on a bound man. "Maybe I was waiting to speak to you."

"I'm flattered," Isaac said. "To what do I owe that honor?"

Hytham considered how far he wanted to take this. He was a dead man after all. He could afford to take a few risks. "Maybe I wanted to discuss a bargain with you."

Now Isaac looked even more intrigued. "Well, now, that depends on what we're bargaining for and if you understand the stakes."

"Leo's life," Hytham said. "No more and no less." He knew

he didn't have to work to show this man what that meant to him. Basim had already seen it written all over him. So had the woman who'd spoken to him earlier.

"I see we were right about that part," Isaac said, his expression unreadable. "I have to admit, I would have rejected this line of conversation entirely had that not been the case. But it isn't often these things become so personal that one of your kind is willing to betray his comrades."

"Those being the stakes you discussed," Hytham said calmly, "can I ask another question out of my own curiosity?"

Isaac laughed. "For your sheer brazenness and the fact that you bruised two of Arman's fingers with your knees, I should say no, and yet I'm too fascinated by these developments to do so." He spread his hands in invitation.

Tread carefully, Hytham told himself. Not too eager. "Why are you so interested in Basim?"

It was not the only question crowding his tongue. Why do you and the Hidden Ones both want him watched so closely? If he is such a powerful threat, why does no one check him? Why does it feel as if you are afraid of him?

Hytham had felt many things in regards to Basim. Respect, brotherhood, a burgeoning friendship – but he had never felt fear. Why did he feel unique in this, and was he just being naïve?

He waited for Isaac's answer. The candlelight carved deep shadows in the man's face. He watched Hytham with a calculating expression. "They haven't told you what he's seeking, have they?" Isaac asked. "You don't really know him, do you?"

Hytham's stomach clenched, but he forced himself not to

react. This was another form of provocation, meant to alienate him from the people he trusted.

But an insidious voice inside his head whispered, *are you trusting the right people?*

His knee was throbbing, his arms had gone numb, and he needed more water. He had thought that his torturers would use more brute force to try to break him. Burn him, scar him, take his eyes and fingers. He'd dreamed of all those horrors. The truth was much worse. Break a person down slowly, make them question everything they've ever believed in, and wait for them to give you exactly what you want.

He was outmatched here, but he pushed on into deeper waters. He had no other choice. "I don't know Basim at all," Hytham said, "and I don't know whether I can trust him."

Isaac nodded, as if he understood that all too well. "A bargain could be made for the boy's life," he mused. "He must never take the throne, of course, but it is possible he could live in exile, visited by his mother. A new identity perhaps, with the rest of the world – and his father – thinking him dead." He looked at Hytham with a cold, flat expression. "This will be contingent on how cooperative and informative you are in the next few hours."

There it was, handed to him like a contract from the devil himself. Everything that Hytham wanted – a chance to save Leo, to get him away from the nest of vipers and the knives in the dark. He could be a normal boy, one who would grow up without a grand destiny, but perhaps he would still have a chance at happiness and prosperity.

Wasn't that what every father should want for his son?

Hytham closed his eyes.

It would be so easy.

He had gone too far in all this, and only now did he see the depth and breadth of his mistakes. Basim had been right all along about him. His affection for Leo had clouded his judgment and endangered their mission. Basim had seen Hytham more clearly than Hytham had seen himself, and yet Basim had let him proceed anyway.

Maybe this was just another lesson.

This time, he would learn it.

The chair creaked, and Hytham opened his eyes to see Isaac on his feet. He approached Hytham, being careful not to get too close. An expression of disappointment lingered around his eyes. "I see," he said. "You've made your decision, haven't you? A shame, really. I thought it was a tantalizing enough bargain that you'd accept. You were tempted, though, weren't you?"

"Yes, I was tempted," Hytham said. He would carry that shame for the short time he had left to live.

Isaac nodded, and with a sudden, graceful movement, he closed the distance between them, aiming a kick at Hytham's injured knee.

Hytham dodged, hurling his body at Isaac, but the restraints held him back. The room spun as he fought to catch his breath. He'd been expecting to die, hoped they might make it quick because they knew he couldn't be bought.

Again, he was naïve. Isaac would keep trying to get his information. He didn't much care whether Hytham bargained for it or broke for it.

So Hytham dredged up a strength he knew couldn't last and *fought*.

Flexing his arms, he lifted both feet from the ground and swung forward, catching Isaac in the chest before the man could get out of the way. Isaac staggered back, tripping over the chair and slamming into the opposite wall. He caught himself before he fell, and his gaze lit on Hytham with a kind of wild glee.

"Oh, this will be interesting," Isaac said, and lunged for him again.

Hytham tried to move, but he was slow, and he didn't see the knife in Isaac's hand until it had sliced open the skin beneath his left eye. Hytham brought his good knee up into Isaac's stomach, but the man had already pulled back out of reach.

Blood dripped down Hytham's face. Had Isaac been aiming to gouge his eye out? The fleeting thought passed through his mind, but Hytham was focused purely on survival now, an animal instinct to last as long as he could, to do as much damage as he could before he fell, so that those who came after him would find their task fighting the Order of the Ancients just a little easier.

A loud crash came from somewhere above them. Both Hytham and Isaac froze. There were shouts. Then screams.

Isaac cursed and drew a second knife from his boot.

"We'll see each other again," he promised Hytham, and left the room, shutting the door so that Hytham was back in the dark.

CHAPTER TWENTY

Hytham's heart still pounded with the aftermath of battle, but a different, shaky excitement gave renewed energy to his body. Was it possible he was being rescued?

He wasn't going to wait around to find out if he was wrong. He couldn't bear to be the animal trapped in the dark anymore. Whatever fight was happening upstairs, he had to take advantage of the distraction it offered.

He yanked on the rope that held him. It was tied to one of the beams that formed the foundation of the building above, old but strong. He wouldn't be able to break it, but he would free himself even if he had to gnaw off his own hand.

He twisted his wrists, trying to take advantage of any flaw or looseness in the knots. The muscles in his arms burned with fatigue, and he felt clumsy and weak. He worked at the ropes until his skin was raw and bleeding, but he could feel he was making progress.

Above him, there were more shouts, footsteps pounding the floorboards, but none of it was clear enough for Hytham to make out who was speaking or how many of them there were. Then he realized the footsteps were coming downstairs.

Someone was coming for him.

Was it Isaac?

No. Hytham wrenched his arms, wrists slick with sweat and blood. He would not meet Isaac again when he was helpless. He would *not*.

With that thought and a red fury driving him, he tore free of the ropes. He was shocked when it happened, his full weight coming down on his feet. His injured knee screamed in protest and his legs gave out as the door to his prison opened.

Hytham staggered, and he would have hit the floor, but arms caught him and held him up. He recognized the soft chuckle in his ear, and his relief was so profound it clogged his throat.

"It's good to see you weren't sitting idle down here, my friend," Basim said, "but you've made quite a mess of yourself."

"I did my best to make a mess of them as well," Hytham managed as Basim pulled him upright and helped him lean against the wall. "How did you find me?"

"With difficulty," Basim said. He had a hand on Hytham's arm to steady him, and was swiftly assessing his injuries. "Can you walk? Fight?"

"With difficulty," Hytham said, "but yes."

"Good, because there's fighting still to do. Come."

Hytham pushed off the wall, taking a second to be sure of his footing. He rolled his shoulders to coax the blood back into his limbs. Basim handed him his sword. Hytham had no idea how he'd managed to recover it, but that was among the least of his many questions.

Outside the room there was a short hall leading to a set of rickety steps. Climbing the steps was fresh agony for his knee, but now that he was free and still feeling the rush from fighting, Hytham believed he could engage the whole world. He knew it was part of the shock and trauma. It would catch up to him and his body would pay the price, but at the moment he didn't care.

At the top of the stairs, Hytham realized by the rooms they passed that they were in a private household, abandoned like the tavern had been, with a strong smell of mildew and dust. Through another door, they came upon Thyra fighting Isaac and a man who had a deep axe wound in his arm. Arman was dead on the ground along with another man Hytham didn't recognize. There was no sign of the dark-haired woman. Hytham gritted his teeth as he waited for an opening to help the Viking woman.

Thyra drove in close to Isaac, her axe handle blocking his lunge with the knife. With her free hand, Thyra grabbed the wrist that held the knife and tried to turn it back to stab Isaac in the chest. They were frozen, bodies trembling, strength pitted against strength. Isaac's gaze went briefly over Thyra's shoulder and met Hytham's. He gave them a faint smile and a nod, then dug in and shoved Thyra back, slashing the air in front of her with his knife to keep her at a distance.

Hytham and Basim moved in. Isaac spun, tossed his other knife to the man with the wound and darted out the front door into the dark street. The man who'd caught the knife placed himself in front of the door to cover Isaac's escape. He faced the three of them grimly, with only one working arm and the knife, but the way he moved and the look in his eyes promised that he would not make the fight easy for them.

"Step back, Thyra," Basim said, putting a hand on her shoulder to draw her away. "Take a rest."

Hytham shifted to the opposite corner of the room, leaning on the wall for support. He had his sword ready, but Basim didn't look particularly concerned. He drew a knife of his own, and then he and the man were fighting, moving so fast it left Hytham breathless trying to follow their battle.

Hytham had been in plenty of street fights, and many of those had been knife fights, but it was rare he saw two people make it an art form the way Basim and the wounded man did. Bleeding but still graceful, Basim's enemy focused on long, sweeping movements to keep Basim away, the edge of the blade catching the light but always in motion, never still, slashing rather than stabbing. A soft singing sound as the blade cut the air added an odd music to the deadly display.

Basim, on the other hand, was the snake in the grass, his movements economical as he dodged the enemy's slashes, but when he found a weakness, he struck quickly and without mercy. He crouched low and came up under the silver arc of the blade, stabbing deep into the man's shoulder. The man grunted and danced back, into the open doorway, still blocking their exit and the path to the fleeing Isaac. He braced his shoulder on the door frame, leaving a bloodstain behind.

He dropped to one knee, and Hytham thought it was over. He stood up straight, muscles tensed to run if he had to. He'd crawl if it meant tracking Isaac down before he escaped.

Hytham had people with him now. The man wouldn't get away.

The hint of movement and the soft rustle of fabric was all he got as a warning.

"Basim!" Hytham shouted as, from the street, the dark-haired woman threw a dagger over the wounded man's head.

Basim dodged it, but only just, and the blade struck the wall two feet from Hytham's face and stayed there, vibrating. Hytham didn't think. He reached over, tore the blade from the wall and flung it back. It caught the injured man in the neck. His eyes went wide, fingers clawing at his throat as he went down at the feet of the dark-haired woman, who'd stepped up to the doorway.

Thyra cursed, aimed her axe and flung it. It bit deep into the dark-haired woman's chest, and she folded around it, the force of the throw driving her back into the street. Basim followed her out. Hytham assumed he meant to finish the job.

He did.

And just like that, it was over. Silence descended on the small house. Hytham sagged against the wall, the blood still roaring in his ears, as Basim dragged the bodies back into the house and closed the door.

"I don't think anyone saw," he said, "or at least no one was in the street."

"Any sign of Isaac?" Hytham asked, taking a moment to recover.

Basim shook his head. "There's no trace of him." If he was surprised that Hytham had just mentioned the leader of the Order in Constantinople being here, he didn't show it. He'd likely recognized the server at the wine bar as well.

Hytham turned to ask Thyra if she was all right. She hadn't yet retrieved her axe from the dark-haired woman's corpse, instead going to the opposite corner of the room, where a table and chair had been overturned near the wall. She got down on her knees and carefully pulled the table back, murmuring something that Hytham couldn't make out. He shifted closer to see what she was looking at.

His breath snagged in his chest, and his body went cold.

There, curled into a ball in the corner, his arms wrapped protectively over his head, was Leo. At Thyra's coaxing, the boy slowly lifted his head and crawled into her arms. She pulled him close, whispering reassuring words into his ear.

"What… is this?" Hytham was having trouble getting the words out. There was a loud buzzing in his ears, his knee throbbed in pain, and for a second, he thought he might pass out. He leaned heavily against the wall. "Why is he *here*?"

Leo had been here for the whole rescue. He'd been crouched in a corner with only a flimsy bit of wood for protection while Thyra fought Isaac, the man who had been trying for months to murder the boy.

Thyra ignored Hytham's question. She was still patting the boy's back and soothing him, though he didn't seem to be crying. He was probably in shock. Basim, meanwhile, had searched the bodies and was now making a methodical sweep of the room to look for anything else of value or interest. He glanced over at Hytham as he worked, his face a cold mask.

"We had to bring him with us to search for you," Basim said. "We have yet to confirm Justin's story, so we couldn't trust him with the boy. The Varangian Guards are also suspect, until Thyra determines which of them are truly loyal to her and not conspiring to murder Leo." A muscle in his jaw worked, the only sign he was concealing strong emotion. "And you, his guardian, were missing."

He was right, of course. This fell on Hytham's shoulders.

But the shame of hearing it spoken by people he respected was so much worse than he'd imagined.

The shame spurred him to anger, for he was only human. "Why didn't you leave me?" Hytham demanded. "You shouldn't have risked the mission to save me."

Basim continued to stare at him, and Hytham shut his mouth. There was something dangerous in Basim's eyes, something even Hytham knew he shouldn't cross. His argument was ridiculous anyway. He should be on his knees thanking both of them for pulling him out of that hole in the ground, not stand here sullen and furious.

But he wasn't wrong. Basim shouldn't have risked the mission just to rescue him. What they were doing was too important. Constantinople was too great a prize to risk on a single member of their brotherhood. It was the very thing Hytham had been told to watch Basim for, signs that his personal obsessions were leading him astray.

Except it was Hytham's obsessions that had ultimately endangered the mission, and standing there, looking at each other in the tense silence of that house, they both knew it.

"We need to get back to the palace before the boy is missed," Basim said tersely. "Can you walk?"

"I can." Now that he was free, Hytham could assess his injuries with a clearer head. He was relieved to discover his knee was badly bruised, but not broken, as he'd feared. There would be a great deal of soreness for the next several days, but right now the worst of his problems was a lack of water.

With his usual preternatural senses, Basim produced a waterskin for Hytham to drink from. The liquid slid down his throat like the finest wine. Hytham had never been so glad for anything in his life. He forced himself to go slowly, but he wanted to squeeze every last drop from the skin.

He handed the water back to Basim and noticed Thyra watching him. When she caught his eye, she leaned down and whispered something to Leo, who was still clinging to her, his eyes very wide. He had his back to the bodies Basim had dragged into the corner.

Hytham felt a renewed flush of shame.

But then Leo was coming across the room to him, tentatively, as if he wasn't sure if he should get too close, and that show of fear came as near to breaking Hytham as anything else he'd experienced these past few hours.

He held out a hand and tugged the boy against his side. "Let's get some air," he murmured, and led Leo into the street.

It was nearly dawn. That gray, misty haze hung over the city, the same as it had the morning he and Basim had sparred, a prelude to the gold light that swept in over the water. Leo wore a nondescript cloak over his normal clothes to let him blend in. Hytham pulled the hood of the cloak up to obscure Leo's face and led him off the main street where they would be unseen while they waited for Basim and Thyra.

There was a moment when he wasn't sure where he was. When he finally got his bearings, it was only to realize that he wasn't actually that far from the closed-up tavern where he'd tracked the assassin from the palace. But for that moment, the winding streets and buildings all looked the same, the open spaces feeling strange and exposed after being in the dark. It was unnerving how quickly it had affected him. Hytham knew with an unsettling certainty that he wasn't going to shake off this experience quickly.

Under other circumstances, this was something he would speak to Basim about. He had a feeling, without knowing why, that the man would understand.

But Basim was the last person he could talk to right now. And Leo needed him.

Hobbling down a short alley, Hytham checked the adjoining streets for any signs of people. He could hear the sounds of the city waking – doors opening and shutting, brooms scraping stone, the snuffling of horses and other livestock slowly coming awake and preparing for the day.

Basim and Thyra were still in the house, probably finishing up searching the bodies and the rest of the building now that Leo was out of the way. The boy was alarmingly silent. He hadn't spoken a word or moved from Hytham's side.

"Leo," Hytham said, crouching in front of the boy. "Are you all right?"

"I… I think so." He was pale, but he stood straight, his shoulders squared – the face he put on when he was trying his best to be brave. Hytham was unspeakably proud of him.

"It's been a terrible night," Hytham said, putting his hands on the boy's shoulders. "I'm sorry I left you."

"I thought you were d- dead," Leo said, his voice quivering. "Basim said that you… that you might be, and that I should be ready in case you didn't come back. He told me to be brave, that he would do everything he could to find you."

That knocked the breath from Hytham's chest. Had Basim truly told the boy that?

He knew on some level that Basim thought he was valuable, despite his cutting words earlier. Hytham may not have yet mastered his emotions, but he was still an Acolyte, a skilled fighter, and an asset to their mission – at least until recently. But for Basim to come after him like this, when he had to have known he was in enemy hands...

When he knew that Hytham had been sent to the city to spy on him.

It would have been easiest just to cut him loose. After their confrontation in the garden, Hytham had expected it. The shock had come when he'd been rescued instead. And Basim had brought Leo along on the rescue attempt, knowing the boy would be exposed, knowing he was bringing the Order's target right to them.

Did Basim actually *care* about Hytham and his fate?

This was yet another revelation in a day filled with them, but for the moment Hytham didn't think of any of that. He focused his attention on Leo. "You *were* very brave," he said, "to come and find me with the others."

"I wanted to come." Leo met his eyes, and there was a flash of defiance and strength in him that Hytham had never seen before. "I can tell you're worried about me, but I wouldn't have let the others leave me behind," he said, "not when you were in danger. I wanted to help you. I didn't want to hide this time."

"And you didn't," Hytham said thickly. "I'm so proud of you, Leo."

"I'm glad you're all right." With those words, Leo's stoicism finally broke under the weight of a child's relief, and he threw himself at Hytham, wrapping his arms around his neck and holding on tight. That relief was an echo in Hytham, who released a long breath and hugged the boy back.

He'd compromised his mission and himself, yet all he felt

was gratitude to whatever powers had pulled him and the boy through.

"It's all right," he whispered, speaking as much to himself as to Leo. "Everything's going to be all right now."

Here he was again, just like a parent lying to a child. Because it wasn't going to be all right. True, they now knew Leo's tutor was the traitor in the palace, but Isaac had escaped, so they were no closer to eliminating the Order's presence in the city.

Their enemy was too powerful for a handful of Varangian Guards and two Assassins to protect Leo forever. The events of this night had proven that. At least they had the letter written in Theodore's hand, condemning himself. Hytham would have to go back to the closed-up tavern to see if it was still there, or if Isaac's people had found and destroyed it. That was the first step. Then they could see what more could be done.

Hytham wished he himself could have done more. He had had Isaac, the leader of the Order in Constantinople, right in front of him. The knowledge burned inside his chest like hot coals. If he'd just been a little bit stronger, things might have turned out differently.

He heard Thyra and Basim's footsteps near the mouth of the alley. Gently, he pulled away from Leo and stood up. "It's time to go home," he said.

CHAPTER TWENTY-ONE

Despite what Hytham had said, they did not return to the palace right away. Once Hytham relayed to Basim and Thyra the existence of the letter, the four of them, moving in furtive pairs through the back alleys of the still-waking city, returned to the courtyard of the abandoned tavern.

Hytham found himself holding his breath, his heart pounding as he sifted through the loose bricks of the courtyard wall where he'd hidden the letter. It didn't look like anything had been disturbed, but there had been so many disappointments, so many setbacks...

No, there it was. Hytham pulled the parchment out and dusted it off before handing it to Basim. He read it while Thyra and Leo sat in the shadows at the base of the courtyard wall so as not to attract attention from passersby. The streets were already filling up, men and women hauling carts and preparing storefronts and wine bars, shouts and curses coming from the multi-story tenements a few doors down as people reluctantly pulled themselves out of bed.

Basim nodded slowly and refolded the parchment. "This is good," he said, perching on the edge of the crumbling wall. "This gives Basil a target for manufactured wrath. After the attack last night, he can no longer pass these incidents off as accidents. He'll have to be seen to take action, and dealing with Theodore will satisfy that."

"That's something," Thyra said. She spread her cloak over Leo, who had fallen asleep against her side. She looked exhausted herself, with deep shadows under her eyes and a grim set to her mouth.

Hytham sat on one of the old chairs, stretching his leg out carefully to give some relief to his knee. "So, the emperor will punish Theodore, and then what? Seek out another conspirator in the palace?" Justin had predicted there would be more awaiting the emperor's command.

"Not among the Varangian Guard," Thyra said, her expression dark. "I will cull the traitors from their ranks. That work has already begun."

Basim gave a nod of acknowledgment. "Hytham will be grateful to you as he sleeps at night." He glanced at Hytham, and there was still that hint of something dangerous in his eyes, something that promised a confrontation, a reckoning. Hytham knew it was necessary, but he didn't look forward to it.

The moment passed, and Basim stood, all business. "We should return to the palace. The empress will be worried, and the rest of the guards will have secured the area in and around the children's wing. It should be safe for the boy to return and get some sleep."

"We need a new plan," Hytham insisted, though he knew

it was risky to push. "We can't just continue as we have been. You know that."

"Then *I* will consider the matter and come up with one," Basim said without looking his way.

The implication, the exclusion, was clear. It was another blow, one more painful than his knee. Hytham tried to hide it, but his hands involuntarily clenched into fists.

"Something wrong?" Basim asked, a challenge gleaming in his eyes.

Was that what was going to happen? Was he going to be dismissed? Pulled from the mission? Maybe Basim had intended that to be his punishment all along.

Hytham shook his head. "We should talk later," was all he managed to say.

Basim smiled a smile that chilled Hytham. "Oh, we will, my friend. We will."

The trip back to the palace was long and arduous. With Hytham's injuries they made slow progress at first, and the constant threat of being watched or tracked by the Order hung over Hytham's head. More than once, Basim ordered them to pause in an alley or behind a church while he scouted ahead to make sure there was no one lying in wait for them. Isaac had been thwarted and robbed of his captive in his own hideout. This would not reflect well on him. No matter what happened, they would have to worry about retaliation from the Order.

So, they were all tense and alert, and the relative safety of the palace seemed very far away.

But Hytham was encouraged. The more he worked his injured knee, gradually increasing the weight on it as they walked, the stronger it became. Standing in one position for hours bearing all his weight had made the pain worse and made him believe the injury was more severe. He would be bruised and aching for a while, but he didn't think there was any permanent damage.

He wondered if Leo would escape this ordeal in the same way. The boy was asleep in Thyra's arms, his head resting on her shoulder. He was young, and had the benefit of a child's ability to forget, but was it possible he'd ever be able to let go of what had happened to him tonight? People had come to kill him. He'd been hunted, chased in the dark while he was all alone. Because Hytham wasn't with him. And then he'd seen people killed during Hytham's rescue. Those things left scars. He could never really be the same after tonight, and Hytham bore some responsibility for that as well.

As if feeling his gaze on them, Thyra glanced sidelong at him. She patted Leo's back gently. "He'll sleep for a day at least. He's exhausted."

It was the first time she'd spoken to him since the rescue, other than to talk of their plans and next steps. Hytham found he was grateful for the chance to get out of his own thoughts. "He's lucky to be alive, though I can't help but wonder what sort of life lies ahead of him after this. So much death can haunt a person, and I can't imagine it in one so young."

He thought of Leo's dreams. A voice in the dark, saying he wouldn't wake up, that he would never escape. How much worse would that voice be to him now?

How much worse would that dark, mocking voice be to *Hytham*?

Thyra was silent for a time, looking thoughtful, though

she never stopped watching their surroundings for danger. "When I was young, my village was raided by a rival clan," she said. "My parents were away, off with a hunting party, and I was left behind."

"How old were you?" Hytham asked.

"Not much older than this one," Thyra said, shifting Leo against her hip. "I was old enough to look after myself but not old enough to fight off anyone who came for me." Her gaze was distant with memory. "I hid in a barn. The adults, including my father, had dug a crude sort of tunnel in the back for the children to shelter in, with a hidden entrance and an exit that came out several feet away outside, in case raiders set the barn on fire. The hope was that if that happened, we could run to the river nearby and get away, though it was a slim hope. Anyway, the children knew to go there, so I went." She frowned. "I remember fire, and screams, blood and running, but it happened so fast that I barely realized what was happening. I thought the battle would be louder, more chaotic, like a grand story told by our fires, but it wasn't. It was just people running around, smashing things up, killing some of us, and leaving." She patted Leo's back again, for his comfort or her own, Hytham wasn't sure. "It wasn't the fire or the deaths that stayed with me afterward," she said. "It was the idea that I knew I wasn't as safe as I thought I'd been up to that point. I'd taken so many things for granted, but after that, I learned how easily everything you have can be taken away. So, I made sure I knew how to protect the things and people I love. It's all any of us could do. Maybe Leo will learn the same lesson."

Hytham could only hope she was right, that the memories Leo would take from this would somehow make him stronger, a better leader for his people. But the part of him that had grown too attached to the boy still felt sorry for that lost innocence. He couldn't help it.

No parent could.

Basim walked slightly ahead of them, to all appearances scouting the streets and surrounding rooftops, but Hytham had the suspicion that he'd been listening too.

Had Basim had his own experiences with lost innocence? Either his own or through a child? If so, he would likely never acknowledge it or speak of it to Hytham.

And after today, if he was dismissed from the mission and Basim's side, it wouldn't matter. Hytham felt the pain of the mistakes he'd made and that subtle, stubborn defiance inside him that insisted that what he'd done hadn't been entirely wrong. That if their brotherhood didn't act out of a caring for others, what was it all worth in the end? Was sacrifice all they represented? They worked in the dark to serve the light, but were they never allowed to exist in it as well?

"Stay sharp," Basim said, and Hytham had a feeling the words were directed at him specifically. His spine stiffened. He was not distracted. He would not fail again.

And somehow, he would find a way to protect Leo from his father, even if it cost him his place in the ranks of the Hidden Ones. He knew himself well enough to know that he'd come too far to turn his back on the boy now.

He just hoped that when the time came, he had the strength to do what was necessary to protect him. No matter the cost.

CHAPTER TWENTY-TWO

They arrived back at the palace in the early morning to a storm of activity and heightened security. The Varangian Guard let it be known that Leo had been hidden away in a safe location while the assassins had been dealt with. Hytham later learned that Thyra had told the empress all that had transpired – leaving out the part where they took Leo with them on their rescue mission – so that Eudocia could help spread the story and so she could tell the emperor when word reached him of the attack.

The emperor, of course, had feigned outrage, and when Hytham had presented the evidence he'd found against Theodore, the emperor had ordered him taken and executed, to no one's great surprise. Basil had no desire for Theodore to be given the chance to speak up in his own defense, in case he tried to accuse the emperor himself of being the man who'd brought him into the conspiracy.

Basil's actions, though, had the added benefit of making it easier for Thyra to regain the loyalty of the Varangian

Guards. After seeing how easily the emperor discarded the conspirators who failed him, none of them were eager to step into Theodore's shoes.

That was the hope, at least.

Hytham had had his wounds tended to and managed to get some sleep, but now in the twilight of the evening, he'd been called to the empress's throne room to speak to Anna and to Eudocia Ingerina herself.

He paused outside the door and straightened the new uniform he'd been given. The old one had been too ragged and bloodstained to be saved. There was a fresh bandage on his hand, and the gash there had been stitched. His torso and knee were a landscape of bruises, and it ached whenever he bent his leg, but he was pleased he could already walk without limping.

Inside the throne room there were fresh flowers arranged in pots on either side of the throne, but the empress was not atop the dais. She stood with Anna near a large window on the opposite side of the room, watching the burning orange sky tinged with purple at the edges.

Hytham went to the empress and bowed. "Your grace," he said simply.

"Welcome, Hytham." Eudocia came to him, taking his wrist to draw him closer to the window. "Let's have a look at you. I'm told you survived quite the ordeal."

He found he had nothing to say to that, so he let her take his bandaged hand and touch the healing cut on his face lightly with her fingers. As she looked him over, Anna stood quietly by, watching him with a wary expression. One side of her face was bruised and swollen from the fight, and her left wrist was wrapped and splinted. She held it protectively against her stomach.

"You also survived an ordeal," Hytham said, addressing Anna. "I've rarely seen someone fight so fiercely."

At that, she smiled, and it was a vicious expression. It reminded him he never wanted to be her enemy. "They came into our home like cowards in the night to kill a child. That they're dead now should be a lesson to anyone else who comes for the future emperor."

"It was a message for you as well, Anna," Hytham said. "You should know that."

The empress glanced at him sharply. "What does that mean?"

"You visited the fortune teller," Hytham said. Anna stiffened, but she didn't deny it. Hytham had considered speaking to her about this in private, but he'd decided that the empress should know about the nurse's activities. "You were trying to contact Isaac. Do you know who he is?"

"No," Anna admitted, "but I overheard Theodore speak the name, so I was trying to find out." The empress gave her an incredulous look, and Anna bit her lip. "I didn't tell you, Honored Empress, because if something happened to me, I wanted you to be able to deny everything and leave me to my fate."

"And you think I would have done such a thing?" The empress scowled at her. "Don't be foolish."

"I was *not* being foolish," Anna said, lifting her chin, proud even in the face of the empress's displeasure. "I became close to Theodore because I suspected either he or Justin – or both – were feeding information about Leo's movements and life at the palace to the conspirators who meant to kill him. I made no progress with Justin, so I focused on the tutor."

"Did you follow him one day to the market and see him go to the fortune teller?" Hytham asked, connecting the timeline in his mind.

She nodded. "I knew something was going on, because Theodore puts no faith in soothsaying or tales of the future," she said. "Such things disgust him. He told me as much."

"You suspected he was conspiring against Leo, so you returned on your own to the fortune teller to see what you could learn," Hytham said. "That's the day Basim and I followed you."

She looked surprised, then resigned. "You are very skilled. I never saw you."

"Thank you." He smiled faintly. "What did you ask the fortune teller?" He'd heard only the end of their conversation, not the beginning.

"I asked to speak to the leader of the conspirators," Anna said, looking down sheepishly when the empress made a noise of disbelief. "I had the token you'd given me long ago, the jeweled comb to trade," she said. "I thought if I told them what I knew and offered a bribe, they would leave Leo alone."

The empress frowned. "If you had confided your plan to me, I could have told you these were not the sort of people to be bought."

"Forgive me," Anna said, bowing her head. "I shouldn't have presumed, but I was desperate. I knew there were people who wanted Leo dead, but I didn't know who all of them were."

"And when I showed up at the palace, you thought I was another who wanted to harm him," Hytham said.

"Yes." Anna looked between them. "I didn't know her grace had hired you specifically to protect him. I apologize for confronting you as I did that first night."

"I should have confided in you," the empress said, smiling ruefully, "but I thought the fewer people who knew what was transpiring, the safer my son would be."

"I understand. You couldn't be sure of my loyalty," Anna said. She held up a hand when the empress made to deny it. "You were right not to trust me. You shouldn't trust anyone here at the palace."

"You're wrong," Hytham interjected. When Anna looked at him skeptically, he continued, "We grew so accustomed to expecting the knife in the dark, to rooting out enemies, we didn't look to who our allies might be."

Hytham's own suspicions had blinded him to Justin's true nature, after all. But no more. They had checked into his story thoroughly and found he'd been telling the truth about everything. His desire to protect Leo was genuine.

"It's the reason you were targeted by the assassins as well," Hytham said to Anna. "They weren't sure how much you knew or how much Theodore had told you about them and their plans. They needed to silence you, to be sure."

"Is she still a target?" the empress asked. "Should I arrange for her to leave the city?"

Anna smiled fondly at her. "You could not make me go from either your side or Leo's."

Eudocia scowled, drawing herself up imperiously. "I will not sit by while those I care about are attacked. I would take you and Leo and live in exile if that is what must be done."

"I hope it won't come to running," Hytham said. "Here, at

least, you operate from a position of strength. And Basil can't spend all his time targeting his son. He must rule the city and consider outside threats as well. He's already risked looking weak by allowing an attack on his own palace."

"You think he will stop, then?" Anna asked, and the hope in her eyes was an ache in Hytham's chest. "You think he will give up this plan?"

"I don't know," Hytham admitted. "I will speak to Basim about what our next moves will be." He looked at Anna. "Guard yourself in the meantime. If they come for Leo again, they'll come for you too."

"I will see to it she is protected," the empress said firmly. She came to Hytham and laid a gentle hand on his cheek. The cool touch surprised Hytham, but he didn't pull away. "Thank you for what you endured on my son's behalf," she said softly. "You kept my son alive, and you found the traitor. Thyra was right about you."

She dropped her hand and turned away before Hytham could ask what she meant by that.

When he left the throne room, he realized he had some time before he had to relieve Thyra with Leo, who was still sleeping and probably would be for the rest of the day. So, he took a different hall past the children's wing. A quick glance in that direction as he went revealed that it had been cleaned sometime during the early hours of the morning. Bodies gone, broken furniture cleared away, new pieces brought in, and fresh flower arrangements left behind to scent the air with sweetness and cover any lingering stench of blood and death.

How quickly everything goes back to normal here, Hytham thought. He would not be surprised to see a new tutor in place in Leo's small library the next day, as if Theodore had never existed at all.

The emperor could create any world he wanted in this place. None could challenge him.

Unless the emperor himself was assassinated.

It wasn't as if the thought had never crossed Hytham's mind before. He'd gone so far as to mention it to Basim at the beginning of their mission. Leo had already been declared co-emperor with his father. If Basil died, in the best scenario, Eudocia would become regent while Leo came of age. He would have years yet to learn the workings of the city and how to feed his people.

But if Basil was eliminated, Leo would still be a target to outsiders who might see the moment as a time of weakness for the golden city and take the opportunity to lay siege to it. Constantinople had never been taken, but it had lain under siege before, and the people had suffered.

Hytham clenched his hand into a fist as he passed through an archway into the sunlight of the training yard. The worst of it was that Basil, by all accounts Hytham had heard since he'd been here, ruled the city well, kept its military strong and trade prosperous. He was viewed as a better leader than his predecessor, Michael the drunkard, had ever been. And in some twisted part of Basil's mind, maybe he truly thought he was doing what was best for the future of Constantinople in wiping away Michael's bloodline, as he saw it.

Even though Hytham would swear Leo was Basil's true son. He knew it all the way to the bone, and knew that no matter what, Leo would be a more than capable ruler if he was given the chance. He would outshine both his predecessors.

He found Justin in the training yard, as he'd hoped. There were a few other members of the Varangian Guard present doing exercises in the twilight coolness. Hytham gave them a nod of acknowledgment, but his focus was on Justin. The other guards seemed to sense something was going on. One by one, they quietly left the training yard, until Hytham and Justin were alone.

Justin was sitting on a bench, his sword across his knees. It looked like he'd just finished sharpening the blade. It was on the tip of Hytham's tongue to compliment him on a fine job, but he was afraid it would sound patronizing to the young man, so he shut his mouth.

He wasn't normally at a loss for what to say. Then again, he was usually a better judge of people, but he'd made a mistake with Justin. If Basim was going to dismiss him from the Hidden Ones and the city, he at least wanted to rectify this mistake before he left.

Justin looked up as he approached. A sardonic smile pulled at his mouth. "I should get Leo to teach me how you do that," he said. "You move like a ghost."

"After last night, I feel a bit like one," Hytham admitted.

Justin's face creased in a frown. "Yes, I heard what happened to you. I should have come back to the palace with you immediately. If I hadn't waited, if I'd done my duty as expected of me, maybe none of the assassins would have got away."

It was strange to think that others might be questioning their actions regarding last night. Hytham had reserved all the blame for the outcome on himself. He hadn't considered that others would be feeling the weight of their responsibilities as well.

"You had a duty to your friend to make sure they were safe," Hytham said. "Whoever they are, they're innocent in all this. They deserve protection too." Hytham moved to the bench and sat down, easing his weight off his sore knee.

Justin watched the movement. "Perhaps now is the time to spar," he said, smiling ruefully. "While you're recovering, I might actually have a chance of beating you."

"I have no doubt you would handle me with ease," Hytham said, with a slight groan. But he appreciated the young man's words, the implication that it was only a matter of time before he was back to his full strength.

They sat for a moment in silence, listening to the night birds chittering at each other in the trees, as the breeze ruffled the dark green ivy along the wall at their backs.

"I owe you an apology," Hytham said at last. It wasn't that he'd been gathering his courage, exactly, but that he was trying to determine all that he needed to say to Justin. Some of it felt too big, too close to the things in his own heart with regards to Leo. It made things difficult to say out loud. "I misjudged you from our first meeting, and I let it influence my subsequent actions and decisions."

Justin glanced at him, lifting his brows in curiosity. "Because you thought I was an assassin in waiting? Or because of my treatment of Leo?"

"I let the latter fuel the former," Hytham said, gripping the edges of the cool stone bench, feeling its rough texture beneath his fingers. "An unforgivable mistake in the world I walk in. We're taught to stay objective and see beneath the surface of things."

"I had become very skilled at my façade," Justin said, and

the bitterness in his voice was impossible to miss. "I had to be, and believe me, I am very aware that I also did unforgivable things." He sighed. "It doesn't matter if you tell yourself you're only pretending to be a bully. You can say you're doing it for the noblest of reasons, but in the end, that's all Leo – all anyone – will remember about me."

"You could confide in Leo," Hytham said gently. "Tell him why you do the things you do. The boy is old enough to know the importance of secrets, and after everything he's been through, he deserves to know the truth as well. He needs to know the people he can trust."

Justin gave a sharp, brittle laugh. "I think I preferred it when we sparred with swords," he said, scuffing his boot in the dirt. "I can't win a battle of words with you either."

"Justin." Hytham took a risk. He didn't enjoy making himself vulnerable, but he sensed in this case it might make a difference to the young man. "In the last day, I've been bound and beaten in the dark in what amounted to a hole in the ground. I was certain I was going to die there, and that experience has given me some clarity. Life can be brutal and short. There's no reason to bring more misery and suffering into it than is absolutely necessary, and that includes the misery we inflict on ourselves."

Justin was silent for a moment, thinking about this. Hytham wondered if he'd said too much, but finally, Justin stood, stretching, looking up at the emerging moon. He turned back to Hytham. "I think this organization of yours has taught you well. I envy you a little, having that firm a purpose and beliefs."

"It's a place you may be able to inhabit as well," Hytham said. "Speak to Basim, if you'd like. He'd be lucky to have you."

"Why shouldn't I speak to you about it?" Justin asked.

Because I may no longer have a place here myself. Hytham couldn't quite hide his chagrin. "Basim holds a higher rank than I do. He's the one you should ask about these matters. But I meant everything I said." He gave Justin an intent look. "Think about it."

Justin nodded. "I will." He gazed at the weapons rack with longing. "You're sure you're not up to sparring with me?"

Hytham laughed. "Give me a few more days, and avoid the knee."

Justin grinned. "Not a chance."

CHAPTER TWENTY-THREE

Hytham needed to speak to Basim, but Basim was avoiding him. Hytham wasn't sure if this was another part of his punishment for disobeying orders, or if Basim had been called away from the palace on other matters. Either way, he wasn't answering Hytham's signals. Hytham even went so far as to go to the Hidden Ones' safehouse in the city to inquire about Basim's whereabouts, but he was given no information there either.

He received a message the following day from Thyra, summoning him back to Demetrios's house. Hytham thought the message came from Basim, but Thyra wouldn't confirm it, and they were not able to speak freely at the time, so Hytham couldn't question her further. The aristocrat's house was an odd choice for a meeting place, but Hytham trusted Thyra, so he went as soon as Thyra started her shift with Leo.

When he arrived, he was shown into a less formal garden than the one he'd seen last time, and to his surprise, it wasn't Basim awaiting him.

Eudocia Ingerina was standing to his left near the garden wall. She was holding a longbow, aiming an arrow at a straw target dummy set up on the opposite side of the garden. Her cloak hood was thrown back, and stray tendrils of hair blew around her face in the soft breeze. Her face was the picture of concentration as she focused on the target. She didn't seem to be aware of his presence, so Hytham watched her quietly, not trying to hide but not wanting to startle her and break her concentration either.

Her chest rose and fell on a breath, and all at once she released the arrow, her brow furrowed. It buried itself deep in the target's neck. The empress lowered the bow, looking pleased.

"I wish I could come here every day," she said, turning to look at Hytham. So, she had noticed his presence after all. "My husband would likely think it unseemly were I to set up an archery range for myself on the palace grounds."

"He might see the value in a partner who could defend herself from attack," Hytham said diplomatically.

Eudocia laughed. "Basil sees the value in many things, but he is blind to others that should be obvious." She picked up another arrow from the pile lying on the ground next to her and refocused on the target. "I didn't summon you here to complain about my marriage, I promise," she said, a hint of humor in her voice. "But I did want to speak to you alone."

"I'm at your service, Honored Empress," Hytham said, inclining his head.

"Oh, please stop with the formality," she said, fitting the arrow impatiently and sighting to the target. "You mean it even less than I enjoy hearing it."

Hytham considered. "The respect is sincere," he said truthfully.

"Yes, I believe that," Eudocia said. She lowered the bow, her fingers toying lightly with the arrow's fletching. "Will you shoot with me? Or do you not favor the bow?"

"I can shoot," Hytham said. "I've been trained in the use of different weapons, though right now I favor the sword."

"Well, I can't duel you with a sword," Eudocia said, "or I'll find myself as humiliated as young Justin." She laughed again at his expression. "Yes, word gets around quickly in the palace. For us it will have to be the bow. Come." She gestured imperiously at a small table by the wall, and Hytham was reminded that though she may not insist upon formality, she could never stop being the empress, not even here in this garden of another man's home.

Hytham dutifully went to take a bow from the table and grabbed a fistful of arrows to go with it. He arranged himself in front of the training dummy and nocked an arrow. Before he could release it, Eudocia made another, halting gesture.

"Wait," she said. "What is our wager?"

"Pardon?"

"First one to strike the heart of our enemy," the empress said, gesturing to the straw man. "If I win, what do I receive?"

Hytham smiled faintly. "I don't have much coin, and I don't believe I possess any object that you couldn't readily acquire for yourself," he said.

"I was thinking of something much less tangible," the empress said. "Let's say if I win, you help me with a moral dilemma. With your advice," she clarified, "not your blade."

Hytham inclined his head, hoping he wasn't putting it in the proverbial lion's mouth. "That's acceptable. And if I win?"

The empress looked intrigued. "Name your boon."

"I only ask to be able to one day tell the story of how I stood in a garden with the empress of Constantinople and talked with her for a while."

She didn't smile, but her eyes warmed. "Very well," she said. "But I get to go first."

Not waiting for him to reply, she faced her target and released, barely lining up the shot. The arrow pierced deep into the heart of the target.

They both stared at the dummy for a moment before the empress said airily, "Beginner's luck, I suppose."

Hytham gave her an amused look. "I'm beginning to think I've been set up," he said.

"Well, life is full of unexpected turns," Eudocia said. "Go on. If you strike the heart too, we'll shoot until someone misses."

Hytham nodded, turned to the target, aimed, and released.

The arrow nestled next to the first in the heart of the training dummy.

"Oh, dear," the empress said. "This could take a while."

It took four more shots, but finally, Hytham's arrow lodged in the target dummy's ribs instead of the heart, and he conceded to Eudocia.

"How can I help with this moral dilemma you have?" Hytham asked as they collected their arrows from the target. Truthfully, he wasn't sad about losing the contest. He was more curious about what Eudocia wanted to ask him.

The empress pulled the last arrow out of the straw man, checking it over to see if it had been damaged. Or maybe she was gathering her thoughts. It was hard to say. Finally, she turned to him. "In your line of work, how do you decide who deserves to die?"

Hytham hadn't been expecting that question. "How is this a moral dilemma for *you*, if you don't mind my asking?"

She looked coy. "Are you saying I can't show an interest in joining your organization? I think I'd make an exceptional Assassin."

"Having seen your skills, I can honestly say you'll get no argument from me," Hytham said, raising his hands.

"Well, that's certainly good to know." The empress walked back to where she'd left her bow. "Does a man deserve to die if he's a monster?" she asked.

Hytham sensed there was more riding on his answer than a simple exercise in morality. "It depends," he said. "We stand for what we believe to be right, but many who've worked to further our cause could be viewed as monsters by the right set of eyes."

"You dodge arrows much better than our straw man," Eudocia said, saluting him with said arrow before she took aim with it and fixed her attention on the dummy. "Tell me, then, how may a person be a monster and still serve a cause such as yours?"

Hytham considered. "Again, it depends on the person," he said. "If they're truly a monster, I have my doubts that their views will align with ours for very long."

"In which case, they'll be cast out of your band," Eudocia said, releasing another arrow, this one going wide of the target and burying itself in the thick trumpet flowers crawling up the courtyard wall. She frowned at it, but her eyes were unfocused, seeing instead something within. "Let me ask you this, then," she said, dropping her voice. "What if, in all other ways, the world sees a man as good, but in just one way, he's a monster?"

Eudocia looked at Hytham then, her expression haunted. It was the first time he'd ever seen vulnerability like this from the empress. Hytham nodded to let her know he knew they were speaking of the emperor, though neither could speak such treasons aloud.

"I can't imagine how hard it would be to reconcile the existence of such a person," Hytham said. "But sometimes removing that person causes even more harm. It's difficult to anticipate all the outcomes of our actions. If we make the wrong choice, many may suffer. I wish I had an easy answer for your dilemma, but I don't."

"It's all right," the empress said. She went to the table and laid down her bow. Apparently, shooting was done for the day. "The older I get, the more I realize there are no easy answers to any of my questions. But I thank you for your honesty, regardless."

"If it helps, Honored Empress, I will continue to do my best to make such questions unnecessary," he assured her, his words coming out more passionate than he'd intended.

She glanced at him sharply. "I know you will," she said. "I could tell that from the day I met you. If I'd felt otherwise, I would never have let you near those I love."

Two of her guards came to fetch her soon after, and there was no more opportunity to talk. Hytham stayed in the garden for a few minutes once the empress had left. His thoughts were a tangle, and he was full of unease. He fired more arrows into the target dummy, but even when his arms burned and the straw man was riddled with arrow wounds, he still hadn't worked off the restless energy.

Could he truly fulfill the promise he'd made to the empress, or were they ultimately fighting a losing battle here in the palace? Isaac was still out there plotting the Order of the Ancients' next move. Hytham felt their mission was now at a critical point.

And where was Basim? Hytham felt the frustration well inside him. He needed to find the Master Assassin. They needed a plan, a way forward out of the dark.

Before it was too late.

CHAPTER TWENTY-FOUR

The Philopation, the vast park that hugged the land walls of Constantinople, was a spot of green leisure away from the hot, dusty urban press of the city. Sculpted pathways ran alongside canals that wound through the park like twisting silver ribbons. Bird calls echoed in the shelter of the trees. But it was also the emperor's hunting grounds, and Hytham had heard that all manner of game lived in the walled space, from foxes and deer to packs of wolves.

Today the emperor was hunting, and he'd brought family and guests along to picnic by the canals while he took his court favorites on the hunt with him. It was, to all outside appearances, a way for the emperor to remove himself and his family from the terror of recent events, to relax and take everyone's mind off what had happened. There were even rumors that Basil intended to hold a special chariot race at the Hippodrome as a way to divert the city's attention.

There was no way to keep so brazen an attack on the palace a secret, and rumors had already begun to spread, questioning the emperor's security, wondering if foreign invaders were trying to topple the city from within by striking at its seat of power.

None of these rumors were to the emperor's benefit. He'd made himself look weak, and now all he could do was try to control the damage.

Hytham had to admit, the emperor's plan was working well, at least among this crowd. People were spread out on the grass, dozens of dots of color on a soft green palette. Servants brought food and poured wine. The sun was high in the sky, but the shade and a pleasant breeze had everyone feeling relaxed and sated while they waited for the emperor and his hunters to reemerge from the trees with some kind of prize.

That was the only part of the festivities that didn't appear to be going to plan. Hytham kept one eye on Leo, who was sitting on a blanket next to his mother, while he watched the tree line and listened for signs of game being flushed from the forest. It had been several hours, but there was no sign of the hunters, either triumphant or defeated.

Thyra came to stand beside him, following the direction of his gaze. "The empress says the emperor is seeking a wolf," she commented. "I've been in this park on and off for years, but I've never seen one. I think they were all hunted out long ago, but the emperor is welcome to tire himself shaking the bushes."

"Ours is the more pleasant way to spend the afternoon," Hytham agreed. They weren't lounging on blankets or eating cheese and meat, but there was a quiet here, a peacefulness that was good for the spirit.

Leo seemed to feel it too. He'd been quieter than usual since the attack on the palace, but out here in the open he seemed to relax. He pointed out birds to his mother and Anna and named them, mimicking their calls – badly – making the women laugh. His new tutor was a lover of nature and often took the boy outside the confines of the library, and gave more encouragement for Leo to run and play, making it a part of the learning process.

It was a relief to get to see him able to be a child again. Judging by the looks on the empress and Anna's faces, they were pleased as well.

The only one who was at a loose end was Hytham himself. Well, Basim too, technically. His superior was still nowhere to be found.

"You're watching for him again," Thyra commented, drawing Hytham out of his reverie.

He turned a startled look upon her. "I was…" he started to say he was just scanning the gathered crowd for signs of a threat. And he was, but he'd be lying if he tried to say that was all he'd been doing. Thyra, perceptive as she was, had noticed.

Ever since the night Basim had promised, rather ominously, that they would talk, Hytham had been searching the shadows for the man, wondering where he'd gone. Wondering when his fate would be decided.

He'd not thought Basim was the type of person to punish with silence, but maybe he was angrier than Hytham had known. Or maybe he was simply taking this long to decide what Hytham's punishment should be.

"I'd like to get it over with and know what my future holds," he said to Thyra.

She shook her head. "Don't try to take all the blame for this on yourself," she chided him. "Besides, Basim isn't just angry at you. I believe he's also angry with himself."

"Why should he feel that way?" Hytham asked, curious to hear her insight. She and Basim had shared more than one private conversation. Of that he was sure, he simply didn't know how it might relate to Basim's personal agenda in the city.

Thyra looked thoughtful, her arms crossed as she watched Leo try to scoop up a frog that was hopping along the bank of the canal. "Basim allowed you to distract from his purpose," she said. "You complicated things for him, I think."

Hytham didn't understand what she was getting at. "I endangered the mission, if that's what you mean," he said, hardly needing or appreciating the reminder.

Again, Thyra shook her head. "No, you complicated his own private mission." She leaned in closer to Hytham, as if she thought Basim might suddenly spring out at them from the underbrush. "I told you before, he's looking for someone, Hytham. I don't know who. I'm not sure Basim himself knows. He seemed very interested in the Varangian Guard, but whomever he was seeking, he didn't find them among my clan members."

Hytham couldn't say he was surprised to hear this. Basim had from the start expressed an interest in the Norsemen and their culture. He'd claimed to Hytham that he was potentially interested in recruiting them, and that might yet be the case. But if Thyra was right, and Basim was looking for someone in particular, what were his reasons? And why did the Hidden Ones care what he sought, as long as he stayed on mission in Constantinople?

He could write to his mentor and relay the information that Basim was seeking someone among the Norsemen, but it was a vague enough lead that Hytham wondered if it would do any good. And he had no idea what his own words would be worth to his superiors, after Basim finished reporting on Hytham's actions.

His gaze moved from Thyra to Leo, and then to the people lounging on the blankets, tracking them all by instinct. He glanced at the tree line and caught a flash of something, like sunlight glinting off metal. He tensed, then relaxed when he recognized a familiar night bird's call. No one else seemed to notice the nocturnal sound or thought it was strange that they were hearing it in the daylight, but Hytham recognized it as the summons it was.

"It's Basim," he said. "He's calling me."

"Go," Thyra encouraged, when he hesitated. "The boy is safe here, and I'm on watch. Better to meet your fate head-on." She smiled at him to soften the words. "You'll be fine."

Hytham wasn't so sure, but it was easy enough to slip away from the crowds, to move along the canal and into a grove of trees, the deep shade immediately relieving the heat of the sun, muffling the sounds of conversation and glasses clinking.

It was like stepping into a different world in some ways. Roots and moss-covered rocks were obstacles he easily leaped over. Old leaves and underbrush sank under his weight but did not make a sound. He wanted to bring Leo here, to show him how different it was to walk the forest floor, to sneak as nature's companion and make yourself a part of the landscape.

Basim was waiting for him in a small glade where filtered

sunlight penetrated the thick canopy of trees and small birds flitted from branch to branch.

At least, he thought it was Basim. He glimpsed the familiar profile, wide shoulders, peaked hood and the dark beard shadowing his jaw. But when the figure turned, angling slightly away, Hytham noticed another shape at Basim's side. He froze.

The wolf was tall and lean, so dark its fur was a strange, blueish black, absorbing the shadows of the forest. Or perhaps it was carved of the shadows themselves. Its lambent gaze fixed on Hytham, one ear flicking as it noted his presence, but otherwise, neither man nor beast moved.

Hytham stayed where he was, barely breathing. It seemed they were caught in this moment, the three of them. Hytham told himself he didn't want to startle the wolf, to give it a reason to attack Basim.

No, that was a foolish thought. Basim was perfectly at ease as he stood there, one hand hovering above the wolf's back, but he did not touch the animal, and the wolf did not touch him. They were simply there, standing as still and ancient as the trees, and Hytham realized it was he who was the intruder, for all that Basim had invited him with his signal.

But there was obviously something here that Basim wanted him to witness.

Was it just the wolf? Hytham listened, and in the distance he heard the sounds of the hunting party. Too far to make out words, but there were raised voices, frustration, all the signs of a thwarted hunt, soon to end. It seemed the day hadn't been a complete success after all.

Hytham felt the swell of satisfaction in his chest at this

latest disappointment for the emperor. Try as he might, he would never find this wolf in the forest.

Not while Basim walked here.

Time ceased to mean anything as they stood there, waiting, Hytham meditating and reflecting on all that had happened since he'd come to Constantinople. He had been so certain of himself when he'd first arrived in the city. Certain of his purpose and his mission. He'd had no doubt that his cause was just and that the decisions he'd made were the right ones. Many things had changed since then, and he was no longer certain of anything, except that he would remember these frozen moments with Basim and the black wolf for the rest of his days.

Finally, the voices of the hunters faded and were gone. The wolf sprinted away with a grace and silence that made Hytham's heart give a kick.

Only then did Basim turn.

Hytham joined him in the glade. "That was incredible," he said softly. "Were you never afraid?"

Basim let his hood fall to his shoulders. "There are much darker things in the world to be afraid of," he said. "How are you feeling, Hytham?"

"I'm well enough." Hytham didn't want to talk about his injuries, which were healing. He'd thought about them entirely too much already. "I was beginning to think you'd never summon me."

"It wasn't a punishment," Basim assured him, as if he'd guessed Hytham's thoughts. He stood half in and out of a shaft of sunlight, the gold cutting across his face and teasing the faintest gray strands from his beard. "I had many things to consider, and I wanted to wait for my temper to cool."

"Has it?"

Basim looked at him, and there was that dangerous light again in his eyes. "Not really," he admitted.

Now Hytham thought he knew why Basim had summoned him to this particular place, far away from prying eyes.

Hytham eased his sword from its scabbard, at the same time Basim drew his scimitar. They were deep enough in the forest now, and with the hunters calling it a day, no one would hear them.

They circled each other, passing in and out of sunbeams, testing the leaf fall for hidden rocks and slippery mud. The birds and small animals in the underbrush had gone silent, as if they too sensed the storm about to break.

Hytham thought he was prepared for it. He was not.

Chapter Twenty-Five

The sun caught the edge of Basim's scimitar, turning it to liquid gold. It shone in Hytham's eyes, temporarily blinding him. He ducked instinctively, and the blade hissed above his head and nicked the tree behind him, sending up a spray of bark. Hytham dove and rolled, coming up behind Basim, but the man turned as if he'd expected the move and dodged Hytham's quick thrust.

Basim backed away, putting the tree between them, and he disappeared behind its slender column. Hytham felt a pulse of alarm. To lose sight of Basim in a duel, even for an instant, was disaster. He'd learned that in the olive grove.

He lunged, coming around the tree, but as he'd expected, Basim was gone. He looked up, and though at first glance there was nothing in the tree, Hytham raised his sword in a defensive move, and was rewarded when a shadow came swooping down on him. Basim put his full weight into the attack, and Hytham could do nothing but absorb it, the sharp ringing of blades loud in his ears. The force of the strike drove him to his knees, and his bad knee protested sharply. Hytham gritted his teeth and held his position. Basim's scimitar was right at eye level.

"Did you think I would hold back because you were injured?" Basim asked, that dangerous gleam still in his eyes. Hytham was further alarmed to note that Basim barely sounded winded, while Hytham's sword hand was beginning to tremble with the effort of holding Basim at bay. He was no longer the silent man shielding the wolf from harm. Now he was the predator on the hunt.

Hytham knew he couldn't win this fight, but in this case, he didn't believe that winning was the point.

"Actually," Hytham said, his voice ragged, breathing labored already, "I think you held off for this long *because* you were worried. You need not be," he added. "I'd rather have every bit of your anger than your silence and pity."

"I'll remember you said that, my friend."

Hytham was not going to go down easy. Jaw tight, he drove himself to his feet, deliberately testing the knee to see if it would hold. It did. Thankfully, he still had strength he could call on when he needed it.

He'd caught Basim off guard with the surge. He could feel it in the man's balance, the swords connecting their bodies like life threads. He shoved Basim back, tossed his sword to his left hand and released the Hidden Blade, aiming for Basim's torso.

Basim pivoted and grabbed Hytham's arm, twisting his wrist painfully. Hytham turned too, putting his back to Basim and coming in under his guard. He threw his head back, and though Basim moved again, he couldn't completely dodge the blow to his face.

Basim released Hytham's wrist and staggered, allowing Hytham to pull free and roll away. He might have pressed his advantage there, but he didn't want to have his back to the tiger for too long.

When he turned to face Basim again, he was both surprised and darkly pleased to see the line of blood running from the man's nose. Hytham didn't think he'd broken it, but it had been a solid blow, one Basim had not been expecting.

And when Basim looked up at him, spitting blood on the grass, his smile was pleased too. "Well done," he said. "There's fight left in you yet."

Is that what Basim thought? That Hytham's encounter with Isaac in that basement had stolen his will to fight?

He didn't have time to consider it. Basim was coming for him again.

The fight went on, the pace of it relentless as they circled the sun-dappled clearing. Again, time seemed to have no meaning. They could have been fighting for hours, though Hytham knew it had only been a few minutes. He was reminded again of that day in the misty olive grove. Basim fought as if he'd always fought, as if he performed the steps of a dance he'd danced for centuries. Maybe that was why Hytham could be forgiven for feeling just a little immortal in Basim's presence. It was that timeless quality he carried with him, absorbing it like their blades absorbed the golden, slanting light of the sun.

But Hytham was not immortal, and whatever its purpose, Basim seemed ready to end the match. He crowded Hytham, bringing the Hidden Blade up, and Hytham realized too late that the move was a feint. Basim hooked Hytham's calf with his foot and tripped him.

And so, arms burning with exertion, Hytham suddenly found himself on his back on the mossy ground. Basim dropped to his knees next to him, mud and damp leaves soaking their clothes. Basim's Hidden Blade sought Hytham's throat, forcing Hytham to drop his sword and hold onto Basim's wrist with both hands. The blade got closer, inches from skin. Abruptly, Hytham jerked Basim's wrist to the side and released it. The blade stabbed the ground, sticking deep in the soft earth.

Hytham groped for his sword, but Basim had kicked it out of reach. It lay half covered in leaves and brush several feet away. Hytham felt around the ground and came up with a rock. He brought it down toward Basim's face, but like an eel the man slipped away again, laughing as he went.

"In the grove you were elegant – the picture of grace," Basim said. "Now you fight like a vicious dog. I can't decide which version of you I like more."

Hytham snorted. He knew Basim was baiting him. Hytham was exhausted, panting, and his knee throbbed. It was the perfect time to make a mistake. But Hytham was determined not to be reckless. He wasn't going to let the emotion of the moment, the need to prove himself, cloud his judgment.

Basim lurched back to his feet. He'd lost his scimitar sometime during the struggle on the ground. He raised his Hidden Blade, and Hytham did the same.

This is how they would finish it.

Hytham knew he couldn't win, but he felt no shame in admitting he loved watching Basim move. Though he was tall and broad, he slipped from shadow to shadow like a creature of another world, evading the light and keeping always just out of Hytham's reach as he thrust and parried with the blade. Sweat poured down Hytham's back, but he would not have stopped this for anything. If this was to be his last fight on behalf of the Hidden Ones, he'd make it a fight to be proud of.

He dodged a slash at his face, felt a small cut open at his chin, a thin line of blood running over his skin. He answered with a low thrust that grazed Basim's thigh, making the other man grunt in pain. Hytham pressed the advantage, backing Basim toward a nearby tree. He hoped that Basim would lose his footing among the knobby roots and creepers, but without even looking, the man's feet found balance, like a fey creature out of a story.

Hytham dodged another thrust, but he was slower now, and not varying his movements as much as he should. The predictability undid him, in the end. Basim grabbed him by the front of his uniform and pivoted, using the momentum to slam Hytham against the tree. It wasn't a hard enough blow to seriously hurt him, but it stole the breath from Hytham's body, dazing him just long enough for Basim to bring his Hidden Blade up and lay it neatly alongside Hytham's exposed throat.

"I have you," Basim said. They were both breathing heavily now, and Hytham leaned hard on the tree for support. He nodded, raising his hands and retracting his own Hidden Blade.

"So you do," Hytham said. "Well fought."

Basim stepped back. Silence reigned in the glade, but it was not the comfortable silence that had followed their earlier sparring matches.

"You disobeyed my order," Basim said curtly, retrieving his scimitar from where it lay next to the tree. "Your duty was to stay at the boy's side, and you left your post to chase our enemies on your own."

"I trusted Thyra with Leo's care," Hytham countered. "He was not in danger at–" He broke off when Basim turned to stare at him with a flat, cold expression, his dark eyes boring into Hytham.

Hytham bowed his head, abashed. "I'm sorry," he said. "Of course, the boy was in danger all of that night. I only meant that I weighed the risk and judged it worth it in order to find the traitor."

"*You* judged it worthy," Basim said. "Who are *you*, Hytham, to make such judgments?"

"I was wrong, and I know it," Hytham said, feeling the flush of shame creep up his neck. "You're right to be angry."

Basim sheathed his scimitar and went to retrieve Hytham's blade. He held it in his hands, examining the weight and balance. Or maybe he was weighing Hytham. "I told you not to form an attachment to the boy. You were to be his guardian, not his father."

Hytham fisted his hand against the rough bark of the tree. He didn't want to have this conversation. He'd rather fight again, or be dismissed. This made him feel too raw, too exposed.

"I was not trying to be a–"

"Don't lie to me, Hytham," Basim said softly. "I know what it is to be willing to die for your children, to commit atrocities that would make the world shake. By comparison, you are painfully transparent – to everyone but yourself, it seems."

"Fine," Hytham bit out. He watched the play of sunlight on the leaves and branches above him, looking away from Basim's too-knowing gaze. "But I did everything you wanted of me," he said, still feeling that defiance, even in the face of Basim's wrath. "I steered the boy and taught him our ways. I worked to make him a tool for our cause, even though he is too young to fully understand what we're asking of him."

"Ah, so you wanted to protect him from *us*, too," Basim said, "from the Hidden Ones."

"You called him a pawn, and you were right," Hytham said. "I wanted to protect him, to give him choices." He hesitated, then met Basim's eyes. "Yes, I came to care about him, even though I was commanded not to." He almost laughed at that idea, that one could be commanded not to love. "I never thought of myself as a father, but I was as helpless as one when it came to Leo."

He held Basim's gaze, daring him to judge, but something in the man shifted, that mercurial light in his eyes dimming, becoming profoundly sad. "The boy was lucky to have you," Basim said. "Fathers can be cruel even when they've no doubt that their son shares their blood." He closed the distance between them and handed Hytham his sword. "My father had no love in him for his son. He had nothing but violence, and he passed that on to me."

Hytham was taken aback at this confession. He had never expected to be given so intimate a glimpse into Basim's past. As far as Hytham knew, it was not in the man's nature to confide in anyone.

"Maybe that's why I feel such fury when I look at you and all you've done," Basim continued. He seemed to be speaking mostly to himself. "You were everything I might have wanted as a child, and as a father I see myself in you so clearly it burns me. Yet I am supposed to stop you, to keep you from pursuing the very thing that…" he trailed off, shaking his head. "It is a strange world that keeps turning and turning and depositing us back at the same places, considering the same choices over and over again."

Thyra had been right, Hytham thought. Not all of Basim's anger was directed at him. Hytham had never realized how many demons Basim carried and all the ways they were tormenting him.

"Why did you come after me that night?" Hytham asked. "Why didn't you leave me to suffer the consequences of my mistakes?"

Basim looked at him in some surprise, as if the answer were obvious. "I didn't want to see you throw your life away for the boy," he said. "You're valuable too, Hytham, to the Hidden Ones, and also to me."

He said it so simply, but Hytham was struck by his tone. He didn't sound like someone describing a commodity or a tool whose only value lay in how it could be used.

"I value your friendship as well," Hytham said after a moment.

Basim gave a nod of acknowledgment, and another silence fell. The shadows of the afternoon were getting longer, the golden light becoming rich and bronzed. Hytham would be missed if he stayed away from the picnic much longer.

"You can't continue on this mission," Basim said, and Hytham's world constricted. He felt the sharp knife of betrayal in his chest. "You're too compromised by your feelings for the boy. You need to leave the city."

"I won't go."

Basim's mouth twisted. "Of course you won't. Ah, Hytham, you're so much like me when I was young."

He was not so very much older than Hytham, but Hytham didn't point that out. His thoughts were tangled and miserable. "I want to see this through, no matter what happens," he insisted. "Afterward, you can do whatever you like. I'll leave the Hidden Ones, and you'll never see me again."

"Don't be dramatic," Basim scolded. "You say you want to see this through, but that's the question, isn't it? What is the endgame? Can we leave Leo in the care of the Varangian Guard? With all that he's risked, will the emperor give up this idea of murdering Leo now that the traitor Theodore has been executed, or will Basil see his obsession through to the bitter end?"

"You know he will," Hytham said. "The emperor turns his attentions – and those of the people – away with other amusements, but he'll remember his hatred eventually. He needs a bigger incentive to give up his plan."

"I believe you're right about that," Basim said thoughtfully. "Isaac, on the other hand, needs no incentive. Losing you as a captive was a blow. He has to kill the boy now, or he can't continue to lead the Order here."

"So we have to end him."

Basim laughed and held out his hands. "A simple matter then. Permanently discourage the emperor from killing his son *and* assassinate the head of the Order of the Ancients in Constantinople." His gaze turned hard. "Which is exactly what we're going to do."

The misery in Hytham's heart flared to hope. "You have a plan."

"Of course I do," Basim said. He paced the clearing, idly toeing at the grass with his boot, as if following the path of their duel in his mind while he thought about what lay ahead. "But you're not going to like it, which is why I would rather pull you off this mission entirely, though a greater part of me wants to leave the choice in your hands. I also know the value of giving people choices."

Hytham appreciated the consideration, but he didn't like the ominous note in Basim's voice. "What do you intend to do?" he asked.

Basim came to Hytham, his expression solemn. He put a hand on Hytham's shoulder. "My plan uses Leo as bait. It puts him in the heart of the maelstrom, and you'll have to let him stay there."

Hytham's breath tangled in his throat. He struggled not to make a denial. "How will this help our cause if Leo dies in the endeavor?" he managed.

"It won't, but better the boy dies than lives his entire childhood under constant threat of assassination and death. The terror of it will eventually take him over, and he won't be fit to rule the city anyway. That's the fate you want to avoid most, the fate you don't want to contemplate for him."

Hytham tried to take a step back, to get air, but Basim kept hold of his shoulder. He was right. Hytham didn't want to see Leo growing up in misery and fear. No amount of protecting his physical body could save him from that, if they didn't make the palace a safer place for him to grow and learn and thrive.

Especially since he would never escape his father's hatred.

"So we put Leo in deadly danger now, in the hope of ensuring his future and his happiness," Hytham said. He sighed heavily. "You're right. I hate it. But I will see the mission through."

Basim's grip tightened, becoming painful, though there was no malice in his gaze. "Do I have your word on that, my friend?" he said, his voice quiet and intent. "Because if we fail in this, we won't have another opportunity. Can I trust you?" He added, "Can you trust *me*?"

Hytham looked into Basim's eyes. Trust was such a tenuous thing between them. Hytham didn't believe Basim truly trusted anyone. Hytham trusted Basim to have his back in battle, but beyond that, there was still the question of whether he truly had the interests of the Hidden Ones at heart.

Except Hytham had been the one acting in his own interests on this mission. Yet Basim had not dismissed him for it. He felt that Basim understood him in a way few had understood Hytham his whole life.

Could Basim trust him? Yes, without hesitation. Hytham would follow his plan if it would save Leo's life. But could he trust Basim? When so many secrets lurked behind those enigmatic eyes?

That was the question Hytham couldn't answer. But he saw no other way out of this situation that didn't end with Leo's death or his suffering.

"I'll follow you," Hytham said. "But I think it will be a miracle if you can accomplish all you say."

"Really?" Basim grinned. "You know I do so love a challenge, Hytham."

CHAPTER TWENTY-SIX

The emperor made good on his promise to hold a race in the Hippodrome.

That he planned to attend personally with his family posed a greater challenge for the Varangian Guard. To ensure the emperor's safety in such an open venue that could accommodate thousands of citizens was no easy task. Still, that was nothing compared to the rumors that circulated that the emperor himself intended to race an exhibition match near the end of the day's festivities.

In hindsight, it shouldn't have been so surprising that the emperor, having been thwarted in his wolf hunt, would look to regain some measure of glory by participating in a race. He'd been the previous emperor's horse master, after all, and he would make a fine figure for the people, strong, capable, with the flush of near immortality that seemed to cling to those in power. They held the absolute confidence of their place in the world.

But the reality of making these events safe and keeping

them functioning behind the scenes was a nightmare for all the lesser players involved.

Hytham stood with Justin and Thyra on the central spina of the chariot track, the sun shining brightly in their eyes, the smell of dust and horsehair strong in their nostrils. Together they surveyed the visible entrances and exits, citing all the places assassins might choose to conceal themselves and finding those with a clear view of the emperor's private box.

They'd been at it for about an hour when Justin gave a bark of laughter, scuffing his boot in the dirt. "It's too exposed," he said. "They're vulnerable to arrows from the moment they sit down. Anyone in the crowd could pick them off."

"We'll be searching and confiscating any weapons the people attempt to bring in," Thyra said, though she didn't sound particularly happy about what this would involve. It would slow the crowd coming into the Hippodrome, resulting in long, hot lines of unhappy people who might choose to take out their anger and impatience on the guards in charge of searching them or their fellow patrons in line. Fights were inevitable in this heat.

Justin scoffed. He turned to look at Hytham, as if waiting for him to weigh in. Hytham had noticed that since they'd declared a truce between them, Justin was more apt to look to him and Thyra, to ask for their opinions and to offer his own more readily. That sullen set to his face was gone as well. Hytham was glad to see the change.

Justin had been avoiding Leo, though. He wasn't hostile or bullying anymore, for which Hytham was grateful, but it was as if now the young man didn't know how to act around the boy, and he was afraid to get too close to him.

Hytham had some idea of how to remedy that.

"There's already a canopy stretched across the emperor's box for shade and privacy," Hytham said. "What if we expanded that and made the material thicker? It'll give more cover and protection from range attacks."

"It would help," Thyra agreed. "The order can come down through the empress, for the comfort of herself and her family. I don't see the emperor arguing."

"So that's it?" Justin shook his head incredulously. "Some extra sun shades and we call everything done? He'll still just be sitting there, the easiest target for anyone who wants to grab him."

He was right, and of course, that was the point. Leo would be a target too good for Isaac and the Order to resist. True, he would be sitting near the emperor and empress during the race, but that didn't mean he would be safe. There were all kinds of ways the Order of the Ancients could strike, distractions they could employ to separate Leo from the others. Hytham's gut churned just thinking about how vulnerable the boy would be.

But that was the risk he'd agreed to take when he'd assented to Basim's plan. Leaving Leo to the wolves, so to speak.

They hadn't shared that plan with Justin, of course. They knew where his loyalties lay now, but neither Basim nor Hytham could be sure that Justin would be able to leave Leo in danger the way they intended. Beyond that, the fewer people who knew their plan, the better. Thyra knew, and she was just as unhappy about the situation as Hytham. But she'd accepted it, following their lead.

Hytham still wondered at the relationship between Basim

and Thyra, and whether Basim had gotten the information about the Vikings and Thyra's clan that he'd desired.

Hytham turned to Justin. "We know it's an impossible task we're facing, but we can't call off the event or tell the emperor that we're unable to guard him or his family. The only thing we can do is prepare as much as possible and be ready if there's an attack."

Justin shielded his eyes against the sun as he swept his gaze over the stands once more. "You're going to be with him in the box?" he asked, for the third time since they'd started working out everyone's positions.

"I'll be there," Hytham told him. "So will Thyra."

"I should be up there with you," Justin said, scanning the box. "I could disguise myself as one of the empress's guests and be in the box right behind Leo."

Ordinarily, that would have been an ideal role for him to play. But not for the outcome they intended. Hytham had to tread carefully here so Justin wouldn't suspect anything.

"I would rather have you keeping watch from afar," Hytham said. "Your eyes are better than most. Besides, there will be another friend close by, should we need him."

The oblique reference to Basim seemed to lift Justin's spirits. Knowing there was going to be another hidden ally nearby gave them a solid ring of protection around Leo.

Hytham tried to imagine the size of the crowd that would fill the Hippodrome. The area they stood in was dominated by an obelisk and other relics from around the world, showing off the treasures amassed by Constantinople over the centuries. The Hippodrome itself was another great feat of architecture, connected to the palace and capable of seating over fifty thousand citizens, each a supporter of a different color faction.

Hytham couldn't help but be reminded of the story Basim had told him during their sparring match at the walls, how the chariot racing teams' supporters had come to the city's defense in repairing its walls.

On racing day, they were going to be a liability, a sea of faces in which to hide assassins. Still, at least this time the Hidden Ones and the Varangian Guard were the ones laying the trap, instead of waiting for their enemies to come to them.

Hytham still had to face Isaac again. He couldn't decide if he was eager to see the man again or if it would cause him to hesitate and doubt himself. Either way, he would find out soon enough.

He banished the thoughts from his mind. Whatever came, worrying would do him no good, and he had different business to attend to today.

"Justin," he said, as the group broke up to go to their separate duties. "Can you spare a moment?"

The young man nodded and fell into step beside him. "Where are we going?" Justin asked, but Hytham didn't immediately answer. He led them to the stables, a place Hytham had only been once before, the day of Leo's disastrous riding lesson. Justin obviously remembered the day as well, because he stiffened as they moved down the row of stalls. He slowed his steps, hanging back as he saw who was at the other end of the room by the last stall.

Leo stood with one of the Varangian Guard, a woman Thyra trusted implicitly. Hytham knew Basim would be nearby as well, though of course he couldn't sense the man's presence.

Hytham had informed the stablemaster earlier of what he intended and told the man his services wouldn't be needed.

As they approached, the woman nodded respectfully to Hytham and left them. When she was gone, Leo came immediately to Hytham's side, smiling. He glanced at Justin's tense form and his gaze shuttered. For his part, Justin just looked miserable, as if he wanted to be anywhere but in that stable.

This would never do, Hytham thought. It wasn't something that would be fixed in a day, but he could make a start.

"Justin, would you please take Sky out to the paddock?" he asked. "I need to talk to Leo for a moment before he starts his riding lesson."

Relieved, Justin practically flew into the stall to bring out Leo's horse and lead it toward the doors. Beside Hytham, Leo had started to tremble. The boy tried to hide it, but the memories of his last riding lesson were clearly still fresh in his mind.

When horse and handler were gone, Hytham pulled up a small stool and sat in front of Leo. Now that they were alone, the boy relaxed. The soft whickering of the other horses was the only sound in the stable.

"You knew that someday you would have to try again to ride the horse," he said, putting his hands on the boy's shoulders. "I think that day should be today. Appropriate, with the racing tomorrow, don't you think? You'll be able to enjoy the event that much more if you understand the ways of the horses involved."

Leo swallowed, his face and neck flushing red. "I don't want to fall off again. Not in front of Justin."

Hytham couldn't blame him. "You and Justin were friends once," he said carefully. "If you give him a chance, I don't think he will let you fall off the horse."

"We used to be friends." Leo shook his head, looking confused and upset, like he didn't want to be thinking of this. "But then he changed." His face scrunched in what looked like anger, a rare emotion for the boy to display. "No, my father *told* him to change," he said.

Hytham's breath caught. "You knew about that?" he said quietly.

Leo nodded. "I knew because it happened after he'd seen my father," he said. He looked at Hytham with those large eyes. "I was afraid it would be the same with you after you saw the emperor," he said. "I was scared he would tell you what he told Justin, that he was supposed to treat me differently."

"I understand," Hytham said, and he felt nothing but bitterness toward the emperor. "Your father threatened to cause you pain if Justin continued to be your friend," he said, wanting the boy to know the whole truth. "Justin didn't want to obey him, but he feared for you and your safety, so he did what the emperor asked. It was a mistake, but sometimes we make errors in judgment when it comes to the people we love."

Leo's eyes filled with tears. "Justin doesn't love me," he said. "My father says–"

"No." Hytham wasn't interested in what that man had to say. "Your father is wrong," he said firmly. "Justin cares about you very much, and I believe he wants you to give him another chance to show you. But he's afraid."

"Afraid?" Leo looked shocked at the notion. "Justin's the bravest person I know besides you, Hytham," he said loyally, and Hytham couldn't help but smile. "He's not scared of anything."

Hytham shook his head. "We're all scared of something, Leo," he said. "That's natural. It's to be expected. It's how we use that fear that makes the difference, how we don't let it overcome us. That's why I want you to try to ride the horse again today. You need to conquer your fear if you're going to move forward."

Leo considered this, then looked at Hytham. "It's not just about the horse, is it?"

Clever boy. He squeezed Leo's shoulder. "No, it's not just about the horse. This is to help you and Justin too."

"How can I help him?" Leo seemed bewildered by the idea that he had anything to offer the young warrior.

"Just be yourself," Hytham said. "I have a feeling you'll both be fine."

Leo didn't look entirely convinced, but he allowed Hytham to lead him out of the stables and back to the paddock, where Justin had brought the horse and a mounting stool. The mare was one of the shorter, calmer beasts in the emperor's collection, but it still towered over Leo when he stood next to it.

Hytham nodded at Justin to begin the lesson, but the young man just stood there, frozen by indecision. He looked around the paddock, as if he expected eyes to be following his every movement.

As if he expected the emperor's wrath to fall on him at any moment.

Stepping forward, Hytham leaned in close to speak at Justin's ear, the words meant for him alone. "There's no one watching," he said. "I made certain of it. You can play the part of the bully to satisfy the emperor, but in these moments, Leo needs to know who you really are. You can do this."

Hytham stepped back, again nodding at the young man to help Leo mount the horse. Justin gave him an unhappy look, but this time he obeyed, stopping twice to check the horse and once more to see if anyone was coming.

"Are you ready?" Justin asked Leo finally.

The boy was clearly not ready, standing still as a statue, knees locked as if to keep them from shaking, but he nodded gamely and stood on the mounting stool. Justin boosted him up into the saddle without issue, and the horse snuffled and nosed the ground, as if bored by the whole affair.

Leo sat rigid in the saddle, clutching the pommel in a death grip and bracing himself as if the horse would suddenly spring into motion and carry him away. Hytham began to question whether this had been a good idea after all, but still he stayed quiet, watching Justin.

The young man stood beside the horse, absently stroking the beast's neck as he considered Leo. Something shifted subtly in his expression, and he sighed as if in resignation.

"All right," he said, "we'll try it this way first."

And he swung up into the saddle behind Leo.

Leo made a small noise of surprise as Justin gathered the reins and adjusted their positions so that Leo settled back against his chest. "What are you doing?" he whispered.

"Giving you a riding lesson," Justin answered. "Rule number one: try to relax. If the horse thinks you're terrified, things aren't going to go well, and I don't want to end up on my backside in the dirt today." But he was smiling slightly, softening the words.

Hytham was not aware Justin was capable of smiling in that way. He slowly backed away as Justin began explaining to Leo how to hold the reins, and he'd faded into the background by the fence as Leo guided the horse in a slow walk around the paddock. From this distance, Hytham couldn't hear what the two of them were talking about, but Leo's body gradually lost its stiff terror, and Justin's expression was no longer so closed off. They rode the horse faster with each turn, until Leo was laughing in delight and holding the reins by himself.

With a pang of something that was both bitter and sweet, Hytham realized he was no longer needed. He could leave them to it and get on with the preparations for the race. Still, he lingered a few extra minutes, watching the two of them ride. His place might be in the shadows, but he could still take comfort from the light.

CHAPTER TWENTY-SEVEN

The morning of the race, Hytham was up with the rest of the Varangian Guard before dawn. Even in the gray, sallow light, it was already warm and humid, promising to be the hottest day he'd spent in the city so far. Hytham's clothes stuck to him in sweaty patches, and as the sun rose the heat intensified.

Yet another thing to worry about. The heat and lack of shade would put the crowds in the Hippodrome on edge. Hytham didn't like the anticipatory tension in the air. The stage was set for an explosion, and he didn't know if they had enough people to contain it.

Thyra was on edge as well when she found him standing guard in the hall outside Leo's room. "Have you seen Basim?" she asked him. Her lips pressed into a thin line.

Hytham shook his head. "Not today, no, but that's hardly unusual." He took a closer look at her pale face, and a tremor of dread went through him. "What's happened?" he asked.

"Maybe nothing," she said tersely. "We were supposed to

meet in one of the formal gardens before sunrise, but he never came."

Another meeting. More questions from Basim about this mysterious person he was looking for among the Vikings. Hytham let it pass. He'd decided to trust Basim. "There's something else, isn't there?" he pressed.

"There was blood on the garden wall," Thyra said. "Not much, but it was fresh. Someone fought there not long ago, but as far as I can tell, there were no witnesses."

Hytham's chest tightened. If Basim had been taken, if the plan was already compromised…

No. If Basim had been taken, there'd have been more signs of a struggle. There'd have been a trail to follow. More likely, Basim had assassinated an intruder in the gardens and concealed the body somewhere, which had kept him from meeting Thyra as planned.

He said as much to her, and she nodded, but she didn't look entirely convinced. "Can you call for him?" she asked. "I've heard you do it before."

Hytham nodded. "Wait here for Leo," he said, and left her.

His thoughts reeled as he walked quickly down the hallway in the direction of the training yard. Had they been focusing on the wrong things, setting this trap for Isaac? Had the leader of the Order shifted his target to Basim instead of Leo?

It made sense, and Hytham cursed himself for not thinking of it before. Perhaps members of the Order were looking for the same mysterious person Basim was. But for what purpose? And why would the Hidden Ones consider it a personal obsession of Basim's if the Order was involved as well?

He came out into the sunlight of the training yard, checking to make sure it was empty before he signaled for Basim using the bird call. He did it three times, just to be sure, and waited.

The moments stretched, and there was no answer, no stirring of the trees or shifting shadows to indicate Basim was nearby. Hytham's unease grew.

A tiny whisper of doubt crept into his mind. What if this had been Basim's plan all along? Use Leo as bait for a trap, keep Hytham, Thyra and the other Varangian Guards distracted, while Basim pursued some other goal of his own? When Hytham truly needed him, would Basim be there?

Hytham dismissed the voice. No. Basim had come for him in that dark cellar. His corpse would still be rotting down there if it wasn't for him. Hytham had chosen to trust Basim. He would stay the course.

But that left the worrying possibility that Basim was in trouble, and Hytham had no way to reach him.

Hytham left the training yard through a side gate and made his way along the stone pathways to the formal gardens. A quick search turned up no signs of a struggle, but he did find the same drying blood patches on the wall that Thyra had.

Where are you, Basim?

Outside the palace walls, the crowds would be filing into the Hippodrome by now. It was still a few hours before the teams would be introduced and the races began, but Hytham needed to get back to the children's wing. He'd be missed if he lingered.

For now at least, Basim was on his own, and so was Hytham.

The imperial family lined up in procession outside the emperor's chambers. Thyra and other senior members of the

Varangian Guard surrounded them, with Hytham and Justin near the rear, as close to Leo as possible.

Hytham scanned the faces of the other guards, looking for anything suspicious. Leo, standing just behind his mother, turned and flashed Hytham and Justin a quick smile while his father was looking the other way. Hytham glanced at Justin and was gratified to see the young man's lips twitching.

They were going to be all right, he told himself.

The emperor gave a curt command to the guards at the front of the procession, and then Hytham had no more time for thoughts of the future. They were moving down the connecting passage to the Hippodrome, past glittering murals of ships on the harbor at sunset, their bootsteps echoing on the marble floor.

At the end of the passage, the guards pulled open the doors, and Hytham was met with a roar of sound and light that felt like a physical force. He fought the instinctive urge to shield his eyes as the procession walked out onto a stone bridge that afforded them a dizzying view of the thousands of people who had packed the Hippodrome, wearing or waving the colors of their team and cheering as the emperor and his family came into view.

The chariots were lined up along the spina, their driving teams standing near the horses. They turned and bowed respectfully to the emperor as he walked to the edge of the bridge, resting one hand on the low railing and raising the other in greeting to the crowd and to the racers.

Hytham watched the emperor's face. Basil wore a small, benevolent smile as he took in the crowd's cheers. Here was a man who was not pretending or playing a part, Hytham thought. The emperor wanted the attention of his people. He wanted their love and respect. Some rulers had no care for those things, but not Basil. Having climbed from the lowliest beginnings to the seat of ultimate power in Constantinople, he wanted everyone to know and believe that he belonged there.

And to all appearances, the people did believe it. They shouted and cheered the emperor and his family as the procession moved on toward the imperial box draped in purple silks. They passed over the bridge, and Hytham scanned the crowd as they went, looking for faces of discontent, hidden weapons, anything that might herald an attack. It was a daunting task, in this crowd. One face blended into the next, the light of the sun flashed off jewelry and buckles, making it easy to mistake them for the edge of a blade or the head of an arrow.

He breathed a sigh of relief when they passed under the extended, thickened awning shading the emperor's box, and the imperial family took their seats. Leo was sitting on his mother's right, leaning forward to get a better view down to the track and the chariot teams.

The emperor lifted his hand again, acknowledging the crowd and the racing teams. People cheered wildly, and the chariots moved into position for the start of the first race.

The crowd settled down while the teams got ready, but already Hytham noticed they were restless. The blazing sun and the excitement of the emperor's presence had emboldened them, especially in one section near the first turn. The people seated there wore blue colors and waved cerulean banners in support of their team, which would be in direct opposition to the emperor's colors since he would be racing for the greens later in the day.

The people were on their feet, alternately cheering and jeering the teams as they arranged themselves at the starting point, horses shifting restlessly as they bunched up. Hytham felt the tension in the air, all that compacted energy of the horses together in a group, waiting for the start as the crowd began to chant for their favorites. It was hard not to get caught up in the anticipation, even though he wasn't rooting for any particular team.

Hytham swept his gaze over the crowd again and kept one eye on the emperor's box in case something happened during the confusion of the start. He didn't think it would. He was almost certain Isaac and the Order of the Ancients would wait until the emperor had vacated his box to strike, but Hytham had been wrong before, and he wasn't taking anything for granted.

A sudden hush fell over the crowd, a collective held breath, and Hytham put his hand lightly on his sword pommel.

The signal came, and the chariots burst into motion, the horses rearing and tearing over the starting line, chariots bumping and roaring behind them.

The crowd erupted, waving their banners, clapping, and shouting at the top of their lungs as the teams careened into the first turn, wheels lifting off the ground as the drivers held the reins in a death grip and shouted to the horses, snapping whips above them to increase speed while keeping a tenuous grip on control. Two chariots came within a hair's breadth of colliding as they came out of the first turn, and the rowdy bunch in the stands were on their feet at the edge of the track.

It was one of the wildest spectacles Hytham had ever witnessed. The drivers and their teams gave no thought to their own safety, instead pouring all their energy into jockeying for position with the other chariots, always looking for a way to gain ground. It was a deadly game with no room for mistakes.

Hytham's heart pounded amidst the roar of the crowd surrounding him. He could only imagine how deafening the sound was down on the track.

He glanced over at the imperial box. Leo watched the race with rapt attention, clutching the edge of his seat as he fidgeted. Next to him, Eudocia looked hot and bored already, and Hytham could see the tension in the tight, unhappy lines around her mouth. Thyra sat behind her. She had seen this spectacle before, of course. It did not move her the way it did some of the younger guards that were gathered at the edge of the box.

Hytham caught sight of Justin moving through the crowd some distance away. It had been agreed that he would be watching for anyone to attack at range, and by the look of things he was doing his job well. He stopped to speak in the ear of several people in the crowd, checking their bags and persons for hidden weapons, giving quelling glares to anyone who looked as if they wanted to start a fight over their preferred team.

And so it went. The first race concluded with a victory for the blue team, although it was a near thing, as the left wheel of their chariot had taken a hit from the greens, and it just barely held on to cross the finish line, the horses stumbling and frothing in the heat. The races were not kind to the beasts, but no one was seriously injured. Still, it set up a rivalry between blue and green that looked as if it would continue through the afternoon.

Hytham relaxed a little as the crowd settled down, some of them seeking out food, wine, and shade between races, chatting about the results in small groups and wiping sweat from their faces. During the lull, Hytham was able to stand for a time in the shade of the imperial box.

Thyra came over to speak to him as the emperor and his family were given wine, and servants came from the palace with platters of fruit and cheese. Others brought fans to create a gentle breeze in the stifling heat.

"I've seen no sign of Basim," Thyra said in a low voice when she came near. "Have you?"

"None." Hytham noted her dark frown. He was worried too. "Can you manage here while I sweep the area outside, just to make sure he's not out there somewhere?"

Thyra nodded, though she didn't look encouraged, and Hytham knew this was a long shot as well. If Basim were nearby, he would have shown himself by now, which either meant he had changed the plan in some way and not told anyone, or he was in trouble and he couldn't call for help.

Either of those options could turn out to be disastrous for their plans.

Hytham took the stairs down to ground level and found one of the long, shaded tunnels that led outside the main arena. He was surprised how many people had gathered in the streets just to listen to the race and socialize. Merchants had set up temporary stalls and sold wine and goods to the crowd, and there was just as much of a festive atmosphere here as inside, though it was perhaps a little more relaxed.

Hytham stood in the middle of the crowd, letting the noise and laughter of the people wash over him, but his mind was distant, meditating, seeking the answer to this latest riddle of Basim.

If he was to trust the man, then he had to assume something had gone wrong with the plan on Basim's end. Blood on the garden wall suggested an unexpected attack. If Basim had come out the victor, he would have hidden the body of his attacker and found either Hytham or Thyra to inform them.

Unless Basim was injured or being hunted. After the attack on the palace, Hytham had tracked his target through the streets to the safehouse where the Order had laid an ambush for him. Basim too, would perhaps lead his attacker away, or at least seek a place to hide so he could tend to his wounds.

Or find a place to die.

Hytham dismissed the curl of dread in his gut at that thought. He refused to believe that would be Basim's fate. He didn't know what premonition told him that Basim would live a long and impactful life, but somewhere deep inside himself he knew it was true.

He shielded his eyes against the sun and looked on the curved edifice of the Hippodrome. Birds circled a tall tower that was situated opposite the spectators. They were too far away for Hytham to see what kind they were. The last time he and Basim had looked upon the Hippodrome from afar, Basim had commented on its magnificent views.

"I wager you can see the entire city from up on its highest point."

A view of the entire city and beyond, Hytham thought, still watching the flock drifting on the wind. A vantage point for a bird of prey – or a secure perch from which to see your enemies coming.

Hytham was moving before the thought had fully formed in his mind, looking for the closest set of stairs.

CHAPTER TWENTY-EIGHT

The stairs that led up to the tower ended in a locked door. Hytham turned in a slow circle, examining his surroundings. Arched windows had been cut into the stone, and a brisk breeze whistled through the openings, carrying the scents of the sea and the distant cry of gulls.

On one of the stone ledges there was a dark smear of blood.

Hytham's heartbeat quickened. He stood on the ledge and leaned out. The city spread below him in a grand, living tapestry, as impressive as Basim had imagined it would be. He could see all the way to the walls from this vantage, and the noise of the crowd below was a distant swell of sound. Up here, it was the domain of the birds and the sky and the ever-present howling of the wind.

The stone wall of the tower was rough against Hytham's fingers. He ran his hands over the wall, fingers seeking and finding purchase. He tested the stone against his weight, making sure there were no cracks or loose patches that would send him tumbling to his death. Again, his training didn't fail him, and he crawled unerringly up the wall.

The wind pulled at his clothing, and the sounds of the birds echoed around him. With a last surge of strength in his burning muscles, Hytham reached the peak of the tower. There, he found Basim tucked into an alcove, sitting in a small puddle of blood and bandaging an angry-looking dagger slash that snaked across his ribs and stained his robes crimson. Relief coursed through Hytham at seeing the man alive.

Basim tutted as Hytham hoisted himself into the alcove, his hands scraped and aching from finding the barest handholds with which to pull himself up the side of the tower. "Took you long enough, my friend," Basim said.

The crowd noise coming from below was even more muted here by the rush of the wind. The height was dizzying, and below them in the harbor, the ships looked like tiny toy boats, the water turned to glittering shards of broken light.

It hurt his eyes, but it was beautiful.

Hytham turned away from the spectacular view and gave Basim an exasperated look. "You could have picked a place that was just as defensible but slightly easier to get to," he pointed out. "And you probably made your wound worse in the climb up here."

He knew that for a fact. He'd followed a trail of blood-slicked stones up the wall to reach this perch.

Basim winced as he finished cleaning the wound with water from a waterskin. "You know why I chose this spot," he said. "I needed to be able to see my enemies if they tracked me. But I grant you, I was almost too late to be of any use in the attack to come."

Hytham crouched next to Basim and took the strips of cloth from Basim's hands and began wrapping the wound. It was a shallow cut, but with a bit more pressure it would have been a death wound. "Was it Isaac's people who attacked you?"

"They were clever to try to isolate and eliminate one of the players from the board while we were all focused on Leo and the security for the race," Basim said, shifting to allow Hytham to wrap the bandages around his body. "I made the mistake of straying too far from the palace alone." He sighed. "You'll be shocked, I'm sure, to learn that arrogance is a fault of mine. I thought I walked unseen, but I was followed and ambushed. I killed one, and the other ran off, but I don't think she went far. Being cautious then, I retreated, making more of a show of being wounded than I actually was. If we're lucky, Isaac thinks he's taken me out of the fight."

"*Should* you be out of the fight?" Hytham couldn't help but observe, as Basim winced again when he tied off the bandage.

Basim smiled at him, and it was not a pleasant expression. "Your sense of humor is one of the many things I like about you, my friend."

Hytham laughed. "Very well, then. Shall we go?" He looked down on the Hippodrome, at the tiny chariots circling the track, the flash of colors, and the birds flying below them, circling the tower.

Basim came to stand next to him. Hytham pointed to the birds. "They were what led me to you," he said.

"What?" Basim asked – too sharply, Hytham thought. He'd been half joking.

"The birds," Hytham explained. "They were what made me think to come up high to find you in the tower."

Basim looked at the birds, a complicated expression on his face. "Sometimes they're just birds," he said, half to himself.

Once again, Hytham had no notion of what he was talking about, and the emotions came and went across Basim's face too fast for him to interpret.

Basim looked down the tower. There was a ledge directly below them, still high but out of the way of people. "Can you make that jump?" he asked Hytham.

Hytham nodded. "After you."

Basim checked his bandages one last time, pulled up his hood, and jumped off the tower. Hytham followed, launching himself into the air, never once doubting that he would find a place to safely land.

The crowd was becoming dangerous.

While Hytham had been gone, there had been upsets in the last two races in favor of the green team, and the rowdy spectators in the first turn sounded murderous, shouting, spitting, and throwing things onto the track. The guards had gone in to try to calm them and throw out the most violent offenders, but that had only made things worse, and two of the guards had gone away bloody from the confrontation.

The emperor could have stopped it. He could have ordered more of the guards down there, had everyone in the crowd at the first turn removed for the safety of all. But he wouldn't. Hytham knew that even before the emperor gave the order to leave the crowd alone. He wanted as many spectators to witness his race as possible.

Vanity and pride were Basil's failings, after all.

And now, with the crowd furious and spoiling for a fight, the emperor descended from his box to take his turn on the racing track.

Hytham's jaw was clenched so hard his teeth ached as he reassumed his post outside the emperor's box. He located Leo, still in his seat next to his mother, then exchanged a glance with Thyra and gave a small nod. Basim had once again vanished, but Hytham knew this time he was not in danger. He swore he could feel the man's presence in the crowd.

It took an age for the emperor to reach the track as he wound his way in a slow procession through the Hippodrome, exciting the crowd into a frenzy. When he reached the starting line, his chariot and horse team was already prepared for him. He raced for the greens, and the other teams lined up beside him, but Hytham noticed they gave the emperor as much space as possible on either side of his chariot.

Which meant the other racers and their horse teams were crowded dangerously close together. The horses tossed their heads, and were Hytham close enough, he knew he'd see the frightened whites of their eyes.

Justin came up beside him near the entrance to the box, pausing in his sweep of the crowd. "This isn't going to end well," he said tersely, nodding to the track.

Hytham gave a small nod of acknowledgment. "Just keep to your duty," he said. "The emperor chose this. Let him deal with the consequences." He hadn't meant to put so much venom in his voice as he spoke, but Justin nodded in grim agreement.

Then a man standing beside the track raised his hand, and a red scarf unfurled on the wind.

The race began.

The chariots once again exploded into motion as the crowd roared its approval. But this time, the horse to the far right of the track, pressed too close between the nearest chariot and the wall, reared and stalled while the others on its team attempted to take off. They came down in a tangle, the violent motion throwing the driver off the vehicle and onto the track. He rolled and came to rest near the wall, his arm sticking out at a wrong angle. It all happened in an instant, and then the other chariots were gone, sailing down the track, oblivious to their rivals' fate.

The emperor was in a narrow lead coming into the first turn. Seeing this, the rowdy bunch went wild, yelling, jeering and climbing on each other's shoulders, while the green supporters waved their banners wildly for the emperor to notice them.

In the second turn, everything went wrong.

Hytham wasn't sure if it was the distraction of the raucous band in the first turn, or if the emperor had seen the shadow of another racer coming up behind him. Maybe there was some debris on the track that he swerved to avoid, for suddenly, Basil grabbed the reins and tried to execute a sharp turn well before he needed to. The horses bucked and protested, and suddenly they were bunched against the wall.

A collective gasp went through the crowd, and the people in the first turn couldn't hold back any longer. Seeing their emperor struggling in the corner, they surged onto the track, scaling the barriers as if they were nothing and running heedless into the path of the other approaching chariots.

Hytham turned, locked eyes with Thyra.

An arrow hissed through the air and buried itself in the wall of the emperor's box. It had been aimed at one of the guards, as far as Hytham could tell, but the bigger awning and uncertain wind made the shot go wide.

Hytham drew his sword and charged toward the box. A

scream came from a group sitting nearby, but it was quickly swallowed by the distress of the crowd as they watched a chariot strike one of the people who'd swarmed the track. Spectators were crowding the aisle to get a better look, blocking Hytham's path to Leo.

Inside the box, Thyra had grabbed the empress and pulled her down to the floor, covering her with her own body to protect her from more arrow shots. Eudocia was trying to push her off, screaming for Leo, but Thyra kept her down.

Leo was alone in the box. The other guards had dispersed to keep the crowd in check. The race was quickly devolving into a riot. People didn't know whether to stay in their seats, run down to the track to help, or just run to get a better view of the chaos unfolding.

Leo was alone in the box.

A sea of people separated Hytham from Leo. The boy's eyes were wide with fear. And he was looking for Hytham. He was looking for his guardian, and Hytham couldn't go to him.

Hytham tore his gaze away when he heard a harsh cry. Above him on the upper seats, Justin was fighting with a man who held a dagger. He was not dressed like a man who'd come to watch the races. He was dressed for stealth, and Justin was barely holding his own.

The Order was here.

Still, Hytham stayed where he was, hidden among the rioting crowd, watching and waiting for – there. A man and a woman slipped into the box and descended on Leo.

Now Hytham moved. He drew his sword and gave a deep-throated shout that managed to carry over the general riot of noise. The woman turned and saw him charging toward them, his sword raised. Eyes wide, she grabbed Leo by the waist and ran for the other side of the box, leaping over the wall. Her companion stood in Hytham's path, but Hytham used his momentum to bowl the man over, tripping him up on the benches in the box. He went down, his sword arm caught under the seats, and Hytham drove his blade into his gut.

But he'd lost valuable time. The woman was escaping, and she had Leo.

Hytham dove into the crowd, shoving spectators aside, ignoring the screams as people saw the body of the assassin Hytham had killed bleeding out in the emperor's box. The panic spread, and people began pouring for the exit, fearing that they were next.

Hytham ignored them all. He kept his gaze trained on the woman holding Leo, who was kicking, biting, yelling in the woman's face, slowing her down as much as he could as she dragged him toward a set of stairs leading down to the ground level. She'd made no attempt yet to kill him, which both relieved and surprised Hytham. Perhaps the Order of the Ancients' intentions for the boy had changed, and this was to be a kidnapping rather than an assassination. If so, every second counted now. He couldn't let the woman vanish.

When Hytham reached the stairwell, he pounded down the stairs and then jumped, closing the distance between himself and the assassin. He glanced up once and saw Thyra and Justin were one flight above him, moving fast. He wasn't alone.

He looked back, and Basim was suddenly below him, stepping out of the shadows, his Hidden Blade leading, closing in on the woman from behind. She swung round at the last second, putting Leo between herself and Basim. Basim only just checked his motion, pulling the blade back, and the woman called out to someone below her on the stairs.

Two men came up to meet her, flanking her on either side, creating a barrier between her and Basim. Swords out, the men and the woman backed away, jumping out a window and dropping the short distance to street level.

Hytham jumped over the rail and dropped two flights, landing next to Basim. They followed the group out the window into the sunlight of the city streets.

The crowd was pouring out of the Hippodrome, a mass of humanity scattering in all directions. More people were coming out of their homes and shops to see what had caused the commotion. Someone yelled that the city was under attack. Others said the emperor and empress had been killed.

The wave of panic that swelled through the streets then was frightening. Some people tripped and fell or were pulled down in the general chaos, the crowd trampling them. There were more screams, then cries by the Varangian Guard for people to be calm.

Hytham caught a glimpse of the woman and the two other assassins plunging into the crowd, trying to get to a nearby group of buildings.

They would find their way into an alley and be gone. Hytham gritted his teeth. He couldn't lose them now. He turned to Basim, but the man had left his side. He'd taken a different route through the crowd, and was moving into position to either cut the assassins off from the nearest alley or to follow them inside. But that wasn't what they'd planned. They were supposed to stay together.

Trying not to panic, Hytham looked behind him for

Justin and Thyra and finally saw them emerging from the Hippodrome. He raised a hand, signaling them to move in the opposite direction. They would flank the assassins and pull the net tight around them.

"Get back!" Hytham yelled at the crowd, raising his blade so it caught the golden light of the afternoon sun. "Move, in the name of the Varangian Guard!"

He drew himself up to his full height. The people right in front of him turned, saw his uniform and expression, and gave way. Across the street, he heard Thyra and the other guards shouting, hustling people aside.

By now, Basim had climbed to the roof of the nearest building, jumping down into the alley so he was in front of the woman and the two men, blocking their escape. Hytham felt a surge of triumph that was quickly dispelled as another man materialized out of the crowd and joined his fellows in the alley.

The man was Isaac.

CHAPTER TWENTY-NINE

Hytham's stomach clenched as he, Thyra, and Justin converged on the alley. It was four on four in a confined space, though the woman holding Leo didn't look like she was going to be part of the fight. It was all she could do to keep the boy still. Leo thrashed and yelled, his cries lost in the shouting crowd nearby, but Hytham could see how hard he was fighting.

I'm coming. Hold on.

Thyra engaged the man closest to her with her hand axe, and Justin attacked the other man with a ferocity Hytham had never seen.

Which left Isaac for himself and Basim.

The crowd noise around the Hippodrome covered the clash of weapons, the deadly, restrained dance that played out in the shadows of the alley. Fighting in such a large group, every movement had to be economical, calculated, and brutal. It shouldn't have worked, with so many of them, but in that moment it was as if the four of them were one. They moved without thinking, blades singing as they clashed, he and

Basim running up the wall and launching themselves at Isaac each by turn, forcing the man to fight them both with knife and sword. Or maybe it was their sheer determination to get to Leo before the woman who held him could take a knife to his throat.

When the combatants began to tire, the fights blended together. It was exhilarating and terrifying. The man fighting Justin grabbed a handful of dirt and threw it in his face to blind him. Hytham drew a knife and hurled it with just a half second to look and aim, and lodged the blade deep in the man's shoulder before he could plunge his sword into Justin, giving Justin the extra seconds he needed to recover.

When Basim drove Isaac close to where Thyra and her opponent struggled against a stack of crates along the alley wall, Thyra locked eyes with Basim and threw her axe at Isaac, striking his knife blade and sending his attack wide. Basim caught the axe in his free hand and threw it back to Thyra, as if they'd planned the move all along.

The four of them had been stalked, trapped, and forced to live in constant vigilance for weeks. Now their enemies were standing in the light of day, and they had the chance to end things. Hytham simply wasn't prepared to lose this fight. None of them were.

And so the assassins were no match for the four of them.

The woman holding Leo, as if sensing the mounting desperation in her companions, pushed the boy into the wall and raised her knife, poised for a killing blow.

"No!" Hytham shouted, his voice raw with rage and fear. He was too far away. He couldn't get to them.

But then, Leo turned his head and sank his teeth deep

into the woman's wrist where she held him by his collar. She screamed, and her grip on him faltered.

It was enough. Leo yanked himself free of her grasp and ran.

Hytham let out a relieved sigh.

The woman gave chase, readying her knife to throw, but in her singular focus on the boy, she came too close to Thyra. The Viking woman spun, ducked a sword strike from her opponent and came up with two quick, dirty slashes to the man's and woman's throats with her axe. They dropped to the ground in a spray of blood, and Thyra gave a cry of triumph, one hand braced against the alley wall.

Leo instinctively ran toward Hytham.

"Don't!" Hytham shouted, holding up a hand to stop him from running straight into the circle of death that was his fight with Isaac.

Luckily, Basim pivoted away from Isaac and intercepted the boy, grabbing Leo's arm before he could get himself impaled on a sword. He shoved him toward the mouth of the alley and the crowd.

"Run!" he commanded.

Leo stumbled, but he righted himself and ran toward the light at the end of the alley. Hytham, distracted watching him go, nearly had his own throat slashed as Isaac produced another knife from somewhere on his person, so fast Hytham wasn't even sure where he'd been keeping it.

Hytham caught Isaac's thrust by the wrist, twisting his arm, tangling their legs, and nearly sending them both to the ground. Pressed close, Isaac smiled at him, sweat pouring down his face, his hands trembling with the effort of trying to bury the knife blade in Hytham's gut.

"I should have killed you before you ever woke in the dark," Isaac lamented. "I misjudged you."

Hytham didn't respond. He was done fencing words with this man. Isaac no longer had any power over him. He looked to Basim, who had turned and was walking back down the alley, releasing his Hidden Blade.

Hytham met Basim's eyes over Isaac's shoulder, nodded once, then shoved Isaac back. The man stumbled, and Basim grabbed him with one hand on his shoulder before he could recover and turn. He slid the blade between Isaac's ribs, holding the man securely as he thrashed.

Blood bubbled up at Isaac's lips, but they were still curved in a resigned smile.

Basim dropped the man's body to the ground.

The man fighting Justin was all that was left of the assassins. When he saw his companions were dead, with a desperate move he shoved Justin away, turned and ran. Hytham thought he was trying to escape, but then he saw Leo at the edge of the crowd outside the alley. The boy appeared to be trying to wedge his way into the swarm of people, to hide and get away, but he hadn't quite managed it.

The last assassin was running right toward him.

Thyra's axe whirled past Hytham's ear, but the throw was wide and clanged off the brick wall. Hytham started to run after the man, but Basim's hand fell heavily on his shoulder.

"Wait," Basim said, and though every instinct in Hytham's body screamed at him to disobey, he forced his body to be still. "Look," Basim said, his voice at Hytham's ear.

Hytham looked. Justin was running after the assassin, moving with a speed that Hytham and his injured knee couldn't match. He erupted from the alley and tackled the man just as he was reaching for Leo. They went down together into the crowd amid shouts and curses, but both sprang up at once, shoving people aside and attacking each other with their swords.

The crowd, seeing the disruption and hearing the ringing clash of weapons, fell back and formed a loose ring around the two combatants. As afraid as they were of being caught in the attack, the fear couldn't hold out in the face of their fascination at the deadly confrontation playing out in front of them.

The brawny man stood before Justin, who had grabbed Leo and pulled the boy behind him protectively. Murmurs of recognition flowed through the crowd. Whispers of Leo's name. Justin was much smaller than his opponent, and both were bloody, their clothing torn, but the colors of the Varangian Guard were still clearly visible on Justin.

A fierce young man fighting against a giant on behalf of the future ruler of the golden city.

Hytham stood in the shadows of the alley with Basim and Thyra, watching the battle play out. They breathed heavily, leaning on each other for support. Hytham felt the tension in Thyra's body. He took her hand and gave it a reassuring squeeze.

Justin would not let anything happen to Leo. Hytham was absolutely certain of it.

His faith was rewarded, because Justin never hesitated. He attacked the brawny man as if he was fresh to the fight, even though blood dripped down his face from a cut on his scalp, and his arms trembled with the effort of holding his sword up. The look in his eyes was something Hytham would never forget as long as he lived.

They thrust and spun and slammed into each other, and it was a brutal spectacle that the crowd drank in as if they were still at the chariot race. Ripples of excitement ran through them at every blocked thrust and complicated swing. They'd never seen anything like this, but they put the full power of their support behind Justin and Leo.

Justin seemed to feel it too. He drew himself up and found a second wind, viciously slashing at the man until he was down on one knee and Justin was above him. He knocked the man's sword out of his hand and ran him through.

The crowd went berserk, cheering and closing in around Leo and Justin as the conquering heroes, kicking aside the assassin's body.

Hytham leaned in to whisper to Basim. "You could not have scripted a better scene. But how could you possibly guarantee it would play out this way?"

Basim whispered back, a ghost of a smile on his sweat-soaked face, "You can guarantee nothing in this life, my friend. But I would wager much on the power of human nature."

Chapter Thirty

The story of the repair of Constantinople's walls, the legend of how the chariot racing teams' supporters protected New Rome from invasion by the Huns, had depended on the competitive spirit of the city's citizens and spoke to the value of understanding human nature. Whether the story actually happened or not, whether the events had been embellished or were outright lies, was beside the point.

Basim knew that better than anyone when he engineered his plan to let the assassins take Leo from the emperor's box. He knew it when he'd planted allies in the crowd on the first turn to sow discontent among them, to work them into a frenzy – and then to throw a spiked chain onto the track in front of Basil's oncoming chariot to sabotage the race and cause chaos, giving the assassins their moment to strike.

Maybe he'd even wanted the crowd to see Basil wrench his chariot out of the path of disaster, narrowly avoiding a crash with brute strength and sheer stubborn will. He wanted those watching in the stands to see Thyra pulling the empress to the ground and shielding her with her body while Hytham fought his way through the Hippodrome in pursuit of Leo, slaying any attacker who got in his path. He'd wanted witnesses to see Leo fighting and shouting at his would-be murderers as they dragged him into the streets.

Most of all, he'd wanted the crowd to see Justin, the young Viking warrior, the Varangian Guard sworn to protect the imperial family with his blade, his blood, and his life, put himself between the last remaining assassin and Leo, to watch the wounded hero stand alone and conquer the perceived foreign invader, cut him down in front of them, striking the blow on behalf of everyone in Constantinople.

Those who had been there to witness the events spread the story through every corner of the city, and it didn't matter if the events had truly happened the way the stories went. That wasn't the point. The important part was that the people of Constantinople took Leo and Justin into their hearts, uniting them against any outside threat that would dare challenge their city or the strength of the imperial family and its protectors.

It was a victory in a war the people hadn't even realized was happening, but a victory was a victory, and they were drunk with it, parading in the streets, selling wooden swords made to look like Justin's blade, and telling stories of how the boy-emperor would make a lion-like ruler one day, for he'd been so young and so small and yet fought like a beast against his attackers.

Their words and cheers and love were stronger than any armor or any guardian the Hidden Ones could put at Leo's side.

Basil could not dare kill Leo now or remove Justin from amongst Leo's protectors. The city loved them too much, and his allies in the Order of the Ancients had failed him one too many times. Beyond that, the emperor was facing enemies and political conflicts outside the city walls that needed his attention. He'd been drawn away too long from the actual ruling of the city, and no matter what else could be said about Basil, he was a canny ruler, and the city was stable under his hand. He would not throw that away for a personal vendetta against a boy who may or may not share his blood. The Order of the Ancients would have to find a new path to power in the city.

All of this Hytham found himself relating to Empress Eudocia as they sat in Demetrios's garden, many days removed from their last meeting there. Hytham had expected Basim to be there also to give the empress a full accounting of the events at the Hippodrome, but he should have known the man would slip out of that particular responsibility in the end, for the empress was none too pleased that her son had been used as bait in this trap. Basim had left Hytham to explain that part and to hope and pray that the empress decided not to have him killed after hearing how close they had come to it all going wrong.

Luckily, she seemed to accept his story and his reasoning for the Hidden Ones' actions as she cradled a glass of wine in her hands and regarded Hytham with a curious expression.

"I confess I'm surprised you agreed to the plan, considering it put you out of reach of my son for so long," she commented. "Do you trust Basim so much?"

Trust. It always came back to that. Yes, Hytham had trusted Basim to save Leo, and that faith had been rewarded beyond his imagining.

Leo was safe. He was safe, and he had Justin to watch over him as he grew to adulthood, the most fearsome protector one could hope for. It was everything Hytham wanted for the boy, and his relief knew no bounds. For all that, Basim would have his loyalty for the rest of Hytham's life. He would gladly follow the man on whatever mission he declared was next for them.

But could he *trust* Basim?

No, he could not. No more than Basim could ever fully trust Hytham. Basim knew the Hidden Ones had sent Hytham to spy on him. With that knowledge, Basim could have acted much differently in their relationship. He could have shut Hytham out, could have left him to die in that basement at Isaac's hands, or exiled him from the city and the Hidden Ones when he'd disobeyed orders.

Basim had done none of those things. Instead he'd made a friend of Hytham, put him back on the right path when he strayed, and helped him when he didn't have to. And maybe all that too was just Basim understanding Hytham's nature and knowing what to do to manipulate him. Maybe nothing of their bond was real, but Hytham chose to believe otherwise. He chose to believe that there was more to Basim than manipulation and subterfuge. Underneath it all, he was a complicated man who worked from the shadows and chased his own demons.

Everyone had their own voice in the dark, taunting them to fail.

Even Basim.

But he hadn't answered the empress's question.

"Leaving Leo to anyone's care other than my own was the

second hardest thing I've ever done," Hytham admitted. His voice thickened. "The hardest thing is what I do today."

The empress's face softened into something almost like affection. She put her wine glass aside and reached across to take his calloused hands in her own.

Holding the hands of the empress of Constantinople, Hytham thought. What a strange and wondrous life this was.

"You don't have to leave," the empress said, looking into his eyes. "There's a permanent place for you in the Varangian Guard if you want it. You deserve much more acknowledgment for the part you played in all of this. At least let me offer you the chance to stay where you clearly want to be."

At Leo's side.

Hytham had thought, during certain moments over the course of the last several weeks, that that was what he wanted. To be the father he would not have the chance to be otherwise. To watch a child grow up and go on to great things, surpassing his parents and creating his own legacy in the world. It was the closest thing he would get to immortality.

But it wasn't his path. His place was in the shadows, and he was content with that role in making the world better. There was much more yet for him to do on behalf of the Hidden Ones.

He shook his head, bowing respectfully to the empress's offer. "I thank you for your consideration, Honored Empress, but my presence in the palace would only be a danger to Leo. It would remind the emperor of how he'd been thwarted in his plans, and it might start his mind down another dark path, and that's the last thing I would want." He gently pulled away. "Leo is in good hands with Justin and Thyra. They'll keep watch over him well."

And Justin was already being watched by the Hidden Ones for potential recruitment. He and Leo could learn together the cause for which Hytham and Basim fought, and they would be formidable allies in the fight against the Order of the Ancients.

At least that was the hope. The future was a nebulous, ever-changing thing, and as Basim had said, there were no guarantees.

The empress nodded her acceptance of his decision, but her brow furrowed in dismay. "Is that why you haven't come to the palace to say goodbye to my son? He was distraught when you didn't return after the race."

Hytham swallowed. It had been several days, and yes, he had deliberately stayed away. He told himself it was better that Leo begin accepting his absence as soon as possible. A long, drawn-out goodbye would be hard on the boy.

He told himself he wasn't being a coward.

But Eudocia was a keen observer. Hytham had forgotten that. She read his face and his silence and said chidingly, "Don't you think the boy deserves the chance to say a proper farewell to his guardian?"

Before Hytham could respond, he heard light, scuffling footsteps and a voice that said, "Mother! I'm here!"

Hytham closed his eyes briefly and opened them to find Eudocia smiling at him, unrepentant. "I did tell you many people at court dislike me," she said. "I am a difficult woman, and I always insist on getting my way."

"So you said." Hytham's lungs suddenly felt too big for his chest.

He turned to see Leo running into the garden. When the

boy set eyes on him, he gasped, and then he was pounding across the stone walkways, jumping over bushes and knocking over flower pots, ignoring his mother's fond admonishments, to launch himself into Hytham, nearly tackling him.

"Ow," Hytham said, absorbing the impact of the small, sweaty missile and reaching out to ruffle the boy's hair fondly. "As surprise attacks go, your technique needs a bit of work."

"I thought you were gone," Leo said accusingly, even as he wrapped his thin arms around Hytham's neck and held on. Hytham glanced over at the empress, but she had disappeared from the courtyard, taking her wine with her, in a fair imitation of the grace and stealth of an Assassin.

Hytham pulled back to look at Leo. He was covered in healing scrapes and bruises, and his wrist was wrapped from a small sprain, but otherwise he was the same bright-eyed boy Hytham remembered from their training sessions. He had not only survived his ordeal, but Hytham had good cause to hope that he would come out the other side stronger for all he had endured.

"What's this?" Hytham pointed to the wooden sword Leo carried – one of the replicas of Justin's sword that had been circulating in the city.

Leo grinned. "Justin's teaching me to use it. You said I could practice with a wooden sword eventually," he added, as if afraid Hytham would take the weapon from him.

"So I did." Hytham laughed. "Justin is a taskmaster. Mind what he says and follow his lessons so you don't get hurt."

Leo nodded, but his expression clouded. "You're not coming back to the palace, are you? You're leaving."

This was going to be just as hard as Hytham had feared. "I'm afraid so," he said. "But I'm not leaving you alone. Justin and Thyra will watch over you. I'd trust them both with my life."

"But where will you go?" Leo asked in a small, trembling voice. "What's more important than here?"

Nothing, Hytham wanted to say, but he swallowed the words and touched the boy's cheek gently. "I would stay if I could, Leo. But it's a very large world outside these city walls, and there are others who need me. I'm sorry."

Leo nodded solemnly. "That was what Justin said." He sighed. "I know I still have a lot to learn, but I won't forget what you taught me."

"Good." Hytham ruffled his hair again, and then his hands came to rest on the boy's shoulders. "I will miss you," he said, and that was all he could manage.

Leo hugged him again, hard, then pulled away at his mother's call from the door. He wiped his face, smiled bravely at Hytham, and said, "Goodbye, Guardian Hytham. Thank you for protecting me."

Then he ran off into the house, his mother following with a last wave and a nod to Hytham.

Hytham stayed where he was, sitting alone in Demetrios's garden, for some time after that.

EPILOGUE

When he stepped outside Demetrios's house after thanking his host for his hospitality, Hytham found Basim leaning against a nearby wall, his hood down, as if he were just passing a fine day in the shade while he waited for his friend.

"You threw me to the wolves," Hytham said lightly as they walked away from the house.

Basim fell into step beside him, grinning. "And yet, you remain in one piece, unmurdered, so I assume that means your report to the empress didn't go as badly as it could have."

"No," Hytham said. "She accepted the mission's outcome, if not how we went about it. But the important thing to her is that Leo is safe, with a bright future ahead of him."

"Therefore, our mission was a success," Basim said. "On to bigger things and bright futures for *us*, eh?"

Hytham nodded absently, but there were still things on his mind. Questions unanswered. "The Order will send a new leader to Constantinople." It was not a fortune teller's prediction, but a statement of fact. "Will they not seek revenge and to finish what Isaac started?"

Basim shook his head. "They won't continue to waste resources there, especially without the emperor's favor. Basil knows the people love Justin and Leo now. He won't risk losing that kind of support, even for his alliance with the Order. He has to be doubting their promises and their strength, considering they couldn't deliver him one dead son."

Hytham winced at Basim's choice of words, but he was correct, of course. It was a victory for the Hidden Ones. The Order would have to accept that and move on to other ways to control the city and bend it to their will.

And they always found ways. It was part of the eternal struggle between the two sides, the shadowy war that never ended.

But Hytham pushed those dark thoughts aside. For now, he was savoring their victory. "What comes next for us, then?" He added, before Basim could respond, "I trust you've noticed there are more Viking tribes arriving in Constantinople daily, beyond those associated with the Varangian Guard."

"I *had* noticed that." Basim glanced at Hytham. "Why would you think I'd be looking at them?"

Hytham almost laughed. "You said yourself we should be cultivating them as allies before the Order takes an interest and gets to them first. Perhaps that should be our focus for a time?"

Basim looked at him, a strange, unreadable expression on his face. Did he recognize this as the gesture Hytham meant it to be? In the name of recruiting for the Hidden Ones, they would continue to seek out the Vikings that came to the city, and in that way, Basim could pursue his personal goals while still working in the interests of the Hidden Ones.

Hytham knew he may not be able to ever fully trust Basim, but he could give the man this. He owed it to him for what he had done for Leo. Hytham would never forget that.

"You may be right," Basim said slowly, as they walked down the city streets. They moved among the people but apart from them, always keeping to the shadows where they wouldn't be noticed. "I believe there are likely candidates who would make great allies of the Hidden Ones. Whether they fully embrace our cause or not, they would still be valuable in what we are trying to achieve."

Hytham wasn't sure whether he agreed with that or not. He'd like to hope that anyone who joined the Hidden Ones did it because they believed in the cause. But for now, this was enough between them.

They walked on in silence for a while before Basim spoke again. "You said goodbye to the boy, then." It wasn't a question. "Are you all right?"

Hytham considered his feelings, then nodded. "It was hard, but don't all children eventually outgrow the need for their parents? It's not so different in this case."

Basim sighed, his gaze very far away, as if sifting through memory. "One hopes they do," he said. "Outgrow, outlive, carry on a legacy. It's not always that way."

"No," Hytham said, "that's true."

Unexpectedly, Basim laughed. It was a warm sound, but there was little humor in it. "We're all living the same story over and over again, Hytham," he said, his gaze turning to the horizon. "That we learn from it each time, I suppose, is the best we can hope for."

Once again, the enigmatic man left Hytham with nothing to say in response, but this time he wasn't worried. Basim had his secrets, and his pain, but he was right. Their stories would continue for now, their bit of history carved into this golden city, though even the mark they left would vanish. Someday, both of them would be forgotten, and even the impenetrable walls of Constantinople could not hold forever against the passage of time.

Acknowledgments

To the team at Aconyte books and wonderful editors Gwen and Lottie, who took turns shepherding this book from proposal to finished product, and who always made me feel I was in good hands. You both rock. To the Ubisoft teams who gave me Constantinople and offered their feedback and support, thank you for letting me play in your universe. It was a privilege and a heck of a fun ride. To my fantastic agent, Sara Megibow, thank you for always having my back and encouraging me to go for it, no matter what wild idea (or how many) I bring your way. And finally, to Tim and to my dad and Jeff, thank you for your patience during that very long and crazy summer. The books wouldn't get written without you. I love you guys.

ABOUT THE AUTHOR

JALEIGH JOHNSON is a fantasy author living and writing in the wilds of the Midwest. Her middle grade debut novel *The Mark of the Dragonfly* is a *New York Times* bestseller, and her other books from Delacorte Press include *The Secrets of Solace, The Quest to the Uncharted Lands,* and *The Door to the Lost.* In addition to the Marvel novel *Triptych* for Aconyte Books, she has written several novels and short stories for the *Dungeons and Dragons Forgotten Realms* fiction line published by Wizards of the Coast. Johnson is an avid gamer and lifelong geek.

jaleighjohnson.com
twitter.com/jaleighjohnson

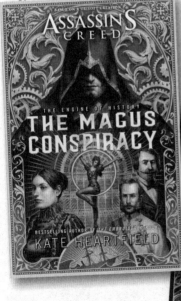
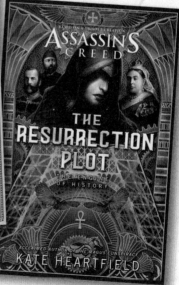

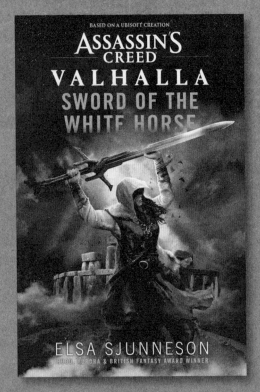
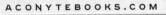

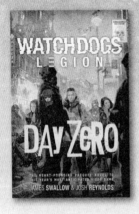